I0612097

EYE OF SALAMANDER

A novel

JOE CASSIUS

Copyright © 2026 Joe Cassius

All rights reserved. No part of this publication may be reproduced or transmitted in any form or by any means, electronic or mechanical including photocopying, recording or any information storage or retrieval system, without prior permission in writing from the publishers.

The right of Joe Cassius to be identified as the author of this work has been asserted by him in accordance with the Copyright, Designs and Patents Act 1988

First published in the United Kingdom in 2026 by

The Choir Press

ISBN 978-1-78963-590-4

Joe Cassius is also a psychotherapist, running a private practice.

ALSO BY JOE CASSIUS

Fiction

All is Wild, All is Silent
This Weirdish Wild Space
NOTTZ '08
Rain on You, Morocco

Drama

Zebra

for Mum

One

Keep Off the Grass

SHE SAID. All the other kids gazed out over the endless plain of brown and green. Their faces blank. It was winter and wet. The kid next to me looked at me to do something, so I did. I ran into it full blast. The teacher's voice shocked me. Just how crazy it was. How crucial it was. Of a sudden I began to fear the grass. What was out there. What did it mean. Why couldn't I go there. Was there something lying in wait. Something I didn't yet know about. Something I didn't understand. An animal, or a trapdoor. Her voice faded as I ran further and further into the clear open space. The winter sun lighting me up. When I looked down I was covered in mud. When I looked back all the faces were on me. The kids' faces and the teacher's face. All the faces were still blank. Except for this one girl. She was kind of smiling, a bit.

Naughty Carpet

IT WAS TECHNICOLOUR with a big cross down the centre. They made me sit on it until Mum came to pick me up.

Way Before That

THERE WAS THE SMELL OF TOAST. A large bright kitchen and a woman who was supposed to be my aunty. She talked different. *Barth* instead of *bath*. I was two years old. I was there because it was something to do with a younger brother being born. There was a row of eggs lined up along a wooden shelf. Everything was big and high up. My aunty was God.

Hating Mum

MUM MUST HAVE took me back because all of a sudden I hated her. I was always being horrible to her. Pushing and pulling her. Trying to make her cry. I was already a master of mind games. I would demand things. Keep her up at night. I wouldn't go to bed. I would see how far I could push her. Eventually she would break and collapse and slide slowly down the wall. Seeing her cry made me cry. I would charge into her arms and say I'm sorry. Hoping she would never let me go.

No One Could Scream as Loud as Me

SOMETIMES she had to. Leave me places. In playschool, on holiday. The pure terror of it all. Being left in a chalet where a ranger with a ranger hat and sunglasses walked from window to window, checking on all the kids. No one could scream as loud as me. While my younger brother Sam slept I screamed and screamed until they brought my mum and dad back.

My House

HAD A SMALL GARDEN at the front and a big one at the back. There were trees and bushes and thorns at the bottom and high fences either side. An old man would throw Club chocolate bars over. Sometimes the chocolates and biscuits would come in little carrier bags.

There was also a shed nextdoor and I would slip through a gap in the fence and climb it. Jump from its roof and land back in my garden. Later Dad put a climbing frame there. It was so high and the top scared me. Later he sent me and Mum out to buy a tipi, like what Indians had, only I came back with a Wendy House instead. It seemed better than a tipi cos I could do more. Like it had different rooms and was more interesting.

He's not a fucking girl, he said.

Cops & Robbers

AT SCHOOL I seemed to be the only one in trouble. I was always being made to stand at the wall. Facing the wall. I would stand there for hours. To pass the time I traced my fingertips around the bricks. One finger would chase the other finger. One would be the cop and the other would be the robber. One day I was standing at the wall for what seemed like all day. Only I wasn't bored because

3

in the back of my mind I knew there was something to be excited about. Only I didn't know what. Then I remembered. It was my brother's birthday.

Temperaments

SAM was behind bars. Watching him behind bars reminded me of being behind bars. Only Sam was better than me cos he could climb over. Sam would scream and fight whereas I was a baby who slept all the time. Only our temperaments were beginning to change.

Bellybuttons

I HAD THESE COUSINS that would come over, only they weren't real cousins. A boy and a girl. There were both blond. They had different bellybuttons to me. My bellybutton was a little hole whereas theirs stuck out. I would stare at them. Fascinated. A really powerful feeling would come over me. Excitement, but dread. Like a big scary too-much feeling. *Down there.* An overwhelm. The sensation was addictive and I wanted more and more. I wouldn't stop asking them to show me.

Why do you want to see them all the time? they'd say.

I don't know.

They began making me do stuff in return. Making me dance and do silly things. The boy would show me more than the girl. I preferred the girl but she was older and seemed to know more. She made me do more things to see it and wouldn't give it up so easy.

Magic

ONE DAY THE GIRL cousin told me she had a magic book and she was going to bring it next time. I was beside myself with wonder. I imagined flying through the clouds or turning invisible. For days my mind was in magic. All week I waited for my cousin to turn up. When she got here we went to my room with the book. Put it on the floor and opened it up. She turned the pages, lines of writing under these pictures. Card tricks and coin tricks. Complicated things with cups and balls and bits of rope. I had been tricked. I had been cheated. Magic wasn't real.

Numbers

DAD asked me how many Rice Krispies I wanted.

Ten! I said.

He counted ten out in the bowl and laughed. I wanted more but I didn't know any higher numbers.

Christmas

I WAS STARTING TO UNDERSTAND Christmas. There was this song they sang in school. A hall full of kids and some teachers. Maybe someone played the piano. This song made me feel good. Made me feel God. Whenever it was sang I would look at all the people, and then at the sky outside. The trees and the clouds and the sun. *O star of wonder, star of light, star with royal beauty bright, westward leading, still proceeding.* I didn't like to sing it cos I wanted to listen properly. Girls were better singers than boys and I wished the boys would shut up. Their soft voices made the hairs on the back of my neck stand on end. Over the weeks they stopped singing the song and it started to disappear. I began to forget what it sounded like. What it was. A real fear grew that it would never come back. That I would never hear it again. Eventually I couldn't take it anymore so I asked her about it. This tiny clever girl with black hair and a sharp voice.

I don't know what you mean, she said.

I tried to sing the song and then she laughed in my face.

You're stupid, that's a Christmas song.

I didn't understand. She told everybody and they laughed.

Introducing the Piss

I WAS STILL GETTING INTO TROUBLE all the time. More than the other kids. I was starting to stand out. Mostly I didn't know what was going on. The headmaster was fat and blond and balding and bearded. He had me in his office and I was terrified. I pissed myself all the way through when he shouted at me. The piss wouldn't stop. My pants, my trousers, my shoes and the carpet.

I Also Discovered this One Thing

OF RUNNING behind kids and pushing them full in the back. What made me laugh was the way their heads snapped back. My laughter was dizzying. I would do this to both girls and boys.

You can't do that to girls, the teacher would say.

One day I did it to this big kid and he got back up and chased me down. Smacking me in the face once he caught me. The pain was unreal and I screamed for ages. The kids all looked at me in this certain way. The teacher asked me if I had learnt my lesson. In the kids' eyes there was a certain knowingness. Something they had understood, way before me.

Three Kids

THERE WERE THREE KIDS that were really fast. I would watch them and wonder which one was the fastest. I'd lay there at night and try to work it out. The next day at school I would try and make them race but they never would. I became obsessed with this and wouldn't leave them alone and soon the boys began to distance themselves from me.

Not This Again

DAD bought me a Superman mug. I pointed at the top shelf and told him that's the one I want.

Oh why did you get him that one, Mum said. He'll never be able to drink out of that. It's far too big.

I took it everywhere with me. Never drank from it but just played with it constantly.

You be careful with that, Mum said. Or it will break.

What's break? I said.

It means it will be *no more*.

I got fascinated with *break*. How can something be *no more*. I wanted to test this out. So in the kitchen I dropped it on the floor. Then I threw it on the floor. Nothing happened. Superman remained as he was. I put it higher on a stool and knocked it off. *Nothing*. Superman can't break. He is so strong. I took it higher, threw it harder. I began to feel something dark inside. A scary feeling. Was thirsty and my hands were starting to shake. I climbed onto the worktop and dropped him some more. Again and again. I couldn't stop. I was possessed by something. Wanted Mum to come and stop me. Take all this away. I threw the hardest. Still the mug wouldn't break. Superman is the strongest. He can't break. He can't ever be *no more*. At last I was up on the ceiling on tiptoes. As high as I could go. It was crazy up here. I held Superman up to the light. Let him go. I watched him spin in slow motion, like a feather floating. All the time looking at Superman's eyes, mine never leaving his. He got smaller and smaller. What are you doing? Mum walked in at the moment of impact. An explosion of a million, trillion pieces. This was *break*. This was *no more*. Superman was dead. And I had killed him.

Like Riding a Bike

DAD was teaching me to ride a bike. He was building me up. He had taken the stabilisers off. We would go in the gravel car park across from our house and go around in circles. He would hold the back of my seat and talk me through it. The moment he let go I would fall straight on my side. I'm sure there was a bit of blood. I'm not ready. I'm not ready yet. I don't want to be near that bike for a long, long time.

Against the Grain

DAD picked me up and put me on the bar.
    This will put hairs on your chest, he said.
    I took a sip and it made me feel sick.
    How do adults do this, I thought.
    You will one day, he said.
    Never.
    That's what we all say.

Still No Magic

I TRIED TO BUILD a castle with cardboard boxes. I must have seen something like it on TV. But as with the magic book what I had in my mind never matched up.

I Was Getting Fast

I COULD BEAT MOST KIDS at school. Even the three fast ones. I wanted to race people at home, only my brother was too small and slow and my dad was too big and fast. One was too far behind and the other was too far ahead. So Mum was a good match. She was a good bet. We would race down the side of our house. I could nearly beat her but not quite. This defeat would send me into a blind rage and I would make her race me again. She kept trying to let me win but I knew it was fake so my rage would get worse so she would go back to the winning and my rage would just continue. Eventually she would sit on the step, tired, and say, I don't know what you want from me, Robin.

Please Don't Go Again

DAD was sometimes a laugh. We had fun and jokes. Sometimes we would wind Mum up. Tell her she was no good. Rubbish at things.

I'll go then, she said. I'll leave.

I'd sit on Dad's lap and say I didn't care. We'd have a better time without her. Dad would tell me all the fun we'd have without Mum. Eat what we want, stay up until what time we wanted.

I'll go then, Mum said. I'll go and stay at Sharon's. Her family will want me.

Good cos we don't, I'd say.

Mum would sit there with this expression on her face.

After this cup of tea then I'll go. Pack my bags. I'll be gone.

Me and Dad would smile and pull faces at her. Go then, go. See ya.

As Mum put her cup in the sink I ran upstairs, into her room. Dived on her bed. Into her bed. From nowhere there was this crash of absolute terror, absolute heartbreak. *Distraught*. I was distraught. Something from the inside out. Devastation. The world ended. No.

The world was *ending*. I was on the edge of it, about to drop. About to fall. I rolled around her bed. In and around the duvet. Tangled up in it. The most silent, violent sobs. I grabbed her pillow and could smell her hair. Put it over my face and wanted to die. To suffocate my way out of this feeling. This eternal doom, eternal damnation. That's what I felt: *damned*. This damned motherless life. I caught myself in her mirror. With her jewellery and perfume all around it. Couldn't believe how crazy my face looked in its reflection. Like my face had melted into a mask. I was all streaked and deformed. My skin was bright and red and wet. I glistened. There was a rabbit sat plump at the base of the bed. The rabbit I had got her for her birthday. Mother's Day. I grabbed it around the neck and pulled it in. Snot ran over its ears. I held it and hugged it and crushed it. Until neither one of us could breathe.

A New House

IT WAS TIME to leave my old house and go to a new one. A babysitter told me enchanting things about this new house. There are steps and a tall tree around the back. It is high up. From your mum and dad's room you can see for twenty miles. There is a loft. But the loft is also a bedroom and one day you might get to sleep in it. I was excited. There was wonder. My imagination went into overdrive. But I had learnt from the magic book and the cardboard castle that most things don't live up to it.

Two

There Was a New School Too

DAD took me to it to meet the teacher. Maybe this was my first love. Probably not. She was beautiful and brown-haired. Slim and smiley and soft. Miss Miller. She took me around Orchard Primary. It was way better, much prettier than my old school. A leafy fairytale with apple trees. The orange-bricked building formed a perfect square. She took me into brightly coloured classrooms and showed me pictures on the wall. One really good one of the Transformer, and leader of the Autobots, Optimus Prime. I wouldn't stop looking up at it. The red and the blue, the perfect lines and the detail.

That's from Andrew O'Reilly, she said.

I want him as a friend, I said.

This made Miss Miller and my dad laugh.

I want him as my best friend, I pushed on.

I'll see what I can do, she said.

She looked closely at my eye. She could tell I was something wild.

Andrew O' Reilly

WAS TALL with dark hair. He was kind and protective. He actually did live up to my imagination. Maybe school life would have turned out different, had I hung onto him a little longer.

It Didn't Take Long

I WAS OUT the class. In the headmaster's. Standing at the wall. Facing the wall. Playing cops and robbers with my fingertips. Chases around the bricks.

Batman

I WORE IT everywhere. I never took it off. For a while people didn't know what I looked like. My babysitter had a friend she brought with her that was horribly cute. She was dark with big curly hair.

Take off your mask, she said.

I didn't. Week after week. She didn't know what I looked like. The mystery drove her mad.

I wore Batman all the time. Even in bed. I even slept like Batman. Put my pillow on the floor and hung upside down. Whataheadrushthatwas.

Spider-Woman

I HAD A TAPE I had to watch again and again. It was of the cartoon Spider-Woman. The scene was where she got trapped helpless in a maze and a wall tried to crush her. She moaned and whimpered. She heaved. Hearing these sounds gave me this really peculiar feeling. Same as the bellybuttons. I was confused. I was small.

Wood Girl

I DON'T KNOW if it was Mum or another family member who asked if I had a girlfriend.

Yeah, I said.

Who, who is your girlfriend? they asked.

Wood Girl, I said.

There was a strange reaction. Something mystified in their expression. Wood Girl. I saw her all the time. Kept seeing her in my dreams. At school. In the woods. She was slightly older than me. With red hair, with brown hair. She had this certain look. She knew I was there.

Christmas Hat

WE WERE HAVING a competition at school. Who could make the best Christmas hat. Miss Miller stood with her arms V-shaped at hips and told us all about it. Her face was always shiny. She would make her eyes big and go around the class. Everything was exciting. Everything was enchanting. She made the room glow. As soon as I got home Dad was on it. I was surprised to see him so fast and focused. He spent time on this. He spent all weekend on this. I wasn't even that bothered but he was. I wasn't even that bothered at first but I was when I could see how much he was. He got an empty crisp box from the shop over the road. Cut it up and somehow made it into the shape of a roof. Then he painted it an orangey-brown and then drew bricks into it. Tidy black lines. Next he placed cottonwool on for snow. He carefully cut out a hole and put an empty toilet roll tube into it. This was the chimney. Next he went out in his car and came back with a little Santa Claus. At first he didn't fit so Dad did more work until he did. Even though it looked perfect he still kept on. Adjusting, finishing touches. By the end it was a masterpiece.

I knew I'd won the minute I stepped into class. Everyone made a fuss. Normally I would show off about things like this but for some reason I didn't. I just stood there while everyone pointed and Miss Miller announced that I was the winner. I stood there smiling. Thinking about Dad.

My First Death

WAS ON Boxing Day. It was Nana. Mum was in front of me, crouching. Matching my eyeline. When she told me the first thing I did was hold down a smile. My first thought was of Nana trying to intimidate me after I was naughty. She was sat in a green chair staring me down with purple eyes. Her skin was frighteningly pale. In the moment of Mum telling me I remember thinking, *who's winning now*. Sometime later I felt different and knew it was different. A real sad thing. Dad spent days and days in bed. I thought he was never going to get out. I would go up and see him. All wrapped up in the sheets like a baby. His foot sticking out.

Miss Miller

WAS CHANGING her name. She was changing both parts of her name. The *Miss* and the *Miller*. The Miss was changing to Mrs and Miller was changing to Myers. I didn't understand because there was already a Myers. A man teacher. Mr Myers was terrifying like my dad. He was short but powerful. He had veins running all up his arms and his body was like a He-Man figure. When someone explained what was going on I began to feel sick. A horrible out-of-place feeling. A small feeling, like I was shrinking. I couldn't look at Miss Miller. I couldn't talk to her. Her creamy skin made me want to run to the toilet. Are you all right, Robin? Her lips were a tight, clueless squiggle.

I hated Mr Myers more and he seemed to notice and make the most of this. Made me piss myself by shouting at me. His veiny arms and Miller's long brunette hair began to melt together in my mind. It was the same thing. Giving me this wrong, weird feeling. The same unusual too-much feeling I had when seeing the bellybuttons. I wanted to stay out of their way. Mr & Mrs Myers. They even brought it all into school one day. In assembly. On a big projection screen for the world to see. Pictures of them. Suit and wedding dress. Cutting the cake. Feeding each other with it. Cream on the end of fingers and falling from mouths. The last one. Last picture. Of them actually kissing. It made me hate them. Their eyes gazing at each other like I never existed.

Storm

I WOULD WATCH THEM from the window. Most kids were scared of them but I was not. Just how they would slash it all open and the rumbling from within. It would turn in my stomach like a washing machine.

There Was Blood

MUM's blood. It came rushing from her finger like the day I was born. She was trying to zip me up in the playground but I wouldn't let her. Knocked her arm down and that's when it happened. A quick, neat tear. I laughed while she cried. *Little bastard*. Even after this she was still waiting for me at the window with the mums. Next to me the boys and girls blew kisses and waved away. As soon as I caught her eyes I drew a fist. The look on her face. The collapse of her expression. The heartbreak in her did something to me. I had to catch a breath. She broke away from the smiling mothers and disappeared out of sight. I swallowed hard, and turned to stone. My fist still where it was, up at the window. Aimed at my own reflection.

Mourning all Morning

I SAT there. Stunned and sad. Wanting Mum, craving Mum. To say sorry. To take it all back. What if she died while I was at school. What if I never got to see her again.

Staffroom

THIS BECAME SOMETHING when Mrs Myers told me to come to the staffroom. I had been to the headmaster's loads but the staffroom was something else. My head began to fill with ideas as I moved towards a door I had never opened, a threshold I had never crossed. This harsh hot stench of smoke and coffee. A cactus plant stood in the centre of the windowsill like a weapon. Suddenly this man I had never seen before stepped into my eyes. A total stranger yet dangerously familiar. A grey and royal blue striped flat cap. Under it a dark face with a sharp nose. It was this nose that gave him away. First thing I wanted to do was wee. Only a deeper fear held it in. Dad's whole being pointed right at me.

Upsetting your mum, he said. Upsetting your mum like that.

Normally it was loud and mad but this controlled menace was worse. Unnervingly solemn.

You ever raise your hand at her again. You *ever*.

A supply teacher then stepped into the room. Looked at us and then walked out.

Sorry, she said.

I Was Always Pissing Myself

EVERY TIME I LAUGHED. They had to take me home from a birthday party. Some blonde girl called Lindsay. Her mum had to take me home to get changed. I was so bothered about the kids knowing and I was so bothered about missing out on everything. The mum was really nice and we thought of ideas of what to tell the kids when we got back.

A Saviour is Born

THE NEXT CHRISTMAS Dad smashed up our main Christmas present. Put it in a bag and then stuffed it in the bin out front. By now I knew Dad had a temper. That was the word they used: *temper*. Having a temper and losing his temper. The word began to confuse me. *Temper*. He was always shouting, throwing things, smashing things. When he started doing something this strong silence would sweep over the house. The second there was any resistance the doors would come off. The world would erupt. This is how our main Christmas present ended up in the metal dustbin on Christmas morning. It was an Atari games console. We unwrapped it and unboxed it. An hour later Dad began setting it up, linking it to the television, only it wouldn't work. And that's when the whole house went up. We watched him from the bay window. Take it down the steps and stuff it in the bin. Then the door was slammed and off to bed he went. The silence that followed. I went out to get it from the bin.

Don't, Mum said. Leave it.

Sam and I just sat there, wondering what to do next. Over the hours I made my way upstairs, step by step, towards Dad.

Leave him, Mum said.

She just went about as always, pottering, doing everything and nothing.

Leave him, she said again.

But I thought we were going to Uncle Ron's.

We are, she replied. We're still going. He's not spoiling it.

But how are we going to get there? You can't drive.

Mum never answered, just carried on making dinner. Putting pots away. Taking them back out. I was still inching my way upstairs. I don't quite know what I was doing but I was doing it. There was some mission deep within me which I didn't understand. Some quest. Something I had to do. By now Mum had left me to it and I was faced with the door. Dad's door at the end of the landing. A big white tomb. I sat outside of it and stared at it. Tried to find meaning there. The handle was a bright golden ball. I knew I had to touch it to open it. Eventually I did. Feeling its cold roundness like a snowball. The door finally falling in, drifting soundlessly open. It was exactly the same as last Christmas. Dad in bed. Wrapped in sheets, mummified. Maybe his foot sticking out. I didn't even know if he knew I was there. We went on like this in the heavy dark of the room. The wavy rectangle curtains. A photo of me and Sam on the bedside table. The real me in the length of the mirror. Startled by how serious I looked. A silly six-year-old out of his depth. Opening a mouth without anything coming out. Shapes and dimensions of these interiors becoming vivid as my eyes got accustomed to the late-afternoon dark.

Dad, I said at last. Dad.

No reply so I sat there longer. Waiting him out. Waiting until I felt to leave so I did. Back downstairs and Mum asked what I was doing.

I want Dad to come Uncle Ron's, I said.

Not sure she said anything. Just put the dinner on the table and the three of us ate.

I want to save Christmas, I said.

Saving Christmas. I had now named my mission. Sam sat watching cartoons while I crept back upstairs and back into the room. Nothing had moved. Nothing had changed. The exact same lump in the bed, same shape. Nothing had changed except for the impression I had made.

Dad, I said once more. Dad.

What?

His voice had impossibly arrived. Something small and surprising from the sheets. This fierce, frightening man. There was a sign from a whiskered face, riding out of the top.

You coming Uncle Ron's?

He said nothing. But turned over onto the flat of his back. Hands, arms. The purple blob of a tattoo. An obscure picture. His blue and red eyes staring at the ceiling.

Are you coming? I said again.

Him saying *no* didn't mean anything to me. I pushed on and talked on. About nothing in particular. I said that Sam and I had got the Atari out of the bin and it's okay because it's not broken.

It can be fixed, I said. It can all be fixed.

He put his leg up and I lost sight of him again. I went back downstairs and gave Mum an update on my progress. She was putting the last pot away.

I think he's going to come, I said.

Her small eyes only looked at me for a second or two. She was still making lots of noise.

Oh I don't care, Robin. Uncle Ron is picking us up. Leave him where he is.

I climbed the highstool and faced her.

But I've almost got him to come, Mum. I can tell because he's just put his leg up.

What are you talking about, she said.

I thought she might smile but she didn't. Sam was still watching cartoons. Back in the bedroom and Dad had changed shape again. His hands were behind his head and he was still staring at the ceiling. Of a sudden I thought of last Christmas. I remembered Nana and wondered if she was a part of all this. I thought about saying this to Dad but stopped myself.

Mum is getting a lift from Uncle Ron but I think you should drive us instead, I said. She's better now. She's talking more. The Atari isn't broken and Sam has been watching cartoons all day. The dinner was all right and I think there might be some left. Shall I tell Mum you're coming down?

Suddenly Dad sat up and this made me take an intake of breath. I was now feeling this all as a game. A game I was almost about to win. A quest, a mission almost accomplished. Him climbing off the bed and coming downstairs was an obsession, bordering mania. It felt like a giant rock millimetres away from being pushed over the ledge. Once he was off the bed the rest would sure to follow. I would have saved Christmas. I would have made everything all right. I would be some kind of hero. If only to myself.

In the car an hour or so later and all was silent. Nothing was talked about. Nothing was mentioned. No explanation whatsoever. I stared at the pattern in my seatbelt. I gazed out of the window. I felt sad and triumphant at the same time. Maybe this will make more sense in years to come. I looked at the back of Dad's head as he drove. I looked at Mum diagonally across the way. My brother Sam had the same expression as he always had. Outside a few families were out walking but not many. Christmas lights passed slowly as we turned one corner and then the next. The hills of suburbia. It was so cold I was surprised it hadn't snowed.

I Was Starting to be Really Cruel to my Younger Brother Sam

I WAS PLANNING TO KILL HIM. I'd lay there at night, in the dark, thinking it over. There were two garages at the top of the close. Close together with only a thin strip of a partition between them. At the end there was a massive drop into some gardens below. I was going to get him in there and tickle him and make him fall to his death. The tickling part would look like an accident. I would get away with it.

Lost Boy

I WAS IN TOWN with Mum, Nana and Sam. Wandering through the dense crowds of Vic Centre. I held on to Nana's hand while Sam was up in the distance with Mum. Some dreary song moaned over the people. The fountain did a little dance on the hour. A thing people gathered around to watch. Plinky-plonky music as the clocks turned and a cuckoo bird popped out of a wooden box. We stood and watched it and then moved on. I really wanted to play on the climb frames. Two or three tunnels. The beams were white and were made to look like bones. It was hard to make out exactly what it was supposed to be. Maybe the skeleton of a large fish. Kids climbed through them and on top of them. I stood still and watched on, longingly.

Go and play, Robin, said Nana.

She was smiling. I looked at the mole on her cheek.

Go on, she said again. *Play.*

There was something in her eye. She smiled more and put her chubby fingers on my shoulder and gave me a light push in the direction of the scene. Mum had been in a tight mood all day and it was good to breakaway. I played. I got lost. A girl with chocolate around her mouth smiled at me. Mothers stood around and talked while their kids played. A little blond boy bumped into me and I had to help him climb the middle part. Two older boys were stood off by the mirrors. Looking at us all and sizing me up. It's like they were about to take my hand and lead me somewhere. Of a sudden I got a dark twist of something and looked out for Mum. I looked for her. I looked for her hair. I looked out for Sam and Nana but nothing. Nowhere. Nana's words were still in my mind. Her lips when she said it: Go play, Robin. It's all right. I walked around the climb frames and looked everywhere. All the adults that were so high up. I stayed and played some more. Hoping she would come back. I felt as if I should be scared but somehow I wasn't. I wasn't because it was only at school some days ago that we watched a video on this. On what to do if we got lost. And it was to keep calm and go straight into a shop and tell someone. The *keeping calm* bit is the bit I remembered the most. The bit that really stuck with me. Keep calm and don't panic and it makes everything much easier. So I did this. I walked through the crowds to the shop we went last: Boots. The fountain thing was doing that dance again. Chiming away as

I moved past it. I felt clear, and with purpose, and was already thinking how proud Mum will be. How well I've done. And then I can tell all the teachers and kids at school and they'll say how clever and brave I was. I might even get a reward. Chocolate or maybe a toy. A woman with curly blonde hair got serious when she knew what was going on. She seemed more panicked than me. She asked my name and age and what my mum's name was. Then she looked at my clothes and wrote things down.

Well done, she said.

Good boy, loads more adults said.

They all stood around me and talked to me and patted my head. While I waited I thought about Sam. So glad this didn't happen to him cos he'd never think to do all this. Part of this made me scared for him. Relieved it was me. Mum was hysterical when she came in. She told me off but squeezed me tight. Like I was good and bad at the same time and this confused me. The other thing that confused me was Nana. She confused me the most. Her face was pale and I could tell that her and Mum had been arguing. She had the same look in her eye. It was a look I couldn't really describe. Other than I didn't like it. It made me feel like there was something else out here. Something I didn't understand. Deep down in this world.

This Time

MUM was teaching me to ride a bike. It was time to try again. She was building me up. We had taken the stabilisers off. We would go in the gravel car park up at Orchard Primary and go around in circles. She would hold the back of the seat and talk me through it. I didn't feel the moment she let go. I just didn't know. When I saw her standing there it was miraculous. Magic. I had separated from her, in some way. I was riding a bike.

I Found Football

IT WAS AT NANA'S house. She bought me a sticker album and taught me to read by breaking the words down. *Liv-er-pool. Ev-er-ton.* When we got to Arsenal she would tell me off for swearing. I opened packets of stickers with faces on. I would find the number on the back and match them to the squares in the book. It was exhilarating and I found myself utterly fixated. I no longer wanted sweets. Just all my money on as many packets as I could get. Other kids at school would do the same. We would meet at playtime and do a game of *got, need, swap*. Sometimes this would lead to fights and the teachers would have to come in and sort it out. Sometimes the stickers would have a *shiny*. Seeing a shiny was miraculous. It wouldn't happen very often but when you did it made you stop breathing for a bit. The rules were you could only swap a shiny with a shiny. Or sometimes you could swap a shiny with five normal stickers. They were worth that much. My first shiny was QPR and this was to be the team I was going to support.

Most kids supported either Nottingham Forest or Liverpool. This made me stand out.

FA Cup Final

BY THE SUMMER I was a full-blown Liverpool fan. At a friend's house I kicked a football around a backyard covered in dog shit. School was getting good too. A giant spider ran up my trouser leg and all the girls couldn't believe how fearless I was. On Saturday we went to a pub and counted down the hour before the FA Cup final. Everybody sitting outside on wooden tables, under the glorious sun. Scent of beer hung in the air. Chunky pint glasses with a handle. Ashtrays. Some kids with weird mullet haircuts played on the broken fence around the back. One of them was called Dwayne.

Liverpool will win, I said.

No, Forest will, he said.

Forest aren't even playing, stupid. It's Wimbledon.

I asked a man wearing sunglasses what time it was and he said two. Only an hour until kick-off. I was stressed at missing it.

Me and Dad had a £1 bet.

We sat in front of the telly.

Even though Liverpool went one-nil down I didn't care cos I knew they were just letting them win. Giving them a chance. Saving themselves. Even when their penalty was saved I knew it was all in the grand plan. I sat casual and cocky and watched, knowing the outcome. Time went on and I felt myself quietly panic. Gripping my legs. Standing up. Sitting down. Pacing. I saw the fraught faces of the Liverpool players. How fast and frantic they were. Foul throw-in. Wild, desperate shots from outside the box. Commentators were beginning to get excited, talking faster. Saying things like, *underdogs, shock defeat, against the odds.* Fans were beginning to whistle and howl. The cockiness in the *grand plan* was beginning to fade. I was slowly becoming beside myself. The world was about to end. I hated Dad. Hated him more when the whistle went and I had to pay him my pound. He was laughing so I threw the coin at him and ran upstairs. Normally I would never dare do such a thing but there were different rules here, today. I lay face down, rigid on the bed. Sobbing into the pillow. I was broken-hearted and vowed to never watch another football game again.

Duplantis

INSTEAD I TOOK INTEREST in the Olympics. Everywhere was this sign with different coloured rings. I was to start a new class with some teacher called Mr Duplantis.

What hell kind of a name is that, I said to my friend.

Teacher heard me so she took me by the arm and led me to another classroom where this tall teacher sat. His long legs reaching out a mile long. He wore glasses and had sticky-up hair. Looked like Clark Kent from Superman. Had the same type of jaw. Small strong eyes. His whole face didn't move an inch. He was serious.

Mr Duplantis, Robin thinks your name is funny.

Oh, he said.

I couldn't look at him so I looked at the floor.

Your name is Robin, he said.

I nodded.

Pleased to meet you, Robin.

When I looked up he smiled. It took me a few moments to smile back.

Three

Ben Johnson

NO CHEATERS on this wall, he said.

Taking down the pictures of Ben Johnson. Everybody loved Mr Duplantis. He wasn't like the other teachers. He didn't look, talk or teach like the other teachers. He was young and energetic. He didn't even try to keep us in line. He just *did* keep us in line.

No cheaters on the wall, he said.

He took down the newspaper clippings of Ben Johnson.

Look at his red eyes, Duplantis said. His red eyes. He took drugs to win and he cheated and now he is disqualified.

It was all over the news. Canadian sprinter testing positive. The first time in Olympic history that a gold medal had been taken away. I had watched the race. All eyes on our man Linford Christie.

After the disqualification I got really excited.

Does this mean Linford Christie is now gold?

No. Carl Lewis.

But Christie was 2nd.

No. He was 3rd.

So now he's 1st?

No. He's 2nd.

Who's 1st?

Carl Lewis.

Is he English?

No. American.

Well can Christie win the Olympics next year?

It's not on next year.

When then?

Four.

Four what?

Four years.

Well that's ages away.

Birthday

BY WINTER I was a full-blown Forest fan and I had the kit for my eighth birthday. My first- ever football kit. A red Umbro with the signature tree on my chest. White and black trim on the sleeve. On my birthday Duplantis called me into the office. Even though he was cool and strict at the same time I would still get in trouble. I didn't think you were allowed to get in trouble on your birthday so I was a bit confused. I followed Duplantis. Before we got to the office he said, what's your favourite sport, Robin? For a moment I was going to say American Football for some reason.

Football, I said.

He turned and faced me. Seemed slightly tense for some reason. He handed me something. It was three little boxes of candy sticks. On them were pictures of footballers. Forest players. And Liverpool and Arsenal and Manchester United.

Happy Birthday, he said.

He looked at me and smiled. A look that said, *don't tell the other kids.*

At home I was so happy I ran at Mum and told her.

Mr Duplantis is the best man in the world!

She pulled a face and swallowed.

Don't let your dad hear you say that.

The Relief She Brought Was Divine

I WAS FINDING it hard to keep up. I was finding it hard to keep it all together. I was finding it hard to work it all out. I was finding it hard to survive. It was small yet big things like the top of my trousers that would dig into my skin and make nasty red marks and cause me misery all day. It would be hell. It would take away any and all enjoyment. One day it got so bad I wanted to cry. When this nameless shy girl who nobody knew came over and simply tucked my shirt in. She looked at me while she did it. She looked at me like I was stupid. It was here I realised that I was behind everyone else. She looked at me again, this slow grin. Yet the relief she brought was divine. The cool soothing of it all. She felt like a nurse. An angel. Taking all this pain away.

A Star is Born

KIDS WERE STARTING to say I was the best player in the class. I wore my Forest kit and played at playtime and dinnertime. I was captain. I always picked the teams. One PE class and Duplantis took us on the field to play a full game. We only ever went on the grass in summer so it seemed strange to be running among the wet and mud. The girls hated it. All the fuss was on me. Kicking the ball. Wearing the red. Duplantis picked the teams and it made me uneasy because all my players were crap. I had most of the girls. The fat kid and a hyperactive French boy who didn't know the rules. We were in position, ready for kick-off. Some older kids watched on from their classrooms. I scored straight away and copied this celebration from a Derby player called Dean Saunders, swinging my arm around like a windmill before pointing at the sky. Duplantis went over to the losing team.

Mark their best player, he said.

Suddenly I was swarmed. Everyone was on me and I couldn't move. It was horrible. I couldn't play properly. No one would pass me the ball. I started becoming frustrated, frantic. My team looked at me to do something but I couldn't. It was then that they scored. One-one. We were drawing. Not winning anymore. I shouted out. I swore. I blamed my team. I blamed Duplantis. I was starting to hate him. How dare he take this away from me. This was my time. I had been looking forward to it all week and now *this*. Still I couldn't budge. Nile Greenaway was on me. Pep Maggio was on me. Robert Marsden was on me. I couldn't *move*. I swore and Duplantis told me off.

All right, Robin, calm down.

The girls looked at me, disappointed. I was supposed to be the best player in the class yet I was doing nothing. I could feel the end in sight. The ball suddenly appeared at the open goal with the French kid running towards it.

Kick it out, I yelped.

I watched him in slow motion. His thin white legs and big sandy hair. Shorts a size too big. He ran up and put the ball in his own net. The cheers went up. Duplantis smiled. Our team was confused, hanging their heads. Frenchy celebrated. I ran up to him and tried to rip his head off.

Wrong goal, idiot. Own goal, stupid.

Duplantis and the girls had to stand in between and stop me.

Robin, stop.

Robin, leave him.

Robin, it's only a game.

I was on the verge of tears and had to use all my energy in not crying cos that would have made it even worse. Duplantis had to talk to me in front of the class.

You can't always win, Robin. Forest don't always win and Liverpool don't always win.

Yeah but it's not fair cos you told them all to gang up on me.

I don't know why Duplantis found this all funny. He was supposed to be on my side.

No, he said. I told them to mark the best player.

I looked around at all the other kids. They were all nodding with serious faces.

Think about that, Duplantis said.

With everyone still looking at me and nodding, I did start to feel a bit better.

Valentine

IT WAS TIME to pick someone to fancy. It was time to choose someone to go out with. Nile Greenaway had picked Amanda Carlton. Pep Maggio had picked Penny Lipman. Gavin Brown was working his way through them. I was shocked no one had even noticed Lauren Makepeace. She was the first beautiful girl I ever saw. Her hair was white. Her skin was pale. She was like milk. But the main thing about her was that she didn't talk. She was too shy to talk. I wondered if this was why no one had picked her. I was the most popular so I assumed she was just going to say *yes*. Valentine was coming so it made sense to wait. I was dead crap at art so I got one of the other girls to help me.

Who is this for? she said.

Mind your business.

I had pink glitter on my hands.

We put them in the post box and waited. The following morning Tess Darby handed them out.

Nile Greenaway had two. Morgan Davenport had six. Gavin Brown had ten. The rest of us had none. Pep Maggio banged on the table and said, this is lame.

I remained calm. I didn't mind not having any. I only wanted Lauren and she didn't know yet. It's still early in the day. As soon as she knows one will come my way.

Now to the girls.

Laura Emerson had the most. Amanda Carlton had some. Lauren Makepeace had one.

She went red. She was dying on the inside and dying on the out. She was scared to death and for a moment I felt guilty. Like I had inflicted something upon her. A small crowd gathered around her table. She stared straight ahead and said nothing. I decided to wait. Give her time.

By afternoon it had gone on long enough so I went up to her.

Where's my Valentine card?

What? she said.

I mean, where's *your* Valentine card?

She looked me dead in the eyes.

In the bin, she said.

Her Word

WAS A KNIFE and she used it without a flinch. After that I decided to make a drama out of it all. I felt kind of adult now. A boy with a girl on his hands. I followed her around. I wouldn't leave her alone. I don't know why but I was getting the feeling she was starting to enjoy some of this. Enjoyed being cruel. People started to notice her more. She strutted instead of walked. She tossed her white hair around. She began to talk. Full sentences now.

Leave me alone.

I was at her heels, following her through class.

We need to talk, I said.

We need to talk.

I had heard this line in a movie and had been wanting to say it for ages.

Lauren, we need to talk.

There's nothing to talk about.

I was so glad she replied with that cos that's what the girl in the movie had said. This is how life was starting to look. The lines. The scenes. It was *all* starting to *happen.*

My Second Death

BRIAN TILSLEY. He wasn't a real person. But a person on *Coronation Street*. A character. I knew he was going to die and that made it worse. Meant I was waiting for him to die. In twenty minutes he will be dead. I watched him and felt sorry for him. How innocent he looked. How unaware. Going about his business, not knowing his fate. The tension was horrific, this build-up. Outside the nightclub I knew it was close. Some woman was in danger in a dark alleyway. Brian ran to her rescue. He was a really great fighter. His punches fast and clean. He also used a headbutt. I had never seen this used before and it looked excellent. Something I must try. I was hoping that he wasn't really going to die. That they had got it wrong somehow. Hoping he would win the fight and save the girl. Only it didn't work out like that. It didn't work out the way I wanted. They eventually got him. Up against the wall, his frightened face in the glow of a red neon light. The sound and the sight of a switchblade. Shining silver. They pushed it in and ended him. Ended Brian. The last thing was some dancing neon in the background as the woman went off to get an ambulance.

The Strategy

SEEING HIM DIE was worse than Nana. Made me feel more and stuck around for longer. It did give me an idea though. I could use this to try and get Lauren Makepeace. I talked Adam Wall into pretending to bully her so I could rush in and save her. Be her hero.

Adam grabbed her wrist but Lauren just looked at him.

What are you doing? she said.

She then looked at me with the same expression.

Leave her, I said to Adam.

My voice was weak and none of it made sense.

Lauren shook her head and walked away.

Adam and I were standing by the bin.

Now what? he said.

Dunno.

The Headbutt

BRIAN TILSLEY came out one last time. I had wanted to try it out. See if it worked like it did on TV. When Anthony Overwood tackled me hard at playtime, I used it. Stuck it on him. I was surprised how well it did work. Dropped him in seconds. He rolled on the floor and wouldn't stop screaming. I felt kind of guilty. I was sent to the back of the class for the rest of the week. Nobody would talk to me.

The Kiss

DECIDED I was going to kiss her. I was going to sneak up behind her and do it. Fearless of all consequences. She was talking to Pep Maggio by the window when I did it. It was just under her cheekbone. My lips against her skin. It was weird. Not what I expected. It was like a peach but not in a good way.

All About Nile

I WAS THE BEST footballer in the class and I was the fastest. I would line up at the edge of the playground and race the boys and win. I didn't realise it was the end of playtime when I challenged Nile Greenaway. Seconds after we started the whistle blew, ending playtime. We might be in trouble for this. A serious quiet fell over the playground. The whole class watched. Duplantis didn't tell us off but rather let us race. Suddenly realising the gravity of this spectacle. One on one. Boy vs boy. This was no longer just a race between kids but an event, a face-off with a full audience, a crowd. Like Sports Day, except for no cheering. By the wall we were drawing but that was all right because I was always a slow starter and a fast finisher. I would use the wall and the turnaround from it as leverage, catapulting myself into the second half of the race. Duplantis and the line of kids were all watching us. It was silent and intense. There was no sign of Greenaway so I must have had him beat. Suddenly there was Lauren. Dead centre of the kids, watching me. Her blue eyes became my focal point. This victory would win her over surely. Still no sign of Nile. Already the giddy explosions in my body as the crowd and the finish line got bigger, drew nearer. That white line. I was laughing as I ran through it, arms up, aloft. As I caught breath I was met with an odd sight. Everyone around Nile, cheering and high-fiving him. Paul Martin was the only one to come up to me.

Not the fastest anymore, Robin, he said.
What?
Nile is number one.

No he is not, I said, panting.

Paul walked away and joined the celebrations. Doom started to fall in on me. I had to get to the bottom of this.

I won, said Nile.

He won, said Amanda Carlton.

I didn't listen to her cos she was biased. But then there was Pep Maggio and Penny Lipman and Tess Darby and Gavin Brown. Nile Greenaway is the new fastest boy in the class. They were all saying it. They were all saying it but they were wrong. I had clearly won. Clearly, obviously, conclusively. Nile Greenaway was alongside me at the wall. But then I had pulled away, eased away. I must of because he was nowhere in sight. I had left him. Left him behind. He wasn't with me as I crossed the finish line. He simply wasn't there. They were all still around him, making a fuss. The only person who wasn't was Lauren Makepeace. She stood at the centre of it all, looking at me. What her look meant I didn't know. But I knew it wasn't good. I kept looking at her and soon I began to read words in her face. In this expression. It said, just accept it, Robin.

The Truth Shall Set You Free

I COULDN'T ACCEPT IT and wouldn't accept it. They were all wrong. There was some trick going on. A vast conspiracy concocted by eight-year-olds. The only person who would give me a straight answer was an adult. The only person who would give me the truth was Duplantis.

You all right, Robin? he said.

His eyes knew too much.

There was a new light in the room. A new sun. It was shining on Nile Greenaway as I watched on from the gloomy corner of the class.

Robin, you all right? he said again.

He knew I needed something from him. This softness and strength all around him.

I wanted to ask Duplantis. Ask him straight up. But I did win, didn't I? I did beat Nile, didn't I? I am the fastest boy in the class, aren't I? They're all lying to me, aren't they?

In that moment I wanted to ask Duplantis the truth because I knew he would give it me.

But, I never did.

Dad Went Mad

DAD picked me up from a birthday party. Mum came to the house and I came out with a goody bag. Some cake and a crappy toy. When we got back to the car it wouldn't start. Dad went mad. The more he tried to fix it the worse he got. Mum got out the car and became a part of it. The voices got louder and maybe someone looked out of the window from the party. They argued and Dad overpowered her. He smacked and lashed out at things. Kicked the car. We ended up leaving the car and leaving Dad and walking home. Through the alleyway that ran alongside the pub. Sam must have been there. Mum said it was over. That we were going to live in a flat, somewhere.

Arsenal

I HAD A FEELING that Mr Duplantis wasn't into football that much but he said he supported Arsenal so I had to too. He had an accent and was from some place called Kent. I knew that Arsenal was London so maybe Kent was near London and that's why he supported Arsenal. I now supported Arsenal.

You can't just change teams, Pep Maggio said.

Why?

You've got a Forest kit and you're *from* Nottingham.

I couldn't wait for my birthday so I could get an Arsenal kit. I was going to get the Away one. A yellow shirt with black sleeves. Only it was April and getting warmer and my birthday wasn't until winter. Ages away.

You can't just support Arsenal cos they're winning the league, Pep pushed on. You can't just support Arsenal cos Duplantis does.

Why?

You're lame.

Being Poorly

I GOT THIS REAL BAD earache that kept coming back. Mostly it was in the night and I had to get Mum out of bed. She would wrap me up and talk me through it. One night it got so bad she had to ring the nightdoctor and he came. A brown man with a funny voice. It was spooky being up in the dead of the night. When everyone was asleep. The pain would go on and on. I would keep on imagining what it would be like without Mum here. It made me want to die.

I Thought About Death a Lot

HOW IT HAPPENED and where I'd go. It felt too enormous to think about. But I wouldn't be here so I wouldn't know. There would be no one to experience death so what's there to be afraid of. But that thought terrified me. This eternal loop of living and dying and knowing and not knowing. The on and on-ness of it all was driving me insane. It made me not want to be here anymore.

Portal

THE ONLY REAL THING I could never explain was when I was little. Like really little and on holiday I remember being at an outdoor swimming pool. It was massive with loads of people. There was some kind of water slide, a climbing thing that had an indoor part. I remember being in there, and then suddenly there were loads of little brown kids, bout my age. Looked not quite human, or from a different time and place, like olden times. They looked like some sort of South American or maybe Philippines. Wearing leaf-like clothes. Jungle clothes. I turned away or closed my eyes for a moment. When I looked again, they were gone.

I Was no Longer the Fastest But Now I Was the Funniest

EVERYONE said so. Nile Greenaway brought his pet axolotls in for showtime. He and Duplantis talked to the class about it and it was dead fascinating.

Anyone know what a Salamander is? Duplantis said.

Yes, I said. It's my street.

Everybody laughed. Even Lauren Makepeace laughed. She laughed and smiled and turned kind of pink. Which was strange because I hadn't thought about her in ages. Months. I had pretty much forgotten about her completely.

'Eternal Flame'

THIS SONG was on all around us when she asked me to ask her out again.

I want you to get me some chocolates, she said.

Okay.

A box of chocolates.

Okay.

We were stood at the top of the steps. Overlooking the rainy field. It was sunny but we still couldn't go on the grass yet. The blades glistened. I watched her little white hand point over to a set of houses.

Mine is the first one, she said.

First what?

All the houses were orange.

Mine is the first one with a different colour, she said.

I looked at a violet house, midway along the cul-de-sac.

I want you to post me a box of chocolates. Either tonight or sometime over the weekend.

Okay, I said.

You will?

I will.

She smiled.

Does this mean we're going out? I said.

She nodded her head, I think. She moved her head very slightly and I'm almost kind of one hundred per cent sure it was sort of a nod.

Gift

IT WAS TIME to take my gift to the wider world. It was time to get famous and play for Forest. Dad knew a bloke at work who ran a football team and I was going to play for them. I was going to be the striker. I was going to be the top goalscorer. Forest would see me and sign me. I would play for them. Then I'd play for Liverpool. Then I'd play for my one true love. Arsenal.

Matchmaker

I TALKED Kev Moss into buying some Matchmakers. Mint chocolate sticks. He was in the other class and didn't know who Lauren Makepeace was but I got him to buy and post the chocolates in the violet house. He had to scrunch the box up to get it into her letterbox.

An hour later we went back and pulled them out. Ate them all at the top of Black Path.

Lauren All the Time

'ETERNAL FLAME' was on all the time and Lauren was on all the time. On my mind. I was scared to death of her yet was loud around her.

You're always showing off and it's annoying, she said.

I didn't quite know what she meant but I had a feeling it wasn't good. I didn't know if we were going out or not. I acted funny around her but at home I felt sick. I followed my mum around everywhere.

Big Fish

DAD took me to the football team. The Bloke at Work's son was the captain. He was loud and confident and had this curly blond hair. I looked at him to like me but he didn't. The other kids were the same. I started as sub because I was new but I didn't mind. The more I watched the game the more uncertain I got. The boys on the pitch weren't like the boys at school. They were faster, stronger, better. They knew what they were doing. They had a position and they stuck to it, and worked it. There seemed to be some kind of system, some *way*. Whereas at school we just ran around and did what we wanted. Kicked and dived in and hoped for the best. Just then The Bloke at Work called my name. He was a big man with a beard.

C'mon then, Robin. Show us what you've got.

The pitch was massive. Bigger than our playground. The goals seemed a million miles away. All eyes were on me. A hundred of them. First thing I did was run on without taking my tracktop off. This made them all laugh. My dad got embarrassed.

Fucksake, Robin.

He unzipped and yanked it off me. It was great to wear an actual football shirt, matching everyone else. In a proper team. Can't wait to tell them at school. Can't wait to tell Duplantis. I wish Lauren Makepeace could see me now. I was looking down at my shirt when the ball struck me hard in the chest and made me fall back. My teammates and the manager was shouting at me. Felt like a telling-off at school. Dad looked mad. The game went on. I started to focus. I started to try. I ran at players and slid into them. I was clearly not the best but I thought if I just kept sliding into them I could pass as good. I thought I was doing well. When I looked up to see if Dad was watching me he was gone. Nowhere in sight. I looked for him and looked for him. The game was still going on around me and my teammates started to tell me off. Of a sudden I didn't like football anymore. I wasn't the best and it was far too hard. I felt like some kind of death, like half of my personality was gone. Of who I was and what I was known for. Still I slid into players. I had dry mud on my knees and on my socks, more than most of the other boys so I figured I must be doing something right. When I looked up Dad was back. Only I was surprised to see him mad. He was shouting but trying to keep his shouting quiet. He was pulling a face. He was embarrassed.

Stop jumping on the fucking floor all the time.

He walked off again, hiding his face.

Eventually, at last, it was over.

At school I hated hearing the final whistle. Here I couldn't wait for it.

I didn't come back the next week.

I didn't play for that team again.

Pisstaker

IT had started ruining my life. The thought of it. The fear of it. I simply should be over this by now. I simply should have outgrown it. Two or three times I had kept it hidden. Gotten away with it. It was nearly always around laughter, laughing. Laughing so much too much I would piss myself. It would come from nowhere. I would fill my pants, cover my trousers. The next time was just before dinnertime. It was glorious now because it was that sacred time where kids were allowed on the field. Everyone making the most of it. The last of the cold wet months, stuck on the concrete of the playground. I couldn't wait to get out and among it. Stretch my legs and make them free. Run into the full freedom of an oncoming summer. Only someone had set me off just ten minutes before break. I ran to the toilet but didn't make it. There was loads this time. A full piss soaking me through. The dark of my trousers, saturated. Oh the anguish and fear and badness of it all. So mad so sad so broken. This huge humiliation. So babyish and stinky. The loss of control. Not knowing what to do or where to go. To lock myself in a cubicle and never come out. Could I get away with that. I wanted to tell a teacher but there was just no way.

I wanted my mum. I wanted my mum. I wanted my mum to come do something.

Fix it. Fix *this*. Make it go away. Instead I got Pep Maggio. Caught me red-handed. Wiping and drying myself down with rolls and rolls of toilet paper and those dark greenish paper towels. I was surprised that he wasn't.

You all right? he said.

There was nowhere to hide, nothing to lie about. I told him and showed him. I expected him to say something. Maybe laugh. Instead he got more paper towels. Told me to use the hand dryer. I kept thinking about the crowd, the other kids. Lauren Makepeace. I looked at the clear dark patch on my trousers and how it just wouldn't go away. I hated that line between the wet and the dry. I wanted that line to disappear more than anything else in the world. Just when I thought it had faded out I would catch more of it. The patch looked like a country on a map. A dark continent. Incontinent. Africa Australia America.

It's going, said Pep. It's gone.

No I can still see it.

I was amazed Pep was helping so much. His calm, patience and efficiency. He was missing his dinnertime. He was missing his vast green and blue outside to be in the piss-stench of a small dark toilet. Occasionally a kid would come in and we'd go quiet.

It's gone, he said.

Holding my arm, putting me at a distance to look me over.

It's gone, he said again. I can't see it.

You sure?

I'm sure.

He splashed his face with water and brushed back his thick black hair. I looked in the mirror and saw a boy even younger than I was. A thin pale face. Frightened eyes.

Come, he said, holding the door.

Sunlight poured through it. Leading the way. I walked through the cloakroom and into the bright afternoon. Full of screams and joy and colours zooming across the field. A massive game on. I wanted more than anything to play but when I looked down it was still there. That evil damp patch covering the entire front of my trousers. As I watched Pep run onto the field I dived onto the flat of my front on the grass bank. Alongside the girls. Tess and Kayleigh and Kerry and Amanda and Lucy and Rebecca and Lauren Makepeace. I kept a certain distance as they picked daisies and made them into a chain. Not really watching the boys who were racing up and down the field, chasing a ball.

I lay hard on the bank. Keeping my groin pressed into the yellow grass. I moved back and forth and in circles. Hoping this motion would do something, dry it. Over time I could feel the girls start to notice me. Wonder about me. Some of the wimpy kids who didn't fight or play football began to notice me too. There was something amiss, off kilter, and this was causing a slight unrest. Something in the air.

What's that smell?

A pocket of giggles. One of the girls stood up and pulled at her skirt.

Dog piss.

She was looking around, pulling at her mate.

Gavin Brown looked at me from the pitch and waved me over. I pretended I was asleep. Sun slowly cooking the side of my face. The school roof always did this thing. Part of it formed into a high red triangle, like an arrow. Wind would get into the beams and make this really spooky blowy sound. No one ever talked about it and I don't know if they even noticed. But I did. I listened to it and listened to the girls. I listened to the boys and someone pull out of the car park in a car. I kept my eyes closed and tried to think the piss stain away. I slowly rubbed my groin on the grass and it must have dried up by now.

Dried up yet?

The voice was loud and clear and casual. I looked through my lashes and through the squinty sun. A fat kid blocking some of it out.

Pep Maggio standing before me.

Dried up yet? he said again. Even louder this time.

I felt Lauren look over. Dread owned me. Total fear. I couldn't work out what Pep was doing. If he was even aware of just how loud he was. Had this been a trick all along or had he changed his mind mid-break. A foe to a friend and then back again. I'll teach Robin a lesson.

Dried up yet? he said a third time.

Now Tess Darby was on her feet. Amanda Carlton too. What's this new fuss? What's going on over there? I stayed where I was. I wasn't going to move. The piss smell was now obvious. I could smell it mingled with the tang of the grass. I looked at Pep's face but still couldn't work out his expression. It was dark in the shade from the sun.

I Had to Walk Off

DAD mentioned it but only sometimes. I still had my heart on being a professional footballer. Playing for Arsenal.

You won't, he said, picking his teeth after dinner. You kept throwing yourself on the floor. I had to walk off. You was embarrassing.

I sat and told my mum I was going to be a professional footballer.

I'm *that* good, I said.

It's like she didn't know what to say in front of Dad.

Yeah but so are lots of lads, she said.

Crash-Bang

I TOLD EVERYONE at school I had a pet spider. It had thick hairy legs and was the size of a dinner plate. We was going around the class, talking about pets. I didn't have one so I made it up.

You just made that up, Pep Maggio said.

I ignored him and pushed on.

It's the size of a dinner plate, I said again.

I loved the reaction this got. Especially from the girls. They got scared and screamed out and distanced themselves from me. I kept threatening to bring him in and they got even more scared. Everyone was looking at me.

You lie, Pep Maggio said.

I told them more stuff. That I kept him in a box under my bed and brought him out at night. Fed him bread and other bugs.

It's not even the season, Pep said.

What?

Spiders don't even come this time of the year. It's not even the season.

Pep Maggio didn't believe me but the girls did and that's all that really mattered. I kept this story going for weeks. My stories got more wild and elaborate. How it had bit my brother and got him rushed into hospital. How the spider protected me, listened to me, knew my thoughts. Did what I told him.

What's its name, then? Pep Maggio suddenly asked.

The question caught me off guard. It wasn't something I had thought about. It wasn't something I had planned for. I tried to answer quick. Say the first thing that came to my mind.

Crash-Bang, I said.

You just made that up. Crash-Bang. That's not even a name. You're a joke. You're lame.

Some of the girls were starting to listen to Pep and I could feel my power begin to go.

Bring him in then, Pep said.

The girls freaked out but Pep looked me dead in the eye. Bring him in.

By chance I found him up Black Path. Running across the grey concrete. It wasn't a scary house spider but one of those garden ones. It was big but far from menacing. Just a beady little body and long brittle legs. It was like a snowflake, but it would have to do. I put him in my lunchbox and took him in.

The girls freaked and ran a mile. Attention was all over me all morning. News got to Duplantis and he addressed the class.

There's a spider in the room, he said.

Again the girls screamed and put their backs against the wall. I held the lunchbox up high but stood at a distance so they couldn't see properly.

But spiders aren't really a pet, Duplantis said. So why don't you do the right thing and take Crash-Bang to the bottom of the orchard where he belongs.

Even though I had only known this spider an hour. I cried and cried. I was heartbroken and I really believed I was heartbroken. The kids crowded the window to watch me. I walked the yellow path to the bottom of the orchard. With my lunchbox. With Crash-Bang. The departure from my pet was a ceremony that lasted all morning. The girls tended to me with kindness. From their hugs I saw Pep Maggio.

You're lame, he mouthed.

26.5.89

IT WAS THE BIGGEST NIGHT of the year. Biggest night of my life. Duplantis explained it all to me. Arsenal had been winning the league for most of the season. They hadn't won it in eighteen years. They had been on a roll, beating most of the top teams. At one stage they were eleven points clear of the defending champions, Liverpool. However in the last five games things had started to go wrong. Things had started to slip, come undone. They had lost Derby. Drew Wimbledon. Liverpool had caught up drastically. Undefeated in eighteen. It was the last game of the season. On a Friday night. It was the first time that the two leading teams played on the final day. It was also the first time to be decided on goal difference. If Arsenal won they would be on exactly the same points. Therefore they had to win by two clear goals. Liverpool hadn't lost by two goals or more at their home ground of Anfield in three years, and Arsenal had not won there in fifteen. The odds were overwhelming. The maths was set. It was a week after Liverpool had won the FA Cup Final. It was a month after ninety-seven fans had lost their lives in the Hillsborough Disaster. The game had a peak British television audience, with over twelve million viewers.

I watched the game at home. It was the same nerves as a year ago for the FA Cup Final. Only now I was supporting the other team. I was older. I was starting to know how it worked. Arsenal came out in their Away yellow. I thought about Duplantis. I wished I could watch it with him. I was starting to know all the players now. The captain, Tony Adams. David Rocastle. Lee Dixon. Nigel Winterburn. Paul Merson. The main guy was Alan Smith. He scored all the goals. The game had this weird quiet about it. I watched games all the time, every Sunday, but this felt different. Almost like there was something else going on. Something I couldn't quite explain. Even though not much was happening there was this atmosphere. This dark wind about it all. At half-time the players came off the pitch. Mum made tea. Dad wasn't really watching it. When the second half started I felt something change. A tilt in the direction of the Liverpool goal. It was in the 53rd minute that Alan Smith scored. A glancing header from a free kick. It almost didn't feel real. An underwhelm. Liverpool players crowded the ref about something but the goal stood. Arsenal were now halfway there. I should have been tense but I wasn't. I should have been on edge like I always was but something out of my hands was playing out so I just let it all be. Like I was there, but not there. It was near the end. It was nearing. It was ending. A Liverpool player held his finger up. He was mouthing at his players, *one minute, one minute, one minute.* I heard the whistle blow in my mind. Yet still there was this weird calm. The keeper, John Lukic, threw away the ball to defender Lee Dixon, who in turn put a long one over to Alan Smith, who flicked it into the path of Michael Thomas. It was here that the world went into slow motion. Twelve million pairs of eyes on this man and on this ball. The hairs on the necks go up. A soundless breathless moment which will be remembered forever.

Duplantis

I LOOKED OUT FOR HIM. The only face I wanted to see. We had done it. Our team had won.

I'm getting the Arsenal Away top for my birthday, I told him.

That's a long time to wait, he said.

He'll probably be supporting another team by then anyway, Pep Maggio said.

Nana Moved to a New House

IT WAS ON A SMALL CLOSE where other old people lived. A small bungalow with hand rails everywhere and chords dangling in every room with an orange plastic thing at the end. There was a patch of grass around the back where I could play football. By the end of the first night of visiting her I had memorised everyone on the close, their names, pets and house numbers.

Tess Darby Brought a Sex Book Into School

IT WAS KIND OF SHOCKING. The girls didn't really make a fuss but the boys did. Even Duplantis seemed embarrassed and joked it off. Girls took it in their stride whereas boys lost their minds. They tried to call Tess about this but she was far too clever and mature. She opened the book and pointed at things and knew all the names. I looked at her white and pink legs. The shape of her body. The more I looked at the shape of her body the more I realised she was not like the other girls. Her chubby face and her eye off-centre. Sometimes she wore glasses or had a face like she should. She wasn't pretty like Kayleigh Highman. Not beautiful and mysterious like Lauren Makepeace although she had a different kind of power. She gave me a different kind of feeling and I couldn't work it out. Her presence was big and confusing.

She sat at my table and opened up the book.

What do you think to this? she said.

I pretended to not hear her. And talked to someone else.

Orchard Primary Five-a-Side Football Tournament

THEY ANNOUNCED IT IN ASSEMBLY. The rules went as follows. The teams were to be picked by having a kid from each year. Except for the goalkeeper. He could be from any. Tommy Philips was known to be the best player in the whole school. A fourth year. He had a pale face covered in freckles. Strawberry blond hair. He didn't talk much but he didn't need to. His football did the talking. Shortly after assembly, him and another fourth year came up to me. His mate was looking me up and down.

We hear you're the best in your class, he said.

I tried to keep the excitement out of my voice. I am, I said.

You sure?

Tommy's mate was Ben Sharpe. A small cold-looking kid with a violent reputation.

Yeah, I am. Ask anyone.

I held out my hands, palms facing.

Tommy was looking me up and down. All of a sudden he produced a football from nowhere.

All right, show us, he said.

He dropped the ball at me feet.

Here? I said.

Here, they said.

So flummoxed I felt sick. I remembered all the goals I scored at playtime. All the kids I twisted and sweated without effort. Then I remembered that awful day with Dad and The Bloke at Work and my confidence fell through. I kicked the ball and turned. Tried to do a few kick-ups but it failed. When I looked up Tommy Philips and Ben Sharpe were staring at me.

He ain't that good, Ben said.

Tommy said nothing.

Kev Moss is better.

Suddenly I felt my world end.

I don't know, Tommy said.

Let's get them to face off, Ben said. One on one. Winner is in.

I didn't like this. I didn't like this at all. I'd never played against Kev proper. He was the best in his class. I was the best in mine. Truth was I had been purposely ducking him for this very reason.

Kev ain't at school today and the teams need to be in by home time. What you thinking?

Tommy was looking right at me. I could see his mind going one way and then the other.

Nah, he said. We'll go with this one.

I Swaggered Back Into Class

I'M IN, I announced. I'm in. I'm in Tommy Philips' team. Being in Tommy Philips' team was instant status. An automatic victory. The kids swarmed me and shook my hand. Patted my back. Ruffled my hair. Minutes earlier, in front of Tommy and Ben, I was powerless, like a pauper waiting to be thrown a piece of bread. Now I was strutting about like Maradona. All the boys were happy for me. Greenaway. Davenport. Brown. Everyone except Pep Maggio.

Upper Echelons

THE TEAMS were read out the following assembly. The rules about the one-from-each-year was pretty much dropped although they tried to spread it as evenly through the ages as possible. We were the immediate favourites and the teachers acknowledged this. These lot will take some beating, they said. *These lot.* Them lot. I was now in the upper echelons. Into the realms of celebrity. Felt like I had the winning lottery ticket. Although our name was a bit shit compared to everyone else's. I wanted to make some suggestions yet I knew not to push it. We were called TB. Simply named after our two top players, Tommy and Ben. The teachers found our name funny although none of the kids knew why.

Ben came up to me after assembly.

Dinnertime, he said. Come up to the field.

What for?

Training. What do you think.

Training

THE OTHER MEMBERS of the team was Arron Rose and Ash Jameson. Arron was a year above me. The best in his class. And Ash was the best goalkeeper in the school. We really were going to be impossible to beat.

We did some passing and we did some drills. Then me, Alan and Ash had a mini-game against Tommy and Ben. They battered us. Then Ben came over onto our team and the four of us tried to take Tommy on his own yet we still couldn't do it. Tommy was unbelievable. His skills. His shots. He was going to be a professional, easy.

The rest of my class watched from a distance. I didn't look over. Just kept my eyes on the training. Eyes on the training yet my head was on all the attention I was receiving. I was so happy.

I don't like him, Ben said.

He was staring at me. This real nasty look.

He's not good enough.

He's only a first year, Tommy said.

He's supposed to be the best first year.

That's what they said.

I want Kev Moss.

Tommy was doing kick-ups. We're going to win anyway, he said.

That's not the point.

What is the point?

I want the best in every year.

Oh do what you want.

I felt my heart break. I looked at Tommy to do something. Arron and Ash turned away. Ben was still staring at me like dirt.

Panic Room

THE NEXT DAY Kev Moss came up to me. Sorry, Robin, he said. But I'm in.

What are you talking about?

I'm in. You're out.

What?

TB. I'm in. You're out.

But I was training with them yesterday.

Doesn't matter. I'm in. You're out.

I ran away, distraught. I locked myself in the cubicle and cried. It was the end of everything. How would I tell the kids in class. How would I tell Mum. Back in class I told Duplantis. Holding down my hysteria the best I could.

No, Robin, he said. The teams have been picked. They can't be changed now.

Light came into my heart. An overflowing relief.

You sure? I said.

Duplantis nodded his head. That smile of his. His small kind eyes. I'm sure, he said.

Tommy Said

I WAS QUIET around TB. Ben wouldn't look at me or kick me the ball. Tommy just smiled.

You're lucky, he said.

That training I did better. With the pressure off I played easier. I even scored.

See he's not so bad, Tommy said.

He's crap.

We'll win anyway, Tommy said.

That's not the point.

I even didn't come last in the sprint race. Even though I was youngest I still beat Ash Jameson. But he was the goalkeeper and he was kind of fat so I didn't show off too much.

The Final Word

THAT AFTERNOON Kev Moss came up to me.

Sorry, Robin, but I'm getting into that team.

I was full of assurance now.

Sorry, Moss, but you're not. The teams have been picked. They can't be changed. Duplantis said.

Well Mr Sharpe, Ben's dad, is coming into school. So I think you'll find otherwise. I'm in. You're out.

There was a confidence and clarity to Kev which petrified me.

The badness returned. My mind into overdrive. Heart about to break all over again. Again I had to get confirmation from Duplantis. Just to make sure.

Don't worry, he said.

The Tournament Started

SOME OF THE GAMES were to be played at dinnertime and some were to be played after school. There were so many teams. Even a girl team. Cos they were girls they were allowed to have the whole team from the Fourth Year. They were tough. This one girl was near-impossible to tackle. She elbowed me in the mouth and dropped me to the floor.

See, said Ben Sharpe. He can't even tackle a girl.

In the end Tommy had to take the ball off her. Tommy took the ball off everyone. He was a one-man team. A one-man machine. Ben Sharpe wasn't even that good. Arron Rose was our second-best player.

The Final

BY THE END of the week we were in the final. The two teams were read out in assembly and placed on the wall in big gold letters: *TB vs The Demolishers*. The teachers were still laughing at our name but we still didn't know why. The final couldn't have been any better. On the very last day before we broke up for summer. It was a massive event. In front of the whole school. A whole crowd. Rows and rows of kids. A trophy on the table. I was taken out of class early so I could get changed with my team. VIP treatment. Special ceremony where both teams were taken out onto the field like Wembley. Ben Sharpe was fired up, slapping us across the face. Getting us hyped. Arron Rose wore proper football boots and shin pads. Our team all looked nervous. Whiteness in the face. The only one who didn't was Tommy Philips. His apple-red cheeks and casual blue eyes. Not a care in the world.

A Trophy

IT WAS WEIRD to play to the roar of a crowd. It put me off. Made me nervous. Too nervous to see straight. I couldn't distinguish between the players and the crowd and the teachers. I couldn't see the ball. All I could do was hope that Tommy, Ben, Arron and Ash weren't as nervous as me. I was relying on them to do their job so I could get my hands on that trophy. The whistle blew and the game kicked off. I ran around in circles. Making myself look busy. I made sure I didn't keep throwing myself on the floor this time. The other team, The Demolishers, didn't have a First Year on their team. It was just me. They were all way bigger. Faster, better. I managed to kick the ball once. Just the once. I think I kicked it out of play and defended well and I think that was all right. I had made it safe. We scored maybe two or three times. They scored once. It was a comfortable win but not a demolition job. We didn't demolish The Demolishers. It was closer than I thought. Tommy was magic but not his best. He did just enough. Just what was needed. Arron Rose did a crazy bicycle kick and was awarded *Man of the Match*. Ben picked up the trophy first. Then Tommy. Then Arron. Then Ash. Me, last. As I did a Fourth Year snarled at me. Mike Zimmer.

You were crap, he said. You didn't even do anything. You only kicked it once.

By this point I didn't care. I was in heaven. I was king. My class all ran around me and picked me up. Carrying me towards the steps, back into the school. Up high and I saw a blonde girl duck under me. Lauren Makepeace. I was expecting her to come out the other side and was shocked when she didn't. Her hands were on my back. Holding me up. She was at the centre of it all.

Next Year

ONCE IN CLASS the kids began queueing to get my autograph.

All right, Duplantis said. Enough now. Back to reality.

Reality wasn't pleasant. Reality was ending our time with Duplantis. There were diamonds in his eyes. A girl was crying. The afternoon began to wind down. It got kind of quiet. A weird emotional atmosphere. Duplantis went into his own world. We found out this was his first teaching job. We were his first-ever class. That had to count for something. I thought about the candy sticks he had given me for my birthday. A secret I had kept. I thought of Crash-Bang. I remembered it all. We were given envelopes to take home. Our parents had to open them. The letters told us what class we were going to be in when we came back. Some were to return to Duplantis and others were going to have another teacher, a new teacher starting in September. We were going to find out through these letters but somehow the kids had already worked it out. The clever adult kids like Greenaway and Tess Darby. They were both happy cos they were with Duplantis next year. So was Lauren. I talked to Duplantis like I knew but there was something in his face. Something in the way he was.

When will you find out, I asked him with fake casualness.

I already know, Robin.

The use of my name. His small and serious eyes seemed to peer over his glasses. With a folding of the lips he told me. Told me straight like he always did.

You won't be with me next year, Robin.

Something Else

I HAD NEVER KNOWN a time where I was half happy and half sad. Happy because of all the glory. I had been a celebrity. My dreams come true. A football star. Although no one was talking about it now. As quickly as it had happened was as quickly as it was forgotten. Lauren Makepeace had moved on to something else. They all had. Sad because I was not with Duplantis anymore.

A new teacher. Starting in September.

Summer Holidays

I WAS TO GO TO NANA'S. Even though I loved the bungalows and the green and the other grannies who had their own characters, I was starting to get bored. I picked on Sam as entertainment. He always cried so easily. Nana was kind of dumb too. She sang songs and forgot things. Made things up. She was hard to read. Hard to keep track of. She was always falling out with people one minute and then loving them the next. She said she was taking me to a Forest game next week even though the season had finished. She told us fanciful stories. She told us bad things about Grandad. How he ran off with another woman so she put a brick through his window. She told us we had to hate Grandad and his wife. She took us out and promised us sweets she never bought. She was always stopping to talk to people on the street. She was dead popular. When out one day at Carlton Square I saw Ben Sharpe. I thought he might smile at me because of our triumph but he did not. His younger brothers Dwayne and Danny spoke to me instead.

Hey wanna come over and watch *Robocop*?

Robocop

EVERYONE had been talking about *Robocop* before we broke up from school. It was supposed to be the best film ever. It was weird because there was *Robocop* toys and sticker albums and movie posters yet no one could watch it cos it was an *18*. It was supposed to be very violent and extreme. Nobody had it on video. Nobody could get a copy. Dwayne looked at me. His tired eyes and face glistening with snot.

Hey wanna come over and watch *Robocop*?

The Sharpe House

NANA didn't seem to mind me leaving the close with Dwayne. Don't tell your mum, she laughed. She sang. There was an awful sinking feeling as I followed Dwayne Sharpe across the busy road and along the rough houses. I wondered if I was going to see Ben. Apparently he had our trophy and I couldn't wait to see it again. The lawn was covered in junk. The door was bust and beat up. One window was cracked and another was boarded up. Ben wasn't there. Dwayne's mum wasn't there. He didn't have a dad and I was confused about what Kev Moss had said. *Mr Sharpe is coming into school.* The only parent-person there was an older sister called Michelle. She had fire-red hair. She wasn't that pretty but instantly she gave me that weird deep tingly feeling that Tess Darby gave me. That insecure out-of-my depth feeling. Hot and sticky.

She put a leg up on the chair and said, so you watching *Robocop* with us?

I nodded.

It's violent you know.

Just then I froze. A massive Rottweiler lazily brushed by me and then barked at the back window. You don't like dogs? she said.

I was bitten by one once, I lied.

Don't worry, she said. He won't bite you. Not unless I tell him to.

Her smile was strange. Her teeth wicked. Her blue eyes turned red for a moment. All of a sudden I hated it here. There was something so wrong about this place. It lived in the walls. It lurked around the corner. There was the smell of dogshit. Of badness. Of decay. There was a hole in the roof.

The Opening Scene Put me on Edge

A DARK CITY SKYLINE. I knew I was about to watch something I shouldn't be. I knew I might not ever be the same again. Dwayne and Michelle barely looked at the TV. Talked through most of it. Fought with the dog. Saliva trailed everywhere. Hung off the battered armrest. Glazed the threadbare carpet. *Robocop* tore through the bad guys. It was nowhere as bad as I thought. A hand was blown off. A gas station was blown up. Someone was shot in the bollocks and a man's face got melted away by acid but the bad guys all got what was coming. I was getting a sense of good and bad. Of good and evil. This room, this house, felt that way. Michelle, Ben and Dwayne weren't evil but somehow they had it around them. They had it harder than the rest of us. I knew that now and counted myself lucky. The only bit of *Robocop* that upset me was the bit where he comes back to his family home. A half-remembered life he once had. The scene played like a dream. Grey with golden outlines. Sad, longing music. That bit disturbed me the most. Loss. I thought about losing my mum and that terrified me. The other scene that made me feel something was when a man tipped white powder over a woman's chest. That's cocaine, Michelle said.

What?

Drugs, she said.

Dwyane looked like he knew what she meant. I was more excited by the chest bit, the breast bit. I wanted to see more but didn't know why. It made me feel sick in the stomach and light in the head.

Pep Maggio

OUTSIDE OF SCHOOL he was an entirely different kid. We hung out. We played. He wasn't into football so we built dens instead. Climbed trees. We came up to school and sat on the grass. At school he was hard and harsh. Here we talked about everything. Opened right up. Mostly he talked about love. He talked about girls.

Who do you like? he asked.

Ugh, no one.

I know you liked Lauren Makepeace.

I didn't know anyone knew about that.

C'mon, Robin, you don't have to be embarrassed.

I was. I couldn't believe he was talking like this. I couldn't stand it.

She's pretty, he said.

I was still embarrassed but kind of angry too. I had hoped no one had noticed how pretty she was. I wanted to be the first and only.

That was until she cut her hair off.

I know, gross.

Ha.

What?

Why do you always talk American.

What?

You always say American words, he said. You talk like the films.

I didn't know what the guy was talking about.

So who else do you like?

He was picking daisies. His chocolate eyes were big. Pep was kind of fat.

I was picking chunks of grass. It sounded like Velcro.

I like Penny Lipman, he said.

I know you do.

I sent her a Valentine card.

I know you did.

You think she's pretty.

No.

Why not?

She's covered in moles.

So?

I felt bad because Pep had a mole. A big one on his chubby cheek.

She's also got weird eyes and goofy teeth.

You've got goofy teeth, he said.

And her face is not straight. And her hair is thin and she's just got too many moles.

Pep's chocolate eyes went even bigger. He looked over at the crashing summer sunset.

I just ... don't see all those things, he said.

He sounded so adult. Pep was way more mature than me. He knew things I didn't.

It was the Height of Summer

DAD took us to this pub. They had this outdoor bit. All the adults sat at wooden tables and drank while the kids played in the park. I had my football and wanted to get a game going. I rounded up some kids and picked the teams. Just then The Bloke at Work turned up with his son. The confident captain kid with curly blond hair. He was staring at me and smiling a bit.

I remember you, he said.

I didn't say anything.

You played for us *once.*

The game behind me continued. I had a feeling I was no longer about to be the best.

Go show 'em how it's done, Bret, his dad said.

Bret joined us and took over. He got more kids to play. He chose the best ones and gave me the crap ones. We had gone from winning to losing. Suddenly I was in the background. Nowhere to be seen. At first I had done everything to make Mum and Dad watch me. Now I was hoping they wouldn't. That they'd look away. This Bret guy was horrible. He took the game by the scruff of the neck and made it his.

More kids came. Suddenly it was a crazy fifteen-a-side battle on this Saturday night. The parents had some background entertainment. Bloke at Work watched his kid take control. Some kids from our team had to go home.

Wait, I said. We're down.

What?

We're two men down.

Bret booted the ball high. Go find someone then.

I left the pitch with my head low. Bret's arrogance was out of control. I caught sight of my reflection in a car window. Shadow of myself moving across the floor. Bret was shouting at some kid. Strutting about in front of his dad. I looked around for kids. New players. Someone who could make a difference and turn this thing around. Just as I entered the arcade a thought flashed into my head. *Imagine if I saw Tommy Philips right now.* No sooner did I receive that did I see him. Up at a computer game. His back to me. The red of his hair and the whites of his legs. The lights of the arcade lit him up. Blue and green and orange. I couldn't believe my eyes. He turned and looked at me. Cherryade all over his mouth from the little Panda pop bottle he was drinking.

Robin, he said.

I took Tommy back out onto the pitch. Bret glancing over sceptically, yet not too concerned.

Found him, I said.

Bret waved us on, only half distracted by the ball. Tommy Philips said nothing. He very rarely did. His football did the talking. Picked up the ball and went through them like he always did. Stepping through the kids. Tangled them up. He was greedy. Didn't pass. Bret went in hard but was left for dust. Tommy scored one, then two, then three.

How old is he? Bret whined.

His dad looked away. Switched seats. Bret's smile changed into a horizontal line of nothing. His face red. His blond curly hair looked sad. I don't think we won. The deficit was too great to catch up. As it got too dark to be playable the game wound itself down. I didn't care about the win. I had my own win. In fact it didn't really feel like *my* win. Just *a* win. Something bigger. A justice in the world. I felt smaller in the presence of it. Like it had taught me something. The night had magic. It was the first time I really felt a force at play, outside of myself.

I didn't speak to Tommy Philips. Didn't even see him go. One minute he was there, next he was gone. He had left for Big School and I doubted that I'd ever see him again.

So Who Else Do You Like?

PEP and I were back up at the school. It was a late Sunday. Almost getting dark. Almost time to be *in*. Pep always told me to leave my football at home.

There's no point, he said. I just won't play.

We had been climbing trees. We were high on sugar and sweets.

What Pep liked to do the most was talk about girls.

So who else do you like? he pushed on.

At first I was dying with shyness but he talked about it so much that I was sort of used to it by now. I was becoming braver, freer. I was starting to say what was really going on.

Kayleigh Highman.

He rolled his eyes. You can't say Kayleigh. Everyone says Kayleigh. It doesn't count. It's a cop-out.

She's in my class next year.

She's an actress and a show-off. She's a drama queen.

I didn't fully know what he meant.

What about Tess Darby, I said carefully.

Ah she's sex mad.

I know.

I could feel my eyes light up.

She's not even pretty.

I know.

Why you like her then?

I was beaming red. There was a buzz in my skin.

Dirty bastard, he laughed.

This was the first time I talked like this and it felt massive, scary and exciting.

You know she will Frenchy you.

Ugh, gross.

Stop talking American.

It is though.

You even know what a Frenchy is?

Of course I do.

She Frenchies Nile all the time.

What?

They're neighbours and they do it all the time. Some older kids force them to do it and watch.

My head was spinning. I didn't quite know what was going on.

I can ask her for you, if you want?

Want what?

If she'll do it with you.

No.

I mean to go out with you. Be your girlfriend and all that.

No.

You sure?

She's not even pretty anyway.

Pep didn't say anything.

She's got a bongy eye.

Pep was looking at me.

And she's kind of fat.

Red came to his face. Pep was kind of fat and I stopped myself from saying any more.

And you're kind of skinny.

His playful tone had dropped. The Pep I knew from school was back.

You're dead skinny, he said. Too skinny.

I looked at my hands, then over at the school. It was strange. It was a Sunday but one of the lights in the classroom just flicked on and off.

You shouldn't talk about girls like that, he said.

Like what?

Penny Lipman and Tess Darby.

Oh I was only joking.

You're not even good-looking, you know.

I looked down.

The only reason you're popular is because of football.

The light went on again in the classroom.

Just don't talk about girls like that. That's all I'm saying.

Okay.

We went quiet for a bit.

Shall I ask her out for you or what?

Who?

Tess.

Nah. She's not in my class next year anyway, I said mournfully.

It seemed like everyone was with Duplantis next year. Everyone. Tess. Nile. Pep. Gavin Brown and Morgan Davenport. If only I was born a month earlier.

What about my sister? Pep said from nowhere.

Zoe?

She's in your class next year.

He was looking right at me. I had to be careful of my next words.

Zoe. I've never really—

Who the fuck is that?

Just then his eyes drifted over my head. He was looking at something else, beyond.

What the fuck is that?

More lights were on in the classroom. All the lights. The tables were moved around and there was a figure moving in there. Up at the walls. White. White face.

Pep stood up so I stood up. Just then the white figure turned slowly and looked straight at us. Without another word Pep screamed and bombed it. Across the field, towards the playground. I was fast and he was fat so I caught and passed him easy. He was still screaming so I did too. All of a sudden I experienced this real fear. Now I knew that ghosts existed. It wasn't up for debate anymore. Halfway across the playground and I slowed down because I didn't want Pep to be alone with this. I knew where I was heading. Through a broken wire fence and across a back garden which led to the top of my close. Just then I turned to take one last look at my school. Only to see a mysterious green light flash across a window. Duplantis' classroom window. Pep and I was through the fence, across the garden. Tiptoeing along the ledge of a rocky wall. It was fully dark now, like the sun had fully dropped in the last five minutes. We were out of breath and on the flats of our backs, down a slanted driveway.

Fuck, he said.

Fuck, I said.

What was that? Who was that?

What was that flashing green light?

What flashing green light?

Fuck.

Fuck.

Four

A New Football Season

A NEW SCHOOL YEAR. A new class and a new teacher. I looked around the room at the kids. Kev Moss. Bart Tucker. Dwayne Sharpe. I considered the girls. Kayleigh Highman. Zoe Maggio. Zara Ellis. Kerry Tromans. Diane Dunne. I was eyeing Kev carefully and he seemed to be doing the same. I knew what was on his mind because he knew what was on mine. Who, indeed, at last, was going to be the best footballer in the class.

America Was Born

IT WAS BORN from a blue book in the school library. A thin hardback with not many pages. It was beat-up and scuffed at the corners. There was a line of something down the centre. The front cover. Big red letters. USA. It was the only book I ever read. Not really read but looked at. Pictures. A New York skyline. Statue of Liberty. The White House. JFK. Marilyn Monroe. Elvis. James Dean. Cowboys. Martin Luther King. An astronaut putting an American flag into the moon. Golden Gate Bridge. Hollywood sign. Mount Rushmore. Basketball and Baseball and American Football. San Francisco 49ers. Carl Lewis.

I was starting to know America but I didn't know what it meant. Just this giant place with a blue sky. The grass was greener and teeth were whiter. Everything was bigger, bolder, brighter. Kids were cooler. Girls were cuter. The way they spoke was sharper, smarter, smoother. Knowing it was out there gave me hope. There was the word *future*.

Mr Michaels

OUR NEW TEACHER only added to the Americanness of everything. He looked American and talked American but he wasn't American. I should have liked him but I didn't. Straight away I didn't like him and I don't know why. He was cool and funny and full of crazy energy but there was something try-hard about him. Something fake. He just didn't give me the same feeling that Duplantis did. Maybe I should give him time. Give him a chance.

Top Lads

NOW WELL INTO OUR JUNIORS the main players were starting to emerge. Boys on the playground. Boys in our year. From both Duplantis' class and our class. Tough lads. My best mates. A gang. Nile Greenaway was the hardest. He was dark and handsome and kind of fat. He did judo and was way more mature than the rest of us. He wanted to be a lawyer. Kev Moss was the best jumper. He was insanely good at jumping. He could jump over anything you put him in front of. Gates. Walls. Fences. Hedges. In PE we played this elimination game on the apparatus and he would always be last to get caught. Sometimes the class would finish and he was still hanging upside down on the highbeam. Untouched. He was blond and his hair would bounce every time he jumped. Gavin Brown was the best with girls. He was light-hearted and didn't seem to care about anything. He had his ear pierced. Morgan Davenport was the best-looking. He was brooding and lethal. He was the only one to go on holiday abroad and when he came back all his skin would be burnt and bubbled yet it never seemed to bother him. He had the best clothes. He would carry five-pound notes and buy everyone sweets. He had two older brothers in prison and his dad was a gangster. He never seemed happy.

We Played Football Every Playtime and Dinner Without Fail

AT PLAYTIME we had the whole playground to ourselves. We used a set of steps as one goal and two trees as the other. Sometimes the ball would go over the fence and that would be heartbreaking. We tried to keep our shots low but sometimes a dumb kid would sky it and we'd hate on him for the rest of the day. A girl lived nearby and at night she would go get the ball for us.

At dinner we had to play with the year above. This wasn't great because they were bigger and better and we just had to blend in. I couldn't show off as much. Trials for the school team was about to start next week.

More America Came Through Films

BACK TO THE FUTURE. Ferris Bueller's Day Off. I began to take on these characters. Marty McFly. Step into their shoes and walk around in their skin. Their mannerisms became my mannerisms. I would take on their facial expressions and copy the very words they used. In my mind's eye I would look like them. Move around the classroom as them. It made life better. The days began to pass with more light and excitement and coolness.

At Home

I LOVED MUM and wanted to be around her all the time. I thought about her death all the time too. I was still being horrible to Sam. Worse now I was bigger and stronger. I also knew how his mind worked. What would get to him. I began to tease him. Tease Sam. Dad knew this too and we would wiggle our fingers at him and for some reason this would send him insane. A weak spot. I was scared of Dad most of the time. He was always smashing things up. Whenever we would go anywhere there was always trouble. Shouting at people in shops. Jumping out the car at people at the traffic lights. Sometimes he was really funny and carefree. He cared about things but didn't care about things. He taught me how to punch and told me to stand up to people. Always hit the leader, he'd tell me. Always hit the biggest one. And always hit them in the nose cos that hurts the most. Pain shoots through their face and their eyes water and they can't go on. Dad was fearless. He'd square up to anyone, even if he lost. When we were out he'd buy us things. Going shopping was funny cos he'd throw loads of things in the trolley like he just didn't care. He made his own rules. When he was good he was the best but when he was bad he was the worst.

Trials For the School Team Started

I WAS HAPPY and relieved that Kev Moss didn't go in for them. He was so wrapped up in the new Batman film and by jumping over things that he didn't seem to care. I was happy about this. More limelight for me. With Tommy Philips now gone, Arron Rose was the best in the school. I ran out onto the pitch nervous. I was starting to realise something. Playing at playtime and playing when the pressure was on wasn't the same. I got into my own head. Felt rigid and slow. I didn't live up to expectations. Mine or theirs. A few more in my year went in for the trials. Even though I was way better than them in *normal time*. Here we were equals. Maybe even lower at certain moments. They could feel that something was wrong, amiss. Even though I pretended otherwise.

You all right, Robin? they'd say.

Yeah, why? I'd casually ask.

Day the squad was put on the wall was nerve-wracking. I was there before everyone else. There every five minutes. Excusing myself to the toilet so much Michaels began to notice.

That's enough now, Robin, he said.

Michaels had begun to sniff out my wants and weaknesses. He knew what I needed and went out of his way to not give it me. Takes one to know one.

The Squad

HE MADE ME wait while the kids crowded the wall, looking at the squad pinned up there. Ink still fresh. My nerves were shot. I felt sick.

It was a cold nauseousmorningtime.

Squad's up, someone yelled.

Michaels levelled me with his eyes. He and Duplantis were both handsome men but Michaels wore his differently. An unattainable smugness. I imagined him having hot girls like America but I can't imagine they'd stay around too long. There was something unsettling about his gaze, unstable in his walk. He was substantial, but only for a short period of time. He was not to be trusted. Not to be counted on.

By the time I got to the wall the kids began to unpeel from it, one by one. My mouth was dry. Palms hot and sweaty and sticky. Eyes all over the names. All the lads in the year above was there. Arron Rose with a (C) by his name. Then set in long agonising moments of deathly panic. Only the small kid next to me snapped me out of this, eased it. Like he could read my mind or feel my energy.

Don't worry, Robin, he said. You're in.

I followed his finger. Seeing myself in black and white. Right there at the very bottom. *Robin Goode.* Slow elation poured right through me. Heartrate decreasing, then increasing again. Relief, then rocketfuel excitement. So much so I needed to piss. My infamous pisses. The blight of my life.

I looked at my name and I looked at my name. I didn't look at the others now because I didn't need to. I was here. I had arrived.

You're the only one in our year too, the kid said.

I was the only one in our year to make the Orchard Primary squad.

Swaggered Back Into Class

ANNOUNCING IT ALL. This time last year they fussed me but now it just wasn't so. No one cared. It was like they were all used to me by now and had turned away. Kev Moss was oblivious. So was the girls. I sat and thought about how bad I was in the trials. How little I had done. Ran around and made myself look busy. Talked a good game and somehow this talk had worked, gotten me through. An invisible talent. Last year this had got me picked for the winning team and the status I got by kicking the ball once in the final. I had a whole reputation based on that. Based on nothing. I was a master of fluke. Big gob, blag job. My achievements underserved. Adulation unwarranted. Like Mr Michaels I was a fake, a phony. I was a hustler.

A straight-up hustler.

Well. That would have to do.

That would have to do *for now.*

Ghostbusters 2

HIT THE STREETS and everyone went nuts on it. Football all of a sudden got put on hold. I insisted that we had a gang. I was Bill Murray's Peter Venkman cos I was the funniest. We convinced everyone that the school toilets were haunted. That if we looked in the mirror and said *ABC* three times a ghost would appear. This caused genuine terror and one girl nearly even had a breakdown and the teachers had to have an assembly and put a stop to it. This was awful for me cos my ghostbusting and chance to save the girls came to an end. I always took the gang thing too far. Made sure everyone stuck to their character traits no matter what. I made us do coded handshakes and high-fives. Writing lines for us to say. I had done this in the past with *Thunder Cats, A-Team, Top Gun.*

Robin, we're bored now. Can we go back to playing football?

Liverpool

BY MY N9NTH BIRTHDAY Liverpool had found me, again. I can't remember the exact moment when Arsenal was put down and Liverpool picked back up. Either way it was decided. I was having the red home kit for my birthday and the grey away kit for Christmas.

They were top of the league.

Pep Maggio.

Our summer bonding of ghosts and girls was long gone. He collared me at playtime wearing my Liverpool.

You're pathetic.

What?

Arsenal, Duplantis, you're pathetic.

What you on about?

Whatever happened to Arsenal?

What about them?

You supported them.

No I never.

At times, to go with my Americanism, I had started adopting this half-attempt at a Liverpool accent.

Yes you did.

No I never.

I'm telling Duplantis.

Telling him what?

You only support whoever is at the top.

You don't even like football.

You're pathetic.

Anyway I've never supported Arsenal. I've always supported Liverpool. *All my entire whole life.*

Liar.

You're not even in my class anymore anyway.

What's that got to do with anything?

Go away then.

Pathetic. Phony.

He stared me out, before turning away.

Gameboy

HIT THE STREETS and everyone went nuts on it. Everyone had one that Christmas. Nothing else mattered. When I looked out the window at the snowless Christmas there was not a kid in sight. Last year there were mountain bikes everywhere but now there was nothing. I felt this was the start of something new. Or if not something new, then something being left behind. The Gameboy was supposed to be for me *and* Sam but he didn't seem to care so I played it all the time. *Super Mario Bros 2* and *Tetris* were the only games I was bothered about. The others were crap. I played it morning and night. Something weird was happening to me. It was like I couldn't put it down. Like I was hooked, possessed by something. I got obsessed with levels. Like I had to always beat the one before. It made me feel sick and dizzy. I got headaches and backache from sitting and staring. I wanted Mum to stop me. Take it away. Give me a break. It got to the point that I dare not pick it up cos I knew I would never put it down. Sometimes my hands would be covered in sweat. A blister started to form on my right thumb. After a while the blister turned to hard skin. The skin stayed and I wondered if this was going to be here for life. A part of me now. There was a quiet kid who lived down the road called Steve Woods. Apparently he was a genius at computer stuff. He had completed both Mario *and* Tetris. I tried to ask him about it but he just looked at me and never really gave me a straight answer.

1990

NANA was settled in. She had all her mates from the close where she lived and was at the centre of it. New Year's Eve was at her bungalow. Me and Sam was staying there the night. Some of the grannies smelled. Some of them had warts with hairs sticking out. Their skin amazed me. All creased and shrivelled up. Some wore thick glasses and others had patches in their hair. They looked like giant babies.

Sam fell asleep before the year turned. As it turned all the giant babies stood in a circle and crossed their wrists and held hands with the next person and bounced their arms up and down. Singing this certain song. I watched their loose skin and folds of flab and thought of meat at the butcher's. I sat by their feet and looked at crusty slippers and confusing kneecaps.

One of the women said, it's not just the end of the year but the end of a decade.

Another one just stared blankly at her. Yellow glue in the corners of her big eyes.

It's 1990.

Daydream Believers

IT FELT WEIRD to write that at the top of the page. 1990. It seemed daunting somehow. I didn't really know about time but it was going fast. I thought back to my old house and the move away from it. Miss Miller felt ages away. Not sure she even works here anymore. Not seen her around and didn't really care. I didn't care about Lauren Makepeace anymore either. I looked around at the girls of today and wondered who to pick. Kayleigh Highman was front runner. She didn't seem as popular now and was within reach. People fussed Kerry Tromans but I didn't see the big deal. Best friends Zara Ellis and Diane Dunne had to be up there too. A blonde and a brunette. It was still so cold out there and I wished it would warm up. I looked out longingly at the school field.

Stop daydreaming, Robin.

Michaels was telling us one of his stories. Walking around the class like it was a stage, clicking his fingers. He talked fast and then talked slow. A built-up drama. Perfected punchlines. Of one of his acting roles. Of when he sang in front of a sell-out crowd. Of when he rode his motorcycle through the desert. He tells me to stop daydreaming.

Parents' Evening

DAD came in first.

That Michaels is an arsehole, he said. I had to walk off otherwise I was going to chin the cunt.

Mum came in second. He's just young, she said.

I didn't quite understand this cos to me adults were just adults. All about the same age. Dad said more about Michaels. He had every religion on the wall except our own.

More America Came Through Music

NEW KIDS ON THE BLOCK. This sound and style. I had a cassette and a Walkman and listened to them when I got home from school and before I went there. Morning and night. I closed my eyes and thought of city skylines and oceans and long locker-lined corridors in cool schools. I thought about a nameless girl with brown hair and a white smile. I was amazed by how far and real my mind could go. Did everybody's imagination have this level of detail? Sometimes by the time I opened my eyes, I didn't know what was real. And what was not.

Michaels vs Goode

MICHAELS and me were beginning to clash. Clashed in the way kids did. He didn't seem like an adult but rather someone my own age. Duplantis used to laugh at my show-off ways. Ask about it. Work with it. Know it. Michaels would pounce upon it, crush it out before it had a chance to start. He would light it up and try to tear it down in front of the whole class. Parts of him felt like Dad, this hard wall. A will to compete with me and drive me out. Kill my spirit.

Kayleigh Highman

I HAD PICKED Kayleigh Highman. We were the loudest in the class and a good match. A boy and a girl. Occasionally I got signs from her. Made her laugh. I was always telling her to look under the table. She would pinch me in the side and fix my collar. I would touch her hair and tell her more jokes. I thought about Valentine's but then I knew what happened last year.

I waited. I watched. I wanted to ask her out.

But then I saw her at the window one day and it killed it.

She had her hand at the window, shouting through the glass at her mate. Her hand horrified me. Palm pressed hard, so hard the white of her skin turned yellow. It was covered in messy blue ink. The sight disgusted me, repulsed me. Put me right off. I decided to not ask her out anymore. I felt not to fancy her. I decided it had to be someone else.

Tuesdays

DAD would come home on a Tuesday. After a long few days on the road. We weren't allowed to talk to him. We would hear the sliding door and in he'd walk. Dark. Silent. A forcefield around him. A certain smell of lorry. A thickness in the air. Sometimes this would spill over. A shout at us. A slipper thrown at the telly. A slamming door. He would talk about work. Someone who was an arsehole. Someone who was a cunt. A wanker, a fucking bastard. Some man who was going to get smacked the next time I see him. Mum would try to calm him but then she'd get it. A raised voice. A boom. The rest of dinner would be silent.

Aiden Beecham

HE SHOT TO FAME by beating Morgan Davenport in a fight. It was unheard-of for someone in the lower year to fight one in the year above let alone win. It was even more unheard-of for someone two years younger to try out for the squad, let alone make the team, the starting line-up. He was a football star and a fighting star. Even though he didn't look the part. A short, scrappy, red-faced ginger kid. It seemed that his secret weapon was judo. He was only eight years old but already a purple belt. He used this skill in both the fighting and the football.

On our first game the year above didn't like it that this little kid had made the team, yet by the end he had won their respect. He was going to be a permanent fixture, for the rest of the season.

Spots on the Wall

THERE WAS A NEW THING he started doing in class. All the kids had their name on the wall. I didn't quite know what this meant or what it was for, until Zoe Maggio took me to one side and said, *look*. She was pointing at my name. Most of the kids had green spots next to their name whereas mine had red. The only other kids with red spots was Kev Moss, Dwayne Sharpe and Bart Tucker. I had the most. Doubling everyone else's. This drummed up loads of fuss in the class and Zoe put her lip out.

You're bad, she said.

I liked that.

The Wonder Years

AT HOME, on Sunday evenings, I had begun falling in love with this show called *The Wonder Years*. It was as American as it could get. The American Dream. It was about a kid called Kevin Arnold and he was about my age or just older and he rode around on a bike and went to school and fancied a really pretty dark-haired girl and his best friend was a geek and his older brother bullied him and his mum was really sweet and kind and his dad was mean and quiet.

Stationery

EVEN THOUGH I didn't like Kayleigh anymore and didn't want her as a girlfriend I was still telling her to look under the table. She told me to look under the table too. We were both looking under the table. On top of the table we moved our hands. Fidgeting. Unable to concentrate on the work. Playing with things. Moving stationery. My pencil. Her sharpener. I put my finger on one side of her ruler and she put hers on the other. We measured the distance between us and pushed. Boys were supposed to be stronger than girls but she kept beating me.

Football in the House

I WATCHED LIVERPOOL at the weekend. I practised the Liverpool accent. I was always kicking a ball. There was barely a time when a football wasn't at my feet. When Dad was away I played football in the house and Mum told me off. When he was here, I did not.

Football Season

ALL SEASON I had watched football from the touchline. Squad did not mean team and I knew this from the start. I watched it from the touchline but I wasn't even a sub. The only time I got to wear the school kit was in the photo. And even then, me and another kid had to wear the old version of the kit while the main players wore the new. That was fair. That was only right. The kit was blue and white stripes, like Sheffield Wednesday but a lighter shade of blue. On away matches I told my class I played even though I didn't. It was amazing to go to other schools. While the game was on I'd go wander. Be in places I shouldn't. Climb fences. Sneak under gates. Hide between trees. No one knew I was there. I made a telescope with my hands and gazed through dark windows into empty classrooms. I imagined kids sat at tables. I pictured their faces. What they'd look like. Was there another Robin Goode out there? Another class clown. Another American boy. I imagined the girls. The pretty ones, the beautiful ones. Girls like Lauren Makepeace and Kayleigh Highman. Maybe they would be even prettier and that scared me for some reason. Knowing they were out there, and knowing that I might not ever meet them.

I'd return to the game and watch on. Mostly I didn't care whether we won or lost. Mostly I'd fixate on someone and study their mannerisms. Imagined their life. Some Italian kid wearing a gold chain. One of the girlfriends in the crowd. A teacher with a funny haircut. Once I watched an old man watching from a high window, overlooking the field, the game. For some reason I watched him more than the match. Standing there in the window. Grey hair with a bald patch. Glasses. He looked like the professor on a box of Weetos cereal. I imagined what the rest of his house looked like. What his life was like. What his wife was like. What was on his mind as he watched us all. What was on his mind *right now*. He's an old man. I wonder when he will die.

I don't know why certain people grabbed me at certain times. I don't know why I became obsessed with them.

I was always hanging around. I was always on the edges of everything.

Sometimes I'd overhear people talk about me, not knowing I was there.

Why does that weirdo come to all the games, he's not even in the team.

He's not even a sub.

He's not even in the squad, is he?

Did you know he's American?

No he's not.

He's in my younger sister's class. She says he's American.

He doesn't look American.

Doesn't sound American either.

My sister says he's always pissing himself.

Worst Piss Ever

'SOWING the Seeds of Love' was all over the place. There was this poorfamily called The Brook Kids. They were like The Sharpe Kids, only not as tough. Like the Sharpe Kids there were loads of them. One in every year. They were pale and had black teeth and they never ate. Always had bigbogies hanging from their noses. They stunk. They were bullied. Kids called them *Fleabags*. They all had that name. All The Brook Kids. Kids said it so much that it wasn't even name-calling anymore. It was just their name. It's who they were. The oldest, Stacey, was in our class. She sat quietly in the corner of the Quietcorner one morning, minding her business when Kev Moss came in singing the song 'Sowing the Seeds of Love'. Only he changed the word *seeds* to *fleas*. I thought this was ingenious and immediately began to fall about laughing. I started to join in, singing the lyrics, alongside Kev. Stacey stared out of the window like she always did. Not knowing if she could hear us or not. Always just that blank look. We sang at her and to the rest of the class. Most laughed, some didn't. My laughing got so much I felt it happen. A twinge. Then cramp. My knees knocked then buckled. I tensed right up. Then an ice-cold fear took hold. The laughing came to an abrupt stop. The breathing stopped next. My face got hot. Crazy dry mouth. I was in front of the whole class. For all the world to see. Nowhere to run. Nowhere to hide. Kev sang on and I wished he'd stop. I tried to fight it but there was no point. Point of no return. Maybe a brief pleasure at the moment of surrender. Then, gush. An unstoppable force. I can't imagine what my face looked like. Silence. Shock. This was my first public performance. There were rumours but now there was proof. Facts. Physical evidence. Reliable witnesses. Caught red-handed. Kev sang on and I started laughing again. A second wave of joy and maybe I didn't care anymore. My trousers had turned dark, a huge expanding patch like it was never going to stop. I was still pissing myself. A kid said something. Another laughed. Another horrified. Another showing kindness. Another saying, *serves him right*. Kids were all different and it was in these moments where we got to see the full range. The wide spectrum of humanity.

Michaels came in and saw me. Made a big deal and pointed it out. Pointed me out.

I looked down at my sopping shoelaces. My soaked socks. Everyone was too shocked to say anything. I stood in the middle, in a puddle of my own piss.

I looked at Stacey staring out of the window. In her reflection, a slow smile moved across her face.

Parkhead Academicals

DAD read it out from the newspaper. *Players wanted.* It was time to try a team again.

Don't throw yourself on the floor this time, he said.

I won't.

Don't embarrass me, Robin.

I won't.

And get stuck in.

I will.

And don't be scared.

I won't.

It was miles away. A long drive on a Saturday morning. The kids were about my age so I might have a chance of getting in the team and not just the squad. No one knew me so the pressure was off so I might play better. Most of the kids already knew each other so it was hard to find an *in*. I tried to be funny but they shut me down. Dad waited in the car, then eventually he came out and watched me. It took me a bit of time to warm up and get into it. I was nowhere near the best but also far from the worst. The one thing I did have was speed. Apart from this black kid I was the fastest on the pitch. I used this and made an impression. After the coach told me that if I come every week I might make the team. In the car Dad seemed mad. I waited for him to say something.

Why did you keep sucking your sleeve?

What?

Every time I looked over you was sucking your fucking sleeve.

We drove on in more silence.

I was good though, wasn't I?

Yeah, he said. Yeah you was all right.

Fast, wasn't I?

I think he might have been nodding his head.

Did you play football at school, Dad?

No but I was fast. Faster than you.

It's like he was trying to get a reaction of some kind.

I was too tired. Instead I looked out of the window at the passing houses. There was a woman at her front door, struggling with a set of keys, trying to get inside.

Snake vs Mongoose

MICHAELS was an actor. He got us doing loads of drama stuff. He got us into these characters and then we would play out scenes. One of them was to choose an animal and then take on that animal. The movements and the sounds. Way of the beast. Then he would get us to form a circle and then make us meet in the middle. I chose a snake. Most of the girls chose their pets. So they would be a cat or a dog or a rabbit or a hamster. I liked this cos it meant I got to scare them in the middle of the circle. They would cower and run away. When I was up against one of the boys it would nearly always end up in a fight. Cos they would choose either a lion or a tiger or a bear. Sometimes Michaels would have to run in and break it up. This would lead to great arguments in the classroom.

A snake is stronger than all of them cos one bite on the ankle and it's over, I said.

Eventually everyone agreed and I got to be the king of the jungle.

The next time we did this Adam Wall chose a mongoose.

What the hell is that? most people said.

Adam had this cunning look in his eye.

It's something that kills snakes, he said with certainty.

The arguments started back up.

Nothing can kill a snake, I said. One bite and it's over.

As me and Adam met in the middle we started to fight.

Michaels stepped in. Sorry, Robin, but Adam is right. Mongooses do kill snakes. It's their *thing*.

So because of this I had to let Adam beat me. I had to let the mongoose kill the snake. I had to die in front of the whole class.

St George's Day

DAD told me to ask Michaels what day it was today. So I did. First thing in the morning. Went up to him as we queued in the playground.

What day is it today, Mr Michaels? I said.

He was looking at me strangely

Monday, he said, after a few moments.

I nodded and then went to the back of the queue.

Birds & Bees

MICHAELS took me by the arm and dragged me out of class. For a moment I thought he was going to hit me. His face was pale and his eyes were small dots of hate. He was strong. His grip was strong. Veins crawled down his forearms. My arms were like twigs. Ready to be snapped with a quick twist of Michaels' wrist. It was his quiet that scared me. He was normally loud. Always normally liked to do this in front of the class. More of an audience the better. Volume. A speech. But now there was this serious silence. The claustrophobic two of us.

You're in trouble, Robin.

What?

I saw you.

Saw me what?

Saw what you did.

What I do?

You know what you did.

Eh?

You know what I saw.

What?

Under the table.

No.

I saw what you did under the table.

But—

I saw what you was doing under the table.

No.

This is serious. You're in trouble. This is serious trouble.

If Michaels was doing his best to scare me, he was doing a good job.

This is not good.

No.

This is bad.

We had been walking the whole time. He was dragging. I was being dragged.

She did it too.

I was being dragged in a certain direction. Through the dinner hall. Through the assembly hall. Towards Mr Murdoch's. Towards our headmaster.

She did it too, I said again. I felt the yelp stick in my throat like a dying mouse fighting for air.

Michaels said no more, nothing now.

She was doing it too.

I didn't want to get Kayleigh in trouble yet her in this with me seemed dire. Like an attempt at some half-hearted survival.

Kayleigh … Michaels stopped me from saying any more by yanking my arm through another door. My body followed.

MR MURDOCH.

His name stamped across the door. The seriousness of this sent me blind. I couldn't see. I saw him on the other side of this door. In my mind. Large in his chair, under his desk. His purple face. His bloated toad-like face. His harsh hair. His black side-sweep of hair. Small sharp glasses. Moth-like powdery hands always fingering things. Pulling at things. His tie, his belt. Michaels dropped me in the corridor. Knocked, waited, listened out for a voice. *His* voice. Before hearing it and then stepping inside. Closing it gently behind him. It had all happened so fast. One minute I was happy in class. Happy and free with Kayleigh Highman. Now I was in the grip of a fist. I began to see other things. My mum. My dad. The police. I could just about make out voices. Not words, just mumbles. A cough. Silence. Dusty funeral quiet.

Okay. It was Murdoch's unmistakable voice.

Mumbles from Michaels.

Okay, all right. Murdoch again. Maybe slightly irritated.

Michaels talked. Michaels was always talking.

Okay, all right.

I could almost see Murdoch shoo him away now, out of the door.

Michaels stepped through it. Never spoke to me. Never even looked at me. Just walked right through me as if I wasn't there. I was left alone with my alone. Ticking of the clock and some girl's distant cry melt through the wall. I was standing next to a fire extinguisher and for some reason I wanted to do something with it. Set it off. Cause a distraction. Break this tension.

Murdoch left me hanging. Kept me waiting. A long hour of slow minutes. The frown of the clockface as the hand ticked and tapped. I felt something on my shoulder. Maybe Duplantis. Mr Duplantis to come and get me out of this. Explain my case. Fight my corner. When I looked no one was there. Just my imagination of wishful thinking. I stood. I stood and I stood. My feet were going numb, toes turning blue. Legs like lead. I moved about on the spot. Too bored to cry and really I just wanted this over with.

Come in!

The boom of his voice dropped through into my stomach.

In!

My shaky hand missed the door.

Come. In.

I thought I might piss myself and was amazed that I hadn't. Part of me wanted to. Something to show how scared I was. How small I was. How sorry I was.

Finally my hand found the handle. Cold and long and silver. I pulled at it and it opened up like a mouth.

Inside and shut it, he said.

I stepped inside and shut the door.

Murdoch at his desk. It felt massive him being here. Like meeting a famous person. Normally he was always at the front of assembly. Big and out there. Up there. Being alone with him gave me some undeserved importance. He was chewing something. He spat it out in a bin. The smell of this room was horrible. Too horrible to even try and describe it. At last he lay his eyes on me.

So, he said. What's this?

I said nothing, just put my head down.

A parent I vaguely recognised walked along the path behind him.

Look at me, he said.

I did.

I expected him to be mad like Michaels but he wasn't.

Are you scared?

I couldn't answer.

I could hear his breathing. Through his nose.

I said look at me.

I did.

You've been showing your bits in class.

His tongue slowly moved across his lip. I nodded.

Why are you doing that?

I wanted to mention Highman but it was all a bit too much so I just shrugged.

You know you shouldn't be doing that, don't you?

I nodded.

Do you know what those bits are for?

He leant back and his big belly rode up the desk. His face was blank. I was confused at what he was asking me.

No, I said.

You know what a man and woman do with those bits?

Make babies, I said.

Yes.

He was nodding and smiling. He wasn't shouting like I expected him to. He wasn't losing his temper and shouting like Dad. I began to relax. Real relief.

And do you know how they make babies?

I moved my head. I thought for a few seconds, wondering whether I should say it.

By having sex, I said, at last.

Now he was leaning right back in his chair. He had something in his hand but I couldn't see what. He was looking at me over his glasses.

By having sex, yes, he said slowly.

I felt weight rise up off my shoulders. I wasn't getting told off and this was great. I had been let off. I felt more grown up. Being talked to and listened to.

You know how having sex leads to having babies?

It was here I got stuck. I shook my head.

Murdoch repositioned himself. I noticed a plant behind him on the shelf.

He told me all about it. He used words I'd never heard before. I knew penis but I didn't quite know vagina. He mentioned things like semen and sperm and eggs. He said that girls had cycles and bled from their private parts. After a while I got confused and lost the thread completely. It didn't matter though because I wasn't being told off or shouted at and this was amazing, miraculous. Like I had struck gold. I felt like I had cheated Michaels, got one up on him in some way. I also felt like a new bond with Murdoch. Like I was special in some way.

So there you have it, he said. Now you know the birds and the bees.

I did. I didn't quite know it all fully but I was in on the secret. Knew more than the other kids. Or some of them at least. Suddenly Tess Darby came to mind.

Your dad never told you? he said.

Slowly shook my head.

Before you go, Murdoch said. Stop sloughing, stand straight.

I did.

The penis and vagina that we talked about.

Yes.

What are some of the names they use?

They?

The other children.

I had no fear now. No shouting. So I had no problem in giving him what he wanted.

Like naughty names, you mean?

He breathed again through his nose and nodded. Watched a gulp in his throat like the swallowing of an egg.

Well, I said. For a penis there is willy. Dick. Cock. Knob. Dong. Todger. Balls. Bellend but I don't know if that counts. Erm …

And for the vagina?

A line of sweat appeared under his hairline. The parent from earlier walked back along the path in the opposite direction.

Well, I started. Suddenly my mind went blank but I wanted to know. I wanted to give Murdoch the answers.

There's pussy. Snatch. Minge. Hole. I hit a brick wall. Can I swear?

He silently nodded. A flower outside his window was swaying. Tapping against the glass.

Twat, I said boldly. I think twat is one.

One?

The fagina, I said. With an F. He smiled.

That'll be enough.

Murdoch repositioned himself again. That'll be all, he said. You can go.

That's it?

That's it.

I put my hand on the handle and pulled. I left the room. I felt relief. I felt grown up. Almost smug in the fact that I had been let off.

Punctured

DAD tried to show me how to fix my puncture but ended up throwing the bike against the garage wall instead. Said it was my fault for passing him the wrong tool. Or not being fast enough. I didn't want it fixing anyway. I just wanted to play football.

Manchester United

FOR TWO WEEKS I supported Manchester United. Not sure how this happened. Maybe they had taken over Liverpool at the top of the league for a few days. I loved the shiny in my sticker album. I loved the badge. A devil. A red devil. I desperately wanted the kit and asked Mum if she would take me into town and buy it for me.

I'll have my birthday present early, I told her.

It doesn't quite work like that, Robin, she said.

On Sunday they played Forest. All this time Dad thought I supported Forest but I didn't. I was lying to him. I sat in Dad's bed and said that I was scared that United were going to beat them.

There's probably a lad in Manchester sat with his dad right now, he said. Saying the same thing.

I thought about that. A father and son in Manchester, talking about the game.

We watched the game. On the outside I was pretending to support Forest but on the inside I was United through and through.

We won one-nil.

At school I teased all the kids. All the Forest fans. I was the only United fan in the class and I got to be above them all for a day.

Michaels 1-0 Goode

DESPITE my more than dubious performances in the trials, I was still considered the best boy in the class. Best footballer. I was the only one to make the squad and I still sweated and scored more than everyone at playtime. I was always captain. I always picked the teams. When Michaels announced we were going to be playing football in PE I got really excited. Girls always did their own thing at playtime and lunch but now they had no choice but to watch me. Watch me play. Watch me go. Kayleigh. Kerry. Zoe. Zara. Diane. They were all going to watch me at work.

I wore my Liverpool away grey. *Candy* splashed across the front in red font. Michaels tried to show off but it was truly pathetic. He could sing, dance, act, play the piano. He was good-looking. But the one thing he could not do was play football. Yet he played like he could. His confidence far exceeded his competence. His delusion was dismal. I just hoped that everyone else could see it. He tried to showcase skill but it didn't work out. There was nothing there. He tried to do kick-ups but it was embarrassing, bordering cringe. His arms out like a dumb bird trying to take flight. His leg straight and stiff. His foot limp. The ball went everywhere. Eventually I had to take the ball off him and show him how it was done. I did ten kick-ups easy, without even trying.

I watched his face go pale with the darkening of expression. His blue eyes so sad.

Are we playing a game then, I said brightly.

No.

What?

No game.

He was sulking and striding away from me.

This was the first twist of torment in my chest. No game. Instead he put a line of orange cones out and told us to dribble around them. Lame, I thought. The grass was damp and loose. It was the backend of winter. A dragging, stubborn cold. Most of the kids found it a struggle to be out here. Bouncing on the spot, breathing into the cup of their little red hands. Michaels shouted at everyone. Something had got to him. Someone had fucked him over. I continued to do kick-ups and fancy flicks. In the eyeline of Kayleigh Highman but she was too bothered about trying to stay warm. I moved around her in circles but she was totally oblivious. I moved on to Zara Ellis but she was much the same. The girls didn't care. Michaels blew his whistle.

Right, he said. Form a line. You are each going to run the length of the field with the ball. Turn through the cones, and then stop at the line. I am going to grade you all out of ten for your level of skill. Whoever wins gets ten green spots on the board.

Fuck. I was trapped. I didn't want green spots, I wanted red. I didn't want to be good, I wanted to be bad. Yet at the same time I had to win this. I *was* going to win this. I was clearly the best boy in the class. I quickly calculated and decided that *this* outweighed *that*. Winning this outweighed the spots on the wall. I was just going to have to take a hit. I was way in front on the red spots anyway and I could always make it up through the year. Michaels blew the whistle. I considered my biggest threats. Only really from Kev Moss and Bart Tucker. Kev hadn't played all winter and seemed not to be bothered by football anymore. Nowhere near the skill he had last year. He was dry and rusty. Bart was only really good at headers. I should have this in the bag, I mused.

Most of the girls were crap. They only got graded three or four. Except for Zoe and Diane who both got six. They even beat some of the boys. Most of the boys got sixes. Kev and Bart both got seven. I had strategically placed myself at the back of the line, waiting it out.

Lay of the land. When I stepped forward one of the boys said, here he comes. That filled me with supreme confidence and I was off. I went fast and for a few seconds the ball ran away from me but I soon had it back under my control. In and around the cones effortlessly. Paul Gascoigne. Diego Maradona. Rolling a full 360 turn at the end before heading back home, punctuating the demonstration with another fancy flick.

Eight, Michaels said.

Of course I was pissed off that it wasn't a ten. I mean what else did he want? It was a masterclass. Not even sure Arron Rose or Aiden Beecham could have done any better. But, it put me in the lead and it was a sure win. There was only two more to go. A girl and a fat kid called Charles Crisp.

Crisp was actually not bad. A red-faced Irish lad who had only been in the school a few months. He had a birthmark on his neck that looked like fire. He was very skilful but was too fat and unfit to make any significance in the flow of a full game. He mostly just stood in the centre of the playground and passed to everybody.

He was last to go.

A wash of unease set in as he pulled away from the first cone. He was slow, half my speed, but the ball was stuck to his foot like glue. Everyone watched on. Kind of surprised.

His slowness felt like a cheat and I wanted to point this out. As he headed the other way I noticed just how dry my mouth was. I watched on. The compact flow of his movement. He rolled like a well-oiled machine. He put the ball neatly on the spot and stepped away. His expression neutral, unaware of the feat he had just pulled off.

Nine, Michaels said.

All eyes on me. I pretended not to hear.

Michaels said it again, without ambiguity. Nine. Blowing the whistle. Charles is the winner.

I Ran Into the Toilets and Wouldn't Come Out

BESIDE MYSELF with grief. Disbelief. It was too much to think about, too much to handle. I ran into the toilets and wouldn't come out. Locked the cubicle and lightly drummed my head against the door. Fraught with rage and altogether heartbreak. Several kids came in and tried to get me out. Luckily they were dumb kids who didn't know what was going on. The real reason. I told them something else. An illness or a death in the family.

Eventually Michaels came in and banged on the door.

I'm sick.

What do you mean?

I've been sick.

You were fine a minute ago.

I've been sick everywhere.

Open up, Robin.

I can't.

Open this door, Robin.

I can't.

I want to help you.

His sudden, surprising sympathy stopped my mind from whirring for a minute.

One minute, I said.

I wiped my mouth with the back of my hand. Flushed, opened.

Michaels was in front of me. His hard American hair. His shell suit, half unzipped. I looked at him and he looked at me. He knew exactly what was going on.

What do you want to do? he said.

I can't go back into class. I'll be sick.

What do you want me to do? he said again.

Tell the nurse to ring my mum and come get me.

He wouldn't stop looking at me. I could see the smile strong in his eyes. Even though his mouth was a perfect straight line.

Sick

I DID THIS at least once a month. Something like that. Say I was sick when I wasn't. Why I did this I didn't fully know. It would just happen to me for no reason. Middle of the morning or early afternoon I would go to Michaels, or better still a dinnerlady, say I was really ill and sick and get them to ring my mum. It meant I had to stand around on my own for hours. Just to see my mum. She would have to take two buses from the other side of town, walking through the door all tired and on edge. Part of her knew I was lying. Through the sympathy there was the cold edge of disbelief. I would

85

wrestle with guilt. But not wrestle hard enough because I kept doing it. Earache. Tummyache. Dizzy, sick. Tired. Ill. Sometimes I would forget which type of sick. I would tell the dinnerlady one thing, the nurse another, Mum something else.

You can't keep doing this, Robin. I'm going to lose my job.

I can't help it, Mum. I can't.

Charles Crisp

PEOPLE were starting to say he was the best in the class. I kept arguing with kids.

Charles is the new best.

No he's not.

Yes he is.

He's not even in the squad.

He wasn't at school then.

So?

So he couldn't go to the trials.

Why?

Cos he was at another school, you moron.

I was arguing with about three or four of them.

He wouldn't have got in anyway, I continued.

Yeah he would.

He's more skilful than you, said another.

He's fat and slow.

So he's still more skilful. All you do is kick it ahead and run. You cheat. You fake it.

Yeah, another kid agreed.

Now more kids joined in, flying in at me, one by one.

Charles *is* better. He keeps the ball closer.

It's simple, Robin. He got a nine and you got an eight.

Yeah only cos Michaels hates me.

You're stupid, Robin, teachers can't hate kids.

Heartbreak Kid

MICHAELS always made sure he had the girls around him when he started on me. He made comments about my ears. Said things about my piss. Jokes about bringing in spare trousers and pants. Sometimes he made me read in front of the class.

The one weapon I had up my sleeve was my dad. Michaels was wary of my dad and one word and it would all be over.

One word to my dad and it will all be over, I said to Kayleigh and Zoe.

The three of us were stood on top of the steps, overlooking the moist field.

Yeah but then your dad will go to prison and you will have to go to another school, one of them said.

I put my head down.

I hope he gets cancer and dies, I mumbled.

This took the girls' breath away.

That's evil, said Zoe.

My grandma died of cancer, said Kayleigh.

So did mine, I said.

It's still evil, wishing someone to die.

Why do you hate him so much?

Because he's a show-off who has to be the best at everything.

Kayleigh and Zoe looked at each other and smiled. It's like they knew something I didn't. One thing was becoming clear to me. Girls were way more cleverer than boys.

Diane Dunne

I HAD HEARD somewhere that girls and boys were the same physical strength up to the age of ten or something. And I found this out in the period where I liked Diane Dunne. I didn't like her until Michaels made us do this acting thing in drama. Diane and I had to pretend we were girlfriend and boyfriend and we acted so well that this seemed to catch on in *real life*. I liked her and fancied her and I wanted to ask her out. But I already fancied her best mate Zara and had asked her out only the week before so it felt kind of wrong. After the acting thing Diane kept looking at me through the classroom and I could tell she liked me too. We pushed each other and called each other names. Then one day when we went swimming this got out of hand. Between the school bus and the baths we got into it. I pulled her hair so she pushed me in the chest. I dragged her down a grass bank and she kicked me in the shin.

Next we were rolling around on the pavement. I hit my head on a railing and she bit my hand. Dad drilled it into me to never hit girls but this was different. I fought her full on and a crowd circled us. I pretended it was a muckabout but it wasn't. Diane fought me off. She held her own. I couldn't get top side of her no matter what I did. Her violence was powerful and even though it looked like a draw I came away with far more injuries.

Red Spots on the Wall

ONE GOOD THING came out of losing to Crisp. I didn't have to endure winning ten green spots on the wall. Red is what I wanted and red is what I was getting. Thick and fast. I was way in the lead by now. The baddest boy in the class. I was the worst which meant I was the best, in my eyes. Every day I made sure I achieved a new red spot. They came easy. Backchatting Michaels. Teasing a girl. Not doing my work. Sometimes it would be for something really bad like smashing something or not coming in on time after lunch. Then I'd get three red spots, sometimes even five. I wondered what it would take to get ten. What lengths would be needed. At the end of the year whoever got the most was supposed to be getting a punishment but I didn't care. It was worth it. Every Friday we had a count-up. Girls had more green spots than boys. Liam Bates and Paul Martin had the most green out the boys. They sat there upright and proud like it was a good thing. It made my skin crawl. It made me want to give them a slap. They had no fire. No fight. In *anything*. As for the red spots I had Kev Moss, Bart Tucker and Dwayne Sharpe as company. Us four were nearly on double figures by now but I was still way in the lead. Everyone looked at me like I was an alien from outer space.

Brothers

ME AND SAM went for long bike rides at the weekends. Rode through the country lanes. Through swarms of flies in the sun. I carried his bike over bridleways. I didn't understand it cos I was only horrible to him at home. In front of people. At school. With the kids on the close. On our bike rides I loved him more than ever. We didn't say much, just rode along. I made sure I kept to the right side of him. Away from the road. If a car was going to hit any of us, it would be me.

Proof of Greatness

I HAD TO QUIETEN them once and for all. I had to prove that I was the best boy in the class. Better than Charles Crisp. When I picked teams I made sure he was in the opposing one. Then I would line myself against him on the playground. Once I had the ball I headed in his direction, hoping all the kids would see me. Watch me sweat him clean and take my title back. Best footballer in the class. As I approached him I knocked the ball around him and ran on. He was too fat and slow to catch me and get the ball. For me this was enough. For me this was confirmation. This would cause massive arguments with the other boys.

You're not better than Crisp, Robin, you're just faster.

You hit it around him and run.

That doesn't make you a better footballer, Robin.

He's more skilful than you, simple.

I don't think I'd ever had a conversation with Crisp but I caught him in the cloakroom one afternoon.

All right, Crisp.

Hey, Robin.

Sorry I sweated you at playtime.

Oh. Yeah.

Fast, aren't I?

Very fast.

Thanks, Crisp. Hey you know what, I'd say you're probably the second-best player in our class.

Really, you think?

After me, of course.

Of a sudden I felt like my dad, trying to get a reaction.

Thanks, man, he said.

His eyes were big and black and his smile was wide. His fire-shaped birthmark glowed in the sun. He was nodding his head, satisfied with life.

A False Sun

THERE WAS CONCRETE, from October to April. Wet, muddy, cold concrete. It was horrible, to try and tie sopping wet laces with red freezing fingers. It went on and on. Then there would be one day right at the beginning of April where one teacher would wander out onto the field. A whole schoolful of tiny faces watching on. The teacher would go further and further into the middle, bend and touch the grass, stand back up, feeling for moisture. Nine times out of ten there would be the smallest shake of the head, in which another teacher would blow a whistle and point back to the playground, back at the concrete. A long moan through the children, before quickly accepting the way it was. But once in a lifetime it would be a nod instead of a shake. A Yes instead of a No. And that's when the kids would roar and surge onto the field like *Braveheart*. This joy was unmatched. This collective rush of giddy bliss. So much land and so much grass and so much green and so much blue sky that we wouldn't know what to do with it all. Football, fight, race or roll. We just wouldn't know. Mostly we would wander with the girls, letting them decide. It would all be over too soon. That impossible premature blowing of the whistle. In class we sat happy. New faces shining in the white of the sun. In the sparkle of the classroom. We would all be happy because it was here. Summer. Was here. Only the next day there was grey and rain. It was a false alarm. A false sun. It was just the one day. A one-off. Sometimes another month or more to wait.

American Blood

I WAS FROM AMERICA, I decided. Decided I was going to be American, from here on in. This was it for me. This is the way it was going to be. I was an American kid. I hadn't figured out the details yet, of how I was and why I was here and how this had happened. All I knew is that I was. Making this decision felt right. It felt good. It was the birth of something. A new beginning and a new identity. It was in the blood and would always be in the blood. A lifetime commitment. Maybe the only thing I'd ever truly commit to.

Strike a Pose

I TOOK THIS TO SCHOOL and told people. Easy at first. Lay of the land. Mostly to dumb kids who didn't know or didn't care. Trying it out to see how it felt. A few asked about it and I built my story slowly, bit by bit, brick by brick.

But the real birth of it came in the springtime when we went on a school trip. It was fine Maytime weather. American weather. A coachload of kids. Madonna's 'Vogue' was all over the place. I was about to let everyone in on it only I didn't want to go at it alone so I cornered Kev Moss on the backseat of the bus.

Why don't you say you're from Australia.

What?

Why don't you tell everyone you're from Australia and I'll tell them I'm from America.

But I'm not though.

Yeah but you could say you were.

Why would I do that?

Cos it'd be fun.

Kev Moss looked confused.

You may as well cos you look like you're from Australia anyway.

Do I?

Yeah.

How?

Cos you've got blond hair.

Oh.

Like someone in *Neighbours*.

Oh.

Like that Donovan guy.

Oh yeah.

Shall we then?

What?

Tell 'em all right now. That you're from Australia and I'm from America.

Do you look like you're from America?

Shall we?

What do people from America look like?

Are you in or not?

I'm in.

Cool.

What do you want me to say?

I looked down at all the hyperactive kids bounding up and down the coach.

Nothing. Just let me do the talking.

It Landed Well

WITHIN A WEEK I was full-blown American. American blood. American by blood. It beat around my body and lived in the mind. Kids crowded me in classroom corners while I told them my stories. Because of the 49ers I went with San Francisco as my city of origin. Mum and Dad were still English and I think my brother Sam was still English but due to a brief period that my family was there, I was born in America. I spoke with an obvious English accent but some words still stuck around. *Banana.* I pretended I didn't like this and told the kids not to tease me but secretly I liked it cos it reinforced my position and strengthened my story. My already-popularity went through the roof. To new exciting heights. An extra level. I made sure to keep it from the ears of the older kids or clever kids who might ask too many questions. There was still more detail to figure out. More work to do.

Kev Moss's Australia lasted no longer than the coach ride. By home it was forgotten but he didn't care and neither did *they*.

They only cared about America.

Kevin Arnold

I WATCHED MORE *The Wonder Years*. Kevin Arnold was becoming my number one guy. Even overtaking Marty McFly and Ferris Bueller. Even gave myself the new middle name of Arnold. He was a template to work from. My American blueprint. Now I just needed my own Winnie. My own

Girl

WHO'S IT GONNA BE? I had gone through 'em all that winter and spring. Started with Kayleigh Highman. Then Zara Ellis and Diane Dunne. I loved Highman's personality and charisma. I loved Zara's brown hair and arse. I kept talking about Zara's arse with Kev Moss. I kept pinching it in class. Then there was the whole Diane Dunne thing. I even fancied Kerry Tromans at one point but that was just cos everyone else did but really my heart was never in it. Then I found her at last. She took me by surprise. She came out of the blue. She arrived out of nowhere. In the middle of listening to New Kids on the Block. I was in the lorry with Dad when she popped in my head and then popped my heart. I was going to choose Zoe Maggio. Just like Lauren Makepeace no one really paid her attention and she felt brand new. She felt *all mine*. She really hit me hard on this Friday road trip with Dad. Weather turning warm and blue. Spring into summer. We were now fully on the field *for good*. I listened to 'Hold On' by New Kids and thought about Zoe Maggio. Zoe in America. Zoe in a skyscraper. Zoe in the centre of an athletics track while I ran laps around her. This love-feeling was all around and it was like Lauren Makepeace was here again. Only this time it was dark hair instead of blonde hair.

'U Can't Touch This'

LIVERPOOL WAS WINNING. Our school team was winning. MC Hammer was all over the place. I left Sam alone. America more than ever. I looked at the USA book every day. Houston Spaghetti Junction. I imagined the ghost of JFK in the school toilets. I hadn't pissed myself in ages. Zoe was getting nearer. At night I lay in bed and imagined how I would ask her out. She was tomboyish with dimples. She could kick a ball in a straight line. She was better than the other girls. Her brother didn't cross my mind once. He wasn't around anymore. Doing other stuff with the older kids.

Dad Taking Me to the Fair

WE started walking. Just me and him. He was silent like he always was and I had to read his mood. This small, big man with diesel breath and purple blobs of tattoo on the backs of his hands. A moustache under his long nose. He walked slow. He did everything slow. I was only ever a heartbeat away from being told off, at any given time. Tonight I ran on ahead, showing him my speed but he never said anything. The night was close, a grey warmth falling off the fading day. We wound through the suburban hills, not knowing where we was going. He told me why Nottingham was called Nottingham. He was always telling me about history. Some story about bows and arrows and missing fingers. I had a hard orange ball with me and I kicked it on ahead. Soon there was the noise of the fair and a green light moved across the sky. I hoped he was taking me here but I never said anything. Just stayed by his side and hoped he would lead the way. Eventually I said this in so many words but he pretended to be oblivious. A restrained smile. The lights got brighter and the fairnoise louder. I kept looking at his face, trying to find something there.

Shoes vs Sneakers

I SLOWLY STARTED to incorporate Americanisms within my daily language. Words casually dropped into everyday life. Things were *pretty neat.* Shopping became *groceries. Guys. Vacation.* I didn't overuse or overkill this. Just now and then. Little nudges. Little reminders that there was an American kid in class. I also found another little edge over the people. Some trainers I saw in Jonathan James. They were pure black and looked just like shoes but they weren't shoes. They had grip and speed and plasticity, and a little Velcro at the top so I wouldn't have to fuck about with laces anymore. Teachers and kids were nonethewiser.

More Red Spots on the Wall

I WAS GETTING MORE and more red spots on the wall and this was great. We did a count-up at the end of the week and now I was way in the lead. Uncatchable. Girls were looking at me in this certain way. Michaels was looking at me in a certain way too. Like he had just figured something out.

Girls' Toilets

SOMEONE dared me to go into the girl's toilets so I did. Maybe I was the first boy ever to do this. Once in there it kind of took my breath away. The boys' was dark and dank, cold and haunted. The mirror was cracked and cancerous damp patches covered the ceiling. There were hard balls of toilet paper stuck to the walls that had been there for years. Puddles of piss on the floor and scabs of shit on the toilets. Graffiti scarred into the cubicle. Bins overflowing. Bullying took place in here. If you ever wanted to *get* anyone then this was the place. Trauma lived in the walls.

The girls' was different. It was clean and warm and sweet, bathed in a pinkish glow. Neat soap dispensers hung from the walls. The taps sparkled and the mirrors were spotless. I caught myself in one and didn't like what was looking back. I was dirtying it all somehow by being here. I didn't belong. I was an intruder.

Zoe Maggio & the Bracelet

IT WAS TIME to make my move. I told Highman cos I knew she would spread this shit in minutes and do the work for me. I would never have to lift a finger. Even though her brother didn't like me I didn't care. Zoe started smiling. She hated it and loved it at the same time. Her dimples. Her black hair. Her boyish walk. All of a sudden we were going out. I didn't even have to talk to her. Kayleigh Highman continued to do all the work. Pass letters back and forth. Even Michaels found out and made a big deal about it. We went out all week. It was strange because I talked to Zoe all the time but now we were boyfriend and girlfriend we didn't talk at all. Not one word. We avoided each other at playtime and dinner. As she entered one door I left through another. If we were ever headed in the same direction one of us would freeze and allow the other to about-faceturn. In assembly we glanced at each other but that was it. I needed to do something to make this love real.

So I went into my mum's jewellery box and stole a bracelet. It was thin and small and way at the bottom. I figured it wouldn't be missed. I put it along the tips of my fingers and inspected it like a dead worm, waiting for it to move. I measured it against my own wrist and hoped it would fit Zoe. Part of me felt guilty about stealing off Mum, and of course I was terrified about Dad.

Love has its price, I guess.

I took it to school and handed it straight to Highman. My messenger. My Cupid. The first thing she did was laugh.

This is your mum's, she said.

I was stunned. My face gave away everything.

No it's not.

How the fuck does she know, I thought. All of a sudden I felt naked. Like she could see straight to my brain.

This is your mum's, she said louder.

Kids started to look over. Zoe was right at the back of the class. She turned her face at us.

I tried to take it back but Kayleigh Highman was off, away with the bracelet. Michaels quieted everything and started the lesson.

At playtime I was cornered by a gang of girls. Kayleigh at the centre, facing me. Zoe at the back with her head down.

This is your mum's.

No it's not.

The fastener is loose. It looks old. It was probably your grandma's in eighteen hundred and something.

Most of the girls laughed. Zoe didn't.

Kayleigh Highman stepped forward and handed me the bracelet. I looked at it on her fingertips. Return it to your mum, she said. Find something new.

I went over to Michaels and told him I was sick.

Can my mum come and get me? I said.

Words are Never Really Needed

WITH THAT WE WERE OVER. Zoe never ended it and I never ended it. It just sort of *went away*. I was feeling this with all things. Most of the time we don't even need words. Things began and ended all the time. All we had to do was listen. There was A Force deep inside that said what was what.

Teenage Mutant Ninja Turtles

HIT THE STREETS and everyone went nuts on it. Football all of a sudden got put on hold. I insisted that we had a gang. I was Michelangelo cos I was the funniest. Nile was Raphael cos he was the hardest. Kev Moss was Leonardo cos he liked blue and Paul Martin was Donatello cos he was a pussy who couldn't fight. I always took the gang thing too far. I insisted that everyone stick to their character traits no matter what. I made us do coded handshakes and high-fives. Writing lines for us to say.

Robin, we're bored now. Can we go back to playing football.

Italia '90

IT WAS *Italia '90* and I made sure we were West Germany. I was Lothar Matthaus and because of the blond hair Kev Moss was Jurgen Klinsmann.

You're a fucking traitor, Pep Maggio said.

What?

We're playing them in the semi-final and you're a traitor.

What's all this *we* business. You're a fucking wop.

Fuck you call me.

Pep chased me around in circles. Around tables and chairs. In and out of girls. Out the firedoor. Through the cloakroom. He was too fat and I was too fast. He was just going to have to accept it. Instead he told the teacher and Mrs Carrol took me to Murdoch's office. All that birds and the bees talk had made me uneasy and I was glad another teacher was here this time.

He called Pep a wop, she said.

This made Murdoch immediately smile.

Wop. Where did you learn that word? he said.

Dunno.

You. Don't. Know, Murdoch said. Speak properly.

His forehead was damp and his eyes were dark behind his glasses.

Yes, don't use Americanisms, Carrol added.

I don't know, I said.

You don't know where you heard that word? Murdoch said, licking the dryness from the corners of his mouth.

My dad, probably.

Carrol and Murdoch looked at each other.

Well, don't say it again. Murdoch was still amused. Off you go, he said.

He waved me off and once back in class I went straight up to Pep and apologised. Sorry for calling you a wop.

I wasn't really sorry. I just didn't want him to get me at playtime. The move was purely strategic.

That's all right, Robin, he said. I accept your apology.

Pep always sounded so grown up.

Fall of the Berlin Wall

I ASKED Dad to get me a West Germany shirt but he wouldn't. He said the same things as Pep. *Traitor. Turncoat.*

I'll get you an England shirt.
I don't want an England shirt.
Why?
Because it's boring.
What do you mean boring?
Well, everyone has an England shirt.
Yes cos we're in England. This is England. You're *English*.
Can I have one, *please*.
No.
You drive a Mercedes.
So?
That's a German car.
Mum had told me to say this.
That's different.
Why?
It just is.

One Night in Turin

I WAS West Germany through and through. This caused mass hysteria at school and I was surprised by how much hatred this brought down on me. They kept mentioning the war for some reason. The semi-final was on a Wednesday. It was a summer's day of undecided weather. Dark and light. Rain and sun. Teachers kept us off the grass and we had to play football back on the concrete. I was still Lothar Matthaus although the rest of the kids on my team couldn't bring themselves to play for West Germany. Not today.

In the evening I took to the foot of the telly. Spaghetti bolognaise followed by a bowl of Neapolitan ice cream. Dad sat behind me.

Robin, move your big tabs, he said. I can't see a thing.

It was strange to see Mum nervous over a game of football. As the players came out I got nervous too. Suddenly I felt a sway in my soul. Seeing the England players line up. Gary Lineker.

Paul Gascoigne. Goalkeeper Peter Shilton. Then the Forest players of Des Walker and Stuart Pearce. A strong sense of loyalty and belonging gripped me. I had supported West Germany all summer but now, here, as the National Anthems was sung, I was taken in another direction. I wanted to stick to my guns and support West Germany but I couldn't. There was something deep in the blood. We were playing in our white, them in green. Already the magic of Gazza early on. Then the other Tottenham boy, Waddle, taking a surprising long shot causing their keeper to awkwardly tip it onto his crossbar. The first half was ours. The commentator used words like *style, class*. At half-time Mum made a cup of tea. Sam was nowhere to be seen. Dad stared darkly into the screen. West Germany started to press straight into the second half. *Frenzied*, the commentator said. *Matthaus coming to the boil.* I watched my hero and wanted him to come undone. There was a definite turning in the atmosphere. I had watched my West German boys long enough to know what was coming. A free kick along the edge of the box. A wall of white and the blond man whipped the ball into it. The ball went up and then down again. A weird deflection. Awkward gravity. I watched silently as Mum said, oh no. Goal. It was a goal. They had somehow got one. Shilton whacking the grass in frustration. I felt the television snap. Dad said nothing. England were going for it. An onslaught. They had to throw everything forward. We watched and waited. Sometimes eyes closed, sometimes open. Now was Gazza in small moments of magic. They say he was the best in the world. There has to be *something*, Mum said. Then, Lineker appeared on the turn. Off his thigh and rounded the defenders. Planting it in the goal. It was an impossible sight to see. We were up and cheering. Going mad. So were our neighbours. Bobby Robson looking so moved and relieved in the dugout. It was 1-1 and there was movement and momentum and more. Another heart-stopping moment of Shilton keeping Klinsmann off the line.

Eventually the whistle gets blown to end the ninety.

It starts again.

Going from left to right.

Gazza alive. The commentator saying, he won't be shaken off. Taking on one German and then another. The ball got away from him and he overextended himself. Putting a German on the ground. Gazza's arms went up, immediately owning it. *Sorry. Sorry.* He kept his head down while he helped him up. Hoped if he ignored it it would just go away. It didn't. The ref pulled a yellow and this was it for him. Already on a yellow from a previous game he will miss the final. The camera squared up to him. Face red. Lost his head. Lineker stepped into the frame. Folding his lips inward, eyes enlarged as he spoke to Bobby off-camera, *have a word with him*. For a moment it was as if Paul and Gary were Siamese twins. One head going one way, the other going the other. I tried to feel what was going on here as the game went on. Who had it and where will it go. Waddle hit the post. An inch of woodwork. But then they did too. Hit the post of their own and it was squared again.

Eventually the whistle was blown to end the two hours.

Penalties.

This was my first World Cup. Felt like my last.

Like all time had stopped and there was just this breathing.

All the players were sitting down in the centre circle.

We won the coin toss and I wondered if this was a sign of things to come. I have experienced this before with moments like this. Other things existing behind the scenes. Lineker was always a good sign and a sure bet. He drew his boot and drew first blood. Next was my man, Matthaus. All summer long I had walked in his shoes, his skin. Played as him at playtime and lunch. Now he stepped up and I needed him to miss, to fail. To put the ball in Shilton's hands or over the bar. He didn't. Dead and buried it like the man he is. Next our Beardsley, no problem. Then them they scored. Next our Platt, a rising star goalscorer in this tournament. Then them they scored. I kept watching the telly and wondered how long this can go on for. Something has gotta give.

The commentator: England would feel pretty good about Stuart Pearce coming up in this situation. He's done the job for Nottingham Forest. Can he do it for England?

He didn't. He put it straight at the keeper.

All is silent. Even the telly was silent like the mute button had been hit.

Before I knew it there was another German. Then them they scored.

Suddenly I saw and felt an end in sight. A form taking shape. A completion of some kind.

Waddle stepped up. He was last to go. A little rat of hair at the back of his head.

I didn't like his face the way it looked. All low and dark and heavy. Like he was not in control of himself. Like he didn't want to be there. His body which was normally so fast now seemed so fragile. He put the ball down like it wanted to hurt him. A turn and run-up. He looked about my age. Like nine years old.

I didn't have to look cos I already knew.

Oh no, Mum said.

Bastard, Dad said.

I didn't see it but I saw it. All over now.

Lothar Matthaus

HE should be celebrating but he wasn't. In the heat of adrenalin in that moment he should've been going insane and ecstatic and jumping all over his teammates like everyone else but he didn't. The captain, instead, went over to Waddle and spoke into his ear. Took his arm and then put his own one around him. Comforted him. Took him into his arms while the world went crazy around them. That was the last thing I had of the World Cup. Maybe I didn't know what it fully meant. But that was the last thing I had.

New Order

I WENT to school and the silence continued there and remained all day. I knew not to disturb it. I knew to allow it, respect it. Let the death live. Kids either avoided me like the plague or they stared me out, daring me to say something. I wanted to tell them that I was with them now. That I had changed my mind at kick-off. That I was England through and through.

Instead I stayed out of the way.

Song 'World in Motion' played on, even though it was over.

Green Spots on the Wall

MICHAELS had found me out. Michaels was fucking me over. He had my balls. He had them good and was squeezing the life out of them every class, day by day. He was slowly, skilfully, filling me up with green spots. I went out of my way to get red but he wouldn't budge. I'd get sent out of class. Sent to the wall. All kinds of punishments and chores but never the red. Maybe every once in a while, just to keep up appearances. Bart Tucker and Dwayne Sharpe were catching me up, week by week. I was getting desperate. Michaels had played it perfect and I was so mad I had given myself away. Now he was giving me green spots for next to nothing. Just for things I was supposed to do. Being quiet for five minutes or turning up on time. Each green spot was a blow to the stomach. I would close my eyes and hold my breath. When I opened them he would be looking right at me. That spiteful smile in the shine of his eye.

The Tournament

ALL THE SCHOOLS in the local area, playing for a trophy. A five-a-side tournament. The team was announced in assembly. Goalkeeper, Lloyd Christian. Defender, Oliver Unwin. Midfielders, Arron Rose and Aiden Beecham. Striker, Richard Docherty. Aiden's fame had now risen to stratospheric realms. Not only had this kid two years younger than everyone reached the team but now he was whittled down to the best five. I followed him everywhere. I looked at him as a god. A god in the form of a 4ft gingernut with a bright red face. There was another ginger too. Docherty. A silent kid who floated around the school. He was so heavily freckled that he even had them on his teeth. Arron Rose was captain, a solid fixture who controlled it all. Unwin was a handsome, muscular kid with cool hair. Whenever I talked to girls I always pretended that I looked like him. I had perfected his squint to such a degree that I was shocked to see my own reflection when I looked in the mirror. Shocked and disappointed. Lloyd Christian was a tall blond lad with a big mouth and big hands. He filled up the goal and was completely at home in the net. Like he'd always been there and always would be. He casually kicked the posts and could jump and touch the crossbar with his head.

So that was the famous five.

I was the only one in our class going to watch them. It was at a nearby leisure centre. Again I lied to Mum about playing. Nile Greenaway agreed to go with me. We walked over South View and headed towards the centre.

Where we going? Nile said.

Calling for Aiden on the way.

We headed towards the bungalow where he lived.

Does he know you're calling for him? Nile said.

I shrugged.

Aiden was surprised to see us but didn't seem to mind too much.

There was always a slight competitive friction between Aiden and Nile. They both did judo. They were both dead hard. And in a few years, one of them was going to be The Hardest in The Whole School. Outside of that they got on.

I was surprised by how normal Aiden seemed. Not nervous or anything. Like it was no big deal. Part of me wanted to scream at him, *don't you realise this is the biggest night of your entire life.*

Instead I asked him if I could wear the school football top.

Yeah, if you want, he said.

It was lying folded up on the back of a chair. I couldn't believe it. How shiny and miraculous it looked. Bold blue and bright white stripes. Aiden and Nile talked in the background, 'bout judo. Aiden's dad was wandering around the bungalow, looking at me every once in a while. He had a look on his face that lots of parents had when they saw me, *a certain concern* that they couldn't put their finger on. Before I put the shirt on I went for a piss, prolonging the anticipation. I washed my hands thoroughly before taking it from the back of the chair. I was going to ask if I could wear the shorts and socks too but that might be a bit weird. Instead I went with just the top. I put it on and stood in front of the mirror. It looked brilliant on me. A perfect fit. Although there was something not quite right. Something amiss.

Just then his dad caught me staring hard into his mirror.

He never said anything, just that look again, that *certain concern.*

You ready, Aiden? he shouted through to his son.

I looked at myself one last time, or my reflection at least, and in that moment I realised what that *amiss* feeling was. It was, that, when it really boiled down to it, I just wasn't meant to be a team player.

The Actual Tournament Itself

I COULDN'T BELIEVE how many schools were out. So many teams. Over a hundred kids, easy. The scene was overwhelming and

I couldn't quite take it in. Even though it was summer the games were to be played inside. Two netted goals stood at opposite sides of a giant hall. From nowhere I saw my cousin. Like me he wasn't in the team but he had come along to watch his school. Normally we were friendly and playful but tonight he just stared me out. Behind him some kids wearing a yellow and black kit passed the ball fluently from player to player. I was dead nervous. I felt sick.

We won the first game quite easily, against a red team wearing different-coloured shorts. I expected it to be all Beecham and Rose but the player who really seemed to be making the impact was Docherty. His freckles shone in the artificial light. He played silent and subtle, weightless. He bagged a hat-trick without even trying. Each goal a replica of the one before. A sharp cut inwards from the left, stroking the ball comfortably, slotting it into the bottom corner. Our goalkeeper, Lloyd Christian, shouting all the way through but he never had to lift a finger. I loitered around the edges of the team in the interval, helping them with a few passing drills. Then Nile and I managed to scam some chocolate bars out the vending machine by pretending they had got stuck. We won the second game 2-0, and the third 4-1. Something magic was starting to happen but I couldn't allow myself to believe it. The hall was starting to empty of teams. Kids were crying and falling out with parents and each other. Cars and minibuses were leaving the car park. I was restless. I kept wandering off. Nile was getting impatient with me. Then my cousin decided to speak to me at last.

Congratulations, Robin.

What?

Your boys have just knocked us out.

My mouth went dry and I felt the sudden drum of a heartbeat in my chest.

And how come all your players are ginger? my cousin said, on his way out.

They weren't *all* ginger although it must have felt like that as Beecham and Docherty was taking everyone apart. Girls pointed at Unwin who cleared every ball coming his way. Lloyd screamed on and on, pointed, ordered then saved a great penalty at the end of the quarter- finals. Now it was the semis. Our shirts were saturated. Dark disks of sweat faded into the blue. Faces red and panting. I brought everybody paper cups of tap water. A few parents were trying to give instructions but it meant little. Our five knew what they were doing. They had worked it all out between them. I could feel it.

Nile Greenaway was staring at me.

Jesus, Robin, you're white. I've never seen you so quiet.

We won the semis but only just. Against some big kids. Again Docherty was on the scoresheet, only now he was starting to look tired. Breathing heavily through his freckled teeth.

Then as they went in for the final something bizarre happened. In the briefest of moments all five turned and looked at me. Looked at me to say something or do something. It was freakish. All of them seemed to do it independent of each other, like accidently on purpose. Lloyd. Oliver. Aiden. Arron. And Richard. Looked at me before running onto the pitch for the final time.

After the whistle blew and the game started, I was off.

Robin, where are you going? Nile yelled.

I hit the door and hit the stairs. My legs and arms numb. My bones cold. My eyes were stinging. I walked fast, then slow, a dreamy tread of water. I didn't know what I was doing or where I was going. Only I knew I couldn't watch this. It was like I had stepped through a portal, like being on the inside and the outside at the same time. I took some more stairs and was back on the ground floor where the final was taking place. Echoes through the walls, screams. I then entered a room that ran alongside the main hall. I could hear it all but see nothing. It was some kind of storage room full of balls and bats and baskets and nets and rackets and straps and mats and poles and pads. I collapsed back on a dusty fold-up trampoline and wanted to go to sleep. I was utterly drained yet I hadn't kicked a ball or ran a metre. Played not one minute so why was this so life/death. I tried to look through the beige-bricked wall in my mind's eye and see what was happening. Unwin had been distracted from the pointing girls and had scuffed a kick and then stubbed his toe and limped away and conceded a goal. Lloyd was screaming at him, which took away his concentration and made him concede another. Rose and Beecham got in each other's way. A bump of heads. The other team had been watching the magic of Docherty and now they were wise to him, onto him. They swarmed the shit out of him and flattened him out, deadened him. Squashed the life out of him. Not one shot in the final. The only game goalless from the redheaded superstar. That was it. This was it. We had lost 2-0, I could feel it. My mind was right. My imagination was always right. I could *see things* and that's why they were all looking at me just seconds before kick-off. My head was thick and heart heavy, heavy and breaking, crumbling. On the other side of the wall now an eerie shivering quiet. A holocaust emptiness. I kept staring at the beam of light above, slowly accepting it all. Starting to move now, one leg and then another. At the end of this storage room was a little wooden door. That was sure to lead me back in. As I got there a new wave of noise rose up. My hand on the handle, having no idea what or where I was opening up to. Now a whistle. An ear-splitting final whistle.

Through the crack of the door I saw Richard Docherty running the full length of the hall. Along the outside with the other four members of Orchard Primary chasing him. Nile Greenaway among it too. His face totally mad. The other team had their heads down and now I knew for certain. Knew for real. We had done it.

The Best of American Fiction

HOT DOGS, COLD CATS. After that it was a blur. All I know is that some teachers and some parents had us all at this diner on the way home. Even though covered in sweat the five couldn't bear to part with the blue and white stripes. Probably sleep in them for the next seven nights if they could. I know I would. The trophy sat in the centre of the table. A gold medal around each neck. Docherty had two for winning the golden boot top goalscorer. Our plates were loaded with burgers, fries and shakes. Somehow Nile and I got free food too. We were a part of it. It was ours. Songs played through the jukebox and the night never seemed to end. Like it couldn't get dark no matter what, just this eternal sunset, going on and on and on and on.

Coventry Friday

MOSTLY I went with him in the holidays but sometimes I would have a sick day and go with him in the lorry. Coventry Friday. A dayrun. Dad was better at work than at home. He would only lose his temper a few times instead of many. We would drive. A small yellow lorry with wood on the back. Sometimes I would help him carry the stacks in. Mostly they would end up being too heavy and he would take it off me. Mum would have made us a pack-up and we would park somewhere and eat. Sometimes he'd say the sandwiches were crap and toss them out. We'd laugh and then go and buy some better food. Wherever

I went with Dad I always looked out for floodlights in the sky. We would drive past the Coventry City football ground. Not like ours, which was over the bridge and across the river. Lit up and shining beyond the water. This football ground was cramped up at the end of a street. It was normal-looking and boring. Coventry was bleak and damp and had no old buildings. Dad told me that this was because of the war. Our afternoon went on. Last drop of the day was at the end of this narrow track covered in potholes. He would make me laugh by throwing himself about as we bounced over the bumps. Then on the way home he'd keep making me laugh by shouting at people out of the window or squirting them with a water gun. Coventry was full of brown people and he would shout *why are you wearing your pyjamas. Why are you wearing a tea towel on your head.*

On the way home he told me all of his stories. Stories ablaze with fights and chases.

When I get back, I thought, I'm gonna make some of my own.

Michaels 1-1 Goode

MICHAELS set us some work to do in class. We were to take a piece of paper and then put two options at the top. Like say, red or blue? Or sleep or food? Dogs or cats? Then we had to go around class and tick the box. See what was most popular. I started with football teams. Then moved on to countries. The task seemed pretty pointless but it was way better than maths or spelling.

Right, Michaels said, do one more and then we'll finish for the day.

I looked at Michaels. Sunglasses perched on the hard scrape of his gelled-back hair.

I took the paper and wrote two names at the top: *Michaels, Duplantis.* Before separating them with a pencil line right down the middle. After I stood and slowly and silently moved around the class. I asked away, and the answers came my way. *Duplantis. Duplantis. Duplantis. Duplantis. Duplantis. Duplantis. Duplantis. Duplantis.*

The results were in.

Duplantis 16 – Michaels 2.

And the 2 came from a pair of kids who had started late. They didn't even know who Duplantis properly was.

Who wants to go first?

I didn't put my hand up straight away cos I wanted to style this out. So I went third.

I stood and read out my results.

First question. Nottingham Forest versus Liverpool. Nottingham Forest 11, Liverpool 7.

A cheer went around the class.

Second question, I said. England versus America. England 12, America 6.

Another cheer.

I looked around the class, preparing my third and final. Kids started to put their heads down and squirm in their seats. I looked at Michaels. His white face, mouth slightly open, maybe sensing something.

Last question, I said slowly. Mr Michaels versus Mr Duplantis. I looked up briefly, his face gave way. Michaels 2, Duplantis 16. I said it loud and strong. Silence. Stone cold. I looked at him in his blue eyes. His world crumbling in them. His face losing another shade of colour, his lips too. The apple in his throat rolled upwards. Squashing his windpipe and making his first words squeak.

No people, he said. I said not to use people.

You didn't, sir, Kayleigh Highman said.

Michaels couldn't stop blinking. Staring at the ground, trying to figure this out.

Another boy shouted out. I asked Winston Churchill versus Adolf Hitler, does that count?

Now the whole class was talking and in disarray. Michaels shouted through it.

Go to Murdoch's, Robin.

What?

Go to the headmaster's.

But why, I just—

Fucking go to Murdoch's!!!

The room was stunned. Only the sound of a pencil dropping to the floor. Rolling back and forth in the silence. I walked past Michaels, his head down, hunched over the desk. His muscled forearm gripped to its side.

I waited at Murdoch's even though Murdoch wasn't in today. Friday. The week was almost done and I didn't mind standing there for the last ten minutes. Warm in the afterglow.

Just then Duplantis appeared. In trouble again, Robin?

Something like that.

What this time?

I told him. I drew it out. Allowing the punchline to hang. Duplantis had his small eyes on me the whole time.

So, Duplantis said, looking over his shoulder, starting to walk away. Who won?

Punchline

WHO'D ya think.

Gave him a wink.

Black & White & Red All Over

DAD was reading the paper and he started telling me about the Berlin Wall. He told me about a guy called Hitler and a guy called Stalin. He told me about East and West Germany and how it was now just going to be called Germany. He told me that there were two kinds of people in this world. Ones that take and ones that make. Two men can be given a wheelbarrow and one can do nothing with it and leave it to rust while the other will collect and save and build and sell.

Do you understand? he said.

Yeah, I said. But who will Lothar Matthaus play for now that the West was gone?

The Mystery of Leon Livesey

HE looked like a banana. Long and yellow. He never talked, just laughed. Laughed at everything. If you tried to pick on him, he laughed. If you were nice to him, he laughed. He laughed when his name was called out at register. No one could work out if he was really smart or really stupid. In summer he wore three sweaters and a duffle coat. Winter he wore a vest. He thought this was hilarious. He hung around with everyone and no one. He was a popular loner. One day he took off running and I had never seen anything like it. His long arms and long legs. His blond arrow-shaped head cutting through the wind. He was double my speed and this terrified me. People tried to get him to race but he didn't. Everyone tried to get him a lane on Sports Day but he wouldn't. All he did was laugh. I couldn't help but think that Leon Livesey had the keys to life.

Losing the Battle

THE RESULTS were in. Bart Tucker had 35 red spots. Dwayne Sharpe, 31. Kev Moss, 28. Robin Goode, 27. I finished fourth. Fourth was the worst place to be. Not a gold or a silver or a bronze. Fourth was horrific. I wasn't bad which wasn't good. Not the best or the worst but straight down the middle. Not standing out in any way. I was decidedly average and this was my worst nightmare. On the afternoon this was to be announced I ran to the school nurse.

I'm ill I'm sick I need you to ring Mum to come and get me. Quick.

Nurse took a stern breath and looked over her glasses.

Not this time, Robin, she said. No more.

But I'm ill I'm sick.

She closed the door on me.

I looked back at my classroom and the kids. Michaels standing there, waiting for me.

I put my head down and looked at my sneakers. I was just going to have to face this one, I thought. I was just going to have to suck it up. I was just going to have to sit with all the other kids and be absolutely ordinary.

Mr Michaels

WROTE, directed and starred in the end of year Rock Concert Play. It was about a teacher who came to a new school but struggled to settle in. So he had to win the kids over by music. It was basically about *him* and *this* but with a fictionised, fantasised version of events. An alternate reality. Duplantis and Carrol stood at the back of the hall with their mouths open. Michaels wore a black vest and tight jeans and played the air guitar to the song 'Johnny B. Goode'. Goode was my name and he looked at me every time he sang it. Most of the mums laughed at him but some of them were really into it. Dads were nowhere to be seen. At the very end of the play Michaels fell to his knees and stared up at the light. He was covered in sweat and was out of breath. Kayleigh Highman ran up to him and hugged his bicep.

Those two deserve each other, I thought, turning away.

My America

IT WAS THE LAST school day of the year. It was the last football match of the season. Last day last year, I was a football hero. It is the last day again and I'm not even in the team. Not even a sub. The school we was playing was over the hill. Not far away but it was somewhere I'd never been before. We took a handful of cars. After winning the tournament and most of the games through the springtime the boys seemed kind of tired. I guess it had been a long season. I found a spare football shirt, one of the old versions I had worn in the school photo. It was dark blue as opposed to the light blue of our new kit.

Hey can I wear this? I asked.

No, they said.

As we rode the brow of the hill, the sight of the school took my breath away. About three times the size of our own. It even had an upstairs. In all the schools I had seen this season it was the first one to have a second floor. I can't imagine how cool that must be to go there. The pitch was bright green and inch perfect, flat and even. Unlike most pitches which ran at a slant and was covered with bumps and bald patches. The other school waited for us. The atmosphere swarmed. I looked at the girls. Our team came back to life. After winning the tournament our blue and white stripes was kind of famous. Captain Arron Rose and the ginger pair of Docherty and Beecham. I sat on the bank alone and watched. I felt tired. I may have slept. When I woke the game was deadlocked at 1-1. This went on for ages. Then in the second half they put one in. Some blond kid with a basin haircut. He ran across the line of fans and family, punching the air. I kind of didn't care. Was more taking in the surrounding area. The trees and the high summer hills. The huge greenness. At the bottom entrance there was a willow tree and a gate. I got curious what it looked like on the other side. It was no longer school hours. The teachers and the kids barely knew I was there. I watched Arron Rose hit the crossbar. He was having the game of his life but he just couldn't find the net. The magic of Docherty just didn't come through tonight. Beecham, two years younger than everyone else, scrapped on but we just weren't going to win this one, I could tell.

I moved on down towards the willow tree, through the gate and out onto a shiny tarmac street with no traffic. The final thrill of solitude. Of wandering off without telling anyone. The houses here amazed me, all neat and clean, rounding off in a curve. I walked and walked. Purposefully got lost. This summer Friday evening. The sun blazed and put everything in high definition but a breeze kept it cool. I couldn't believe this place I had stepped into. This place I had found. How did I not know it was here? How could I live here for so long and have no idea. It was all on top of me. A new universe. A frontier to a new world. It was America. It looked like America. These perfect lawns. A sprinkler turned in the green. A shooting fountain of water. I was keenly aware of everything. I was as pin-drop clear as the blue bowl of sky I walked under. Barbeque smell. Sound of a lawnmower melting with the sound of an ice cream van just two streets away. I walked on further. Trees everywhere. A rope swing. Parks and grassy cut-throughs. A stream. Barely any people. This aloneness, this newness. It was all so soothing. More I got lost the better. The disorientation was delicious. Turning every corner was a treat. I imagined the people to have a new accent, maybe even an entirely different language. Men and mothers. Brothers. Girls, girls, girls. Maybe I would meet one at the next corner. A dark girl, a blonde one. Someone to show me the way. Despite this vision the avenues were empty. It had all the dusky mystery to fill my imagination with. It's like I could have walked for hours and never run out of new lands to tread. I could no longer hear the sounds from the school. The football noise had faded away. Leaving this insect hum. A sweet scent of something from the flowerbed. I didn't know the name of the school. I didn't know the name of this new kingdom where I walked. I had stepped through a portal. It was as simple as that. An endless vista, surrounded by the climb of hills, etched with rooftops. Soon it all got bathed in orange sunset. Then pink. By the time I found home I was on the edge of dark. A soft twilight.

Mum was at the door as soon as I walked through it.

Where the hell have you been?

Football, like I told you.

But it's nearly eight o' clock. I've been worried sick.

Sorry, Mum.

Sick to my stomach.

I'm sorry.

Sick to my backteeth.

I said nothing.

Soon she seemed too tired to tell me off anymore.

I was watching football, I said.

In this moment I felt no need to lie about saying I played. I was a watcher, not a player.

From being on her hips, she dropped her hands down her sides.

You could have dropped me a text.

A what?

Something strange came over her face like she didn't know what she'd just said. She stared into space for a few moments, before blinking out of it.

I'm going to my room, I said.

Wash and then get your dinner.

I did. I washed. I ate. Then I went back to my room and lay on top of my bed, by the open window. I was tired but not sleepy. Body heavy, but mind light and alive. I fell into a long evening daydream. My mind seeing pretty pictures. Of scenes, people, places. Girls.

I had found America. Only it was better than America. It was my America.

intermission chapter

Soft Slow Summer Sunday Rain

NO ONE was around. Mum was quiet. Dad was quiet. Sam was nowhere.

I was already far out walking when it started to rain.

An old woman waddled up the long hill as I walked down it.

We met in the middle and took shelter under a tree.

An ice cream van landed on the corner.

Do you want me to buy you an ice cream? she said.

She had a baby voice. And cracks in her face and empty blue eyes.

It's like she was an old woman and my age at the same time.

Her heavy breasts hung around her waist in a pink Minnie Mouse t-shirt.

Nah, I said. It's not the weather.

The ice cream van moved on. The battery was low so the faded chime droned through the high urban area.

Yeah, but it's only a soft rain. She smiled her black teeth at me.

It'll soon pass.

Five

A Smashing Time

IT WAS THE SOUND of it. Smashing glass. Devastating. Like breaking out of this world. Over the summer holidays I found myself a new best friend. Bart Tucker. He had won the red spots on the wall. It was strange him being called Bart because he was just like Bart Simpson. Spiky hair. Always in trouble. He was starting to give me a run for my money. Dares. Pranks. Escalating vandalism. The thing he liked to do the most was smash glass. Smash windows. We started with milk bottles. Steal them from the crates around the back of school and off we went. Popping them against the wall. Then on Black Path. Then on people's driveways. Next we put them on doorhandles and knocked. Hid behind a bush and heard it break, followed by an adult shouting and swearing. The feel it gave me was exhilarating. A thrill, a high. I wanted this feeling more and more so me and Bart started smashing windows. First the garage at the top of my close. My brother Sam watched us. Then a deserted house and an abandoned car and a caravan at the end of a long driveway. Next we wanted a real house with people still living there. We collected bricks and rocks. The fear was real. The enormous explosion of glass made me piss myself as I ran away. Bart was fearless. I tried to keep up with him but it was hard.

As the summer went on we did bigger windows with bigger bricks. Stood by the road and threw rocks at passing cars. Dropping boulders off a bridge. We were only very little so it didn't feel like we could get into any real serious trouble yet what we were doing felt out of proportion. It had something life-and-death about it.

Right at the end of summer Bart and I took Sam on a long walk. Up and down hills, through parkways. We ended up at that school that beat us on the last day. That big school with an upstairs. The grounds were big and set away from the houses. We climbed a fence in the alleyway and we were in. We walked past a painted wall. First thing Bart did was kick over a plantpot. We went about our business. Looking for a rock or large stone. Bart had already found himself on the roof. He used a fence and drainpipe and up he went. I found it a little harder and Sam had to give me a push up. The view was massive. I looked for my house among the distant dots of scenery. We had come a long way. I expected Sam to be some kind of scared but he wasn't. His face was white and blank, like he didn't really know what was going on.

Here, Bart said.

A large clean window in the centre of the roof. We put our mucky hands on it and peered through. A huge hall. Dark and low. I imagined what it must look like on a busy Monday morning. Schooldays now seemed ages away. Like the holidays were going on forever. We knew what to do next. Bart and I stepped back and drew the rocks. A quick catching of the eyes before hurtling them into it. The smash was louder than I could ever anticipate. It shattered around the large silent school. Bart slid down the drainpipe like it was a fireman's pole whereas I had to clumsily shimmy. We were off and running, into a nearby bush. We waited and looked. Amazed no one had come out. Sam was staring at me, maybe some fear now in his eye. Bart wasn't done. He stepped out into the space and found another rock. Stood in front of a new window, at the end of a path. Don't know why but I had a feeling this was the headmaster's office. Something about the way it looked, at the foot of the school. Had something important about it. Regal red curtains draped either side. I took Sam by the wrist and started running. Down towards the football fields. The smashing went on all around us. I was laughing yet petrified. We were way in the open. Across the centre of the grass. I ran slower so as not to leave Sam. At the bottom of the school we clambered over a short wire gate.

Think anyone saw us, I said.

Nah, said Bart.

Which way is home? I said.

I have no idea.

No Air

THE ORANGE FOOTBALL I'd had since forever was deflated and I didn't think to get a new one. With the season over and the World Cup over football went away. I wanted to miss it but I didn't. I didn't wear my Liverpool top, or my Forest. The pain of Italia '90 was completely gone. It didn't mean anything anymore.

The Chase

BART, Kev and I had found a new area. Top of the hill, through the twitchels. A view of the disappearing pit. Black then green then blue. It was a high far-off view. We cut down a long avenue. Every twenty yards there were sets of steps which linked the road to a stony path overhead, across grass. We got Kev Moss to jump these steps, from wall to wall. The further along we got the higher and wider the gaps became. Kev pulled it off each time. It was spectacular. He didn't jump, but floated. The wind carried him. The last one was really hard and Kev had to take a run-up but he still made it. I loved seeing new places. New houses and alleyways. New twists and turns. Hidden worlds. It always did wonders for my imagination. Down at the bottom of the green there was a new park, overlooking a line of flat maisonette roofs. There was a school I hadn't seen before, behind a big black gate. Kev and Bart were already down at the park, climbing and swinging.

C'mon, Robin, what you staring at?

Kids always caught me in daydreams, snapping me out of them. Sometimes I didn't know where I was or where I'd been. Adjusting myself to a new emerging world. We played the park to death. Right to the stretch of late afternoon. A late August orange filling the sky. A new cold in the air. Hint of autumn. And so some big boys blindsided us and entered the park from the left. Sound of the gate, a deep dong of rubber against metal as they let it shut. Startled, we looked up. Straight away I knew there was trouble. Tall thin boys with hard eyes. A blond one and a brown one. One threw a can in the bin and the other put his yellow racer against the bars of the fence. I looked at the racer. Its skeletal frame and the ram-horned handlebars. It looked fast. The boys were staring us out and one mumbled something. I was already off. Like I could sense something Bart and Kev couldn't. At last they joined me at the top of the hill. I felt the thrill of fear. A twist in the guts like I had to do something and *was* about to do something. A moment too tantalising to pass. The two big boys were now glaring at us, daring us.

Your bike is crap! I shouted.

What?

Kev and Bart went white in the face and started running.

And your mum is a slag.

My own words made me laugh. Laughter cut my throat in two. I was scared to death yet hysterical. *Your mum is a slag.* I didn't even know what this fully meant. Just heard Morgan Davenport say it loads at school. I knew it was really bad. Probably the worst thing I could find, in that moment. The boys went nuts. Brown boy ran immediately in my direction, through the gate, attacking the grass bank. Blond went straight for his yellow racer. I didn't quite know why I had done this. Bart and Kev were way in the distance. Two tiny dots of colour, disappearing between patches of green. My whole being was fear. My whole being was survival. Yet all of it amounted to exhilaration. I knew if the boys caught me they were going to kill me. I ran on. The road had no end. The colours of the cars blurred on by. My eyes searched for something. An alleyway or a garden. Anything that would hide me. There was nothing. Somehow, miraculously, I had caught up with Kev and Bart. Both were panting, gasping for air. There were trying to say my name. All the time I had my head pointing forward. Not taking the risk to waste a second by foolishly looking around. But now I did. A quick sideways glance on the road and here was the yellow racer, winking in a ray of light. His blond head down, going for it. Suddenly my head started to fill with things I could say when they caught me. How to talk myself out of this. I ran on and all of a sudden I could feel the atmosphere change around me. It quietened and seemed to free up, empty out. When I stopped and turned I could see that both boys had a hold of Kev and Bart. They were mad. Bart appeared to be crying and Kev was looking at the ground. I crouched and watched on. Hiding lower into the bush. Ducking deeper every time they looked up. Eventually they let them go and I breathed out. My friends heading towards me. It was not over yet as the boys loitered, still on tiptoes, trying to catch a glimpse of me. I stayed squat. Looking over at that great view. Praying it would all go away and set itself straight. Bart and Kev with me now, I carefully stepped out of the bush. Before I could say anything Bart curiously took me by the wrist. His eyes sharpening around his white face.

You're not going anywhere, he said.

Shock took me and the fear returned. I looked over his shoulder to see the big boys gather. I slapped him so hard across the face. Releasing his grip. The chase felt like it was back on although I really didn't know if they were in pursuit or not. Just this continuing dire feeling to get away at all costs.

We ran down the huge steep hill and into the safety of Kev's backyard. Now there was thirst. A thirst I have never felt before and not since. All day we had gone without a drink and with everything in the last twenty minutes my thirst raged. Kev ran in and got three large glasses of lemon dilute. Mostly water but with the tiniest pinch of citrus.

The first contact with the liquid made my face explode. We gasped and glugged, pouring it through our faces. After we lay back on the grass, silent for ages, our chests heaving. Waiting for our breath to come back. After, I looked at Bart and he looked at me. We both had some serious questions to ask of each other. But that could wait, until another day.

There's a Knock at the Door

MUM opened it. She seemed to draw in a breath as she did so. First thing I heard was radio squabble. First thing I saw were two police officers standing there. They seemed massive even though they weren't particularly. Their uniforms made them taller and wider. They were packing – radios, cuffs and other stuff. The man did all the talking. Everything about him was thin. His facial features looked like they had been drawn on. His face was full of lines and squiggles. Nose, eyes, a slash of a mouth. His hair too was black and thin. He looked like a pencil. The woman was blonde and round with a bright red mouth. Her eyes were large and white and round. She looked like a potato.

The policeman was full of lines and the policewoman full of circles. They made me think of noughts & crosses.

Mum was an absolute mess. Like she was about to faint at any minute. She tried to offer them a drink but only half the sentence fell out. She couldn't stop shaking and had lost all coordination and the colour in her face was gone. Potato had to comfort her while Pencil kept his eyes steady on me.

Some property has been damaged at Hope Plains Primary School. Several windows have been smashed and we have been given your name.

They asked me my name. They asked me to say it in full.

Then Potato asked Mum my date of birth. Only she was still too petrified to talk.

December twelfth, I said. I think I was born in nineteen eighty.

You're nine years old? Pencil said.

Yes sir.

Saying *sir* softened him.

You're very young, he said.

I nodded.

Potato was now looking at me, her head to one side. Oh, Robin. You shouldn't be breaking your mum's heart like this.

I was trying to work out how they knew. Bart and I had made a pact to tell nobody.

Who was you with?

Bart Tucker.

They didn't have to write anything down. It's like they already knew.

Anyone else?

I tried my best to not look at Sam.

No, I said.

Why did you do it, Pencil said. Why did you smash all them windows?

How many windows? Mum could eventually speak.

A lot of windows, Pencil said, regrettably.

They beat us at football, I said at last.

They beat you at football? The lines in his face changed shape.

Yeah.

You in the team?

I'm in the squad.

I saw words in his mind, *strange boy.*

Okay, he said. Okay. He went into business mode. There is quite a significant amount of damage here. There will be costs.

Will I go to court? I said.

Pencil looked at me.

Will I go to prison? I pushed on.

He let out a soft, nasal laugh which he had been holding in for the last few minutes. He crouched to my level. Dead in the eye. No, but you will do one day, if you carry on this road.

Lads Being Lads

I NOTICED that Mum and Dad were bothered about different things. Dad would turn the house upside down over a dirty cereal bowl or the toilet not being flushed or a light left on yet the big things he didn't seem to care about. We had to meet Bart's parents about the windows and it seemed to be the same in his house. While both mums sat with faces slicked and streaked with tears and trembling hands the dads didn't care.

I think Bart and Robin need to be apart, the mums said. They're obviously no good for each other.

Whereas the men shrugged and didn't see the fuss.
At the end of the day, they said, it's just lads being lads.

Black Path

WASN'T black. But a bleached grey. It seemed like I was grounded
for the rest of summer. By the time I was back on the streets there was
a new dark and cool in the air. A leaf on the ground. Tess Darby had
scalped her knee at the bottom of Black Path. Only Nile Greenaway
had seen it. He described her knee as a flap. It flapped open, he said.
That made me want to be sick and faint. I looked for Tess's blood at
the bottom of Black Path but couldn't find any.

Black Cat

SHE FOLLOWED ME home one night after dark. This small black
cat. I heard her noise at the intersection of the roads. At first I tried
to shoo her away but she followed so I eventually knelt and stroked
her. She rolled through my arms and her tail went straight up and
pointed at the small moon. We were in the middle of the empty
road. The large trees above made a soft whooshing sound. She was
doing laps around me. Purring as she rubbed against my arm. My
sleeve was covered with her fur, which lit up in the nightlight. I
stood and walked and still she followed. She was following me
home. I walked dead centre of the street. Along the whitelines. She
tightroped them. Her tiny paws moving fast but her body looked
slow. I liked her following me and I wanted to take her home. Make
her a pet. I wondered if Mum and Dad would let me. I'm sure I
heard somewhere that Mum was allergic. Just then I noticed other
creatures of the night. A fat badger scuttling along the fence edge.
A fox stalking the corner. I thought about calling my cat Jessica
and watched her green eyes every now and then. When she stopped
under a car, I waited. When she dipped into a garden for a few
moments, I waited. We were work in progress. I had never had a
pet before. Apart from that spider. But mostly that was imaginary.
Now there was a black cat following me on this warm night. At my
house the cat began to moan again and I figured it was scared and
hungry. So I crept into my house and made up a white bowl of milk.

Because of the white on white I couldn't see how full her bowl was and I spilt some down my arm. She was still there. At the bottom of my steps. I put the bowl down and she immediately began to lick at it with her small pink tongue. While she did I went back in and brought her a banana, cut it up with a spoon and placed the slices next to her. She sniffed at it a little but did not eat. After some time I decided to try and pick her up and take her in my house for a while. Only she got scared and did something with her double-jointed body and escaped. I went to close the door on her but she began to moan again. It's like Jessica wanted me but didn't want me. Instead we just stood and looked at each other. In the dark. Both of us waiting for the other to do something.

Mr Murdoch

HAD US in his office. Bart 'n' me. Somehow he had found out about the police. On the first morning of the first day and here we were. Already before him.

Not a good start is it?

No sir, we both said.

Bet you're wondering how I know this?

He took off his glasses and twirled the tip of them around his grey tongue. His eyes looked weird, crossed and lost and intense.

Well Mr Williams is a good friend of mine, he said. We were at a headmasters' meeting only last week.

It felt like he made that bit up.

And you can imagine my shame when he told me that two of my pupils had smashed *his* window.

We both put our heads down.

Look at me when I'm talking to you.

We did.

He was looking more at Bart than me. Which was a relief.

Now I get it, he said. Young boys. Young bodies. Full of explosive energy. Needing to get it out.

He was staring hard at Bart.

But vandalism is no way to relieve that tension.

Bart and I were both lost as to what he was talking about.

He took off his glasses again and wiped them. Pulled his red tie tight across his flabby chest.

I take it the police were informed? he said.

We both nodded.

You two are quite the pair. Pair of troublemakers. Troubled twins. Now he was smiling.

And, he said, it's a good job you two are not in the same class this year.

This was true. Bart was back with Michaels. I was with Carrol.

This is an out-of-school matter so be lucky I'm not giving you my own form of punishment.

It's like I could smell his hot breath from here.

But, he said, rest assured. I will be watching you both, very, very closely.

He moved his tongue across his lips and smacked down on the table, making us jump.

Dismissed.

Mrs Carrol

LOOKED LIKE A BOY. She was an old lady but wiry and agile. She had short sandy hair and a clean white face. There was something powdery about her hands. Feathery fingers. She didn't have the same whimsical ways of Duplantis and Michaels. She was solid, sound, straight down the line. She made us feel more adult which was good cos I guess we were heading in that direction. The thing about her more than anything was that she hated America and Americanisms. She was always stomping it out. This was going to make my life difficult. Kids were still on it. Considering me as *an American Kid.* It was too late in the day to backtrack. Terrified at being exposed my days took on a new edge of tension and worry. I began to devise backup plans to get me out of it.

Some of the old bunch was back. Nile Greenaway and Tess Darby and Gavin Brown and Morgan Davenport. It was going to be nice to have a break from Kayleigh Highman.

Michaels now was no more than a dirty ghost of the past.

Wishbone

SUNDAY AFTERNOONS, Sunday roasts. Mum and Dad would drink in the kitchen while slowly working on the dinner. Mum would cook it and then Dad would cut up the chicken. I loved the skin. The shiny, crispy golden skin. For me this was better than the actual meat of the chicken. I could eat sheets and sheets of this. All day every day. Then we would give Sam the arse part of the chicken to eat and we'd laugh and he'd have not a clue. Then me and Dad would pull at the wishbone with our little fingers. The wish I made was nearly always to do with a girl. To marry either Amanda Carlton or Zoe Maggio or Kayleigh Highman or Diane Dunne or whoever it was at the time. Or maybe the blonde girl in *Neighbours* who was now in *Round the Twist*. As dinner was nearly ready it would happen. Dad would decide to be *off*. Usually with a comment around the dinner. Overcooked. Undercooked. Too much of something. A quiet would fall over the kitchen. Mum would make it worse by trying to make it better. Some brushing-it-under-the-carpet which would just make the quiet all the more quiet. A timebomb silence. Sam would be paralysed with fear. His hands shaking so bad he couldn't pick anything up.

The dinner would pass this way. One word away from the table going up.

Then from nowhere, Dad would make a small joke somewhere, and everything would be back to normal again. As if nothing had happened.

Swastika

I WAS doing this more and more and it was kind of getting out of control. Someone had crayoned a swastika on the side of our wall. It had been there years now and it was so faded you would barely see it but I knew it was there. Every time I passed it I had to trace it with my fingers otherwise something bad was going to happen. I had to do this three times. Then five times. Now ten. It took so long yet I had to do it otherwise something really bad was going to happen.

What are you doing? Mum said.

I played it down as a joke but this was becoming an excruciating thing. If I was with a friend I had to pretend I had forgotten something and go back. Then I had to start doing it in reverse. Ten one way. Ten the opposite way. Next I had to touch each step on the way up. I didn't know what this was or what it meant but I knew it wasn't normal. The pissing had stopped but now I had *this*.

Vanilla Ice

HIT THE STREETS and was everywhere. Only I took it further by having tramlines in the back of my head, just like him. I managed to get hold of a tape and listened to it constantly. He quickly took over New Kids on the Block. I watched him on *Top of the Pops* and practised his moves. I even told some of the kids in class that I was related to him. A young uncle or an old cousin. I'm seeing him next time we go home. I found out he was from Dallas so I said I was from there.

Thought you said you was from San Francisco?

No Dallas.

Is San Francisco near Dallas?

Kind of, I said.

Hulk Hogan

IT TURNED OUT to be a day we'd always remember. Sam and I rode our bikes for miles. Way longer than Mum and Dad knew. I was nine nearly ten and Sam had turned eight last week. For one month almost exactly, I was only a year older. We were so young and small and so far out on our bikes. Way up into the countryside. Riding the long lanes. Cars whipping past our handlebars and sometimes beeping. We would stop at a field to pet Black Beauty.

This is the actual horse they use on TV, I told him.

Sam just nodded his head and looked at her. I remember thinking how their eyes were the same. Big and black and bottomless. We rode on. A huge loop back to our house. It seemed like we had been gone all day and making it home was something that had been *achieved*. A mission accomplished. Covered in mud. Legs heavy and numb. Dying of thirst and starving too.

Dad's mate Tall Paul was here. A big scary man who was the hardest man in town. He brought us stuff. Taught us to punch. Took the piss out of our hair. Our clothes. The way we talked. But we liked him.

I've brought you a tape, he said.

What is it? we asked.

You'll love it, he said. Next week I'll bring you another.

When he was gone and Mum was upstairs, we put it on. Shoved it into the machine.

Survivor Series 1990, it said.

It was so blurry and jumpy that we could barely make it out. Mostly colour but parts were black and white. It had the first hour missing but that didn't matter because we were hooked. We watched it again that night and again first thing in the morning. Life as we knew it was over. We would never be the same again.

Sam & I

WERE NOT quite the first but there weren't many. A kid in my class and new friend of mine Jack Glass knew all about it. He had a magazine. Most kids didn't know about it and I liked that yet at the same time I was determined to spread the word and get everybody onto it, into it. It was like waves on the beach. They got bigger and bigger.

First-Ever Proper Girlfriend

LEANNE MORTON. Kind of pale and kind of thin and kind of blonde but not proper blonde not golden blonde or white blonde but a sort of dirty blonde. She had a mole on her cheek. She was dead quiet and shy. She was plain and nice and sweet. I didn't fully know how this had happened but now we *were* and of course I was really into it. Really into *her*. She lived not far away. In between my house and Orchard Primary. The real reason it was my First-Ever Proper Girlfriend is because we actually talked and held hands a bit. Within a week I was going to her house. All this felt miraculous. A sudden unfolding adultness. Seeing her open a door and stand on her doorstep. Wearing real clothes in real time. Not the school uniform. Sometimes her mum would answer. A ginger woman with big dark glasses. She didn't shout her daughter but rather quietly go get her.

I'll go get her, she said.

And then she'd appear. A thin view of her through the crack in the door. The more I talked the more she opened up. By the time the autumn dark came in we were sat on the floor talking the world through. I wanted to talk about wrestling but girls don't like that so I talked about other things. Told her how great my dad was. How crazy and fearless he was. I talked about My America and how one day I will live there. Come with me if you want? She'd smile and nod. She was a listener. A great listener. And it was amazing what my mind had to say once I got going. I'd never really had this before and it felt brand new. I was surprised how I could talk about people. How I knew about people. Their characters. I liked talking about all the main players like Greenaway and Davenport and Darby and the Maggios. Moss and Highman. The teachers. Leanne listened. And said very little. As the days went on we moved our conversations *around the back*. Sat at her back door instead. I felt like I had moved up a level. Got closer to her. Letting me in. It was here that I noticed that her house had *a certain smell*. It wasn't a good one and it wasn't a bad one. But it was one I had never smelled before. A tang. Maybe lemon, maybe orange. Yet something else was there, in the air. Wood, maybe. It lived in the walls and was everywhere. I loved it and it was a Leanne smell. It gave our doorstep hours certainty, identity. Like I knew I was here and couldn't wait to smell it again when I was gone.

Shell Suits

HIT THE STREETS and everyone went nuts on them. Everyone had one. They came in all colours. I had black and purple. Sam had orange. Moss had blue. Greenaway green. Gavin Brown red. Morgan Davenport was rich so he had about five different ones. His brothers sold them from the back of a van. Girls wore pink and turquoise. They were crisp and light so you could run really fast in them. Mrs Carrol thought they came from America so she put a ban on them. Duplantis didn't wear one but Michaels did. I asked Mum and Dad to buy me a new one and they said, you always want more, Robin. Never satisfied with what you have.

Terrorising the Old Man Which Led to the Subsequent Fall of My First-Ever Relationship

MORGAN DAVENPORT and I did it all the time. Terrorise the old man who lived next to Black Path. He started it. The old man stole our ball so now we were onto him. He ran out of his house the second we put a foot on his drive. For an old man he was fast. He was thin and wiry. Wore glasses and had white hair around a big shiny bald patch. In the centre of his face was the large red O of his screaming mouth. He was always screaming at us. So we danced around him and taunted him. We did this on the way to school and on the way home. Every day, without fail. It was weird cos it was like the old man was getting something from it. He never called the police. He never called school. Just came tearing out of his house. Mostly he was down to a white vest, even though autumn was creeping to the edges of winter. Waving a red fist on the end of a thin sinewy arm. Morgan and I made it a competition with each other. Who could get the closest to him. Like matadors with a bull. Morgan won this by actually getting close enough to slap him across the head. People watched this and found it funny. Even the girls. Especially the girls. They're mad, they said. I wanted Leanne to see so I got the timing right one Monday morning. Ran up his drive, kicked his garage, and out he came. Fist, vest, and the screaming circle of his red and raging mouth. When I got to school I was met with something I wasn't prepared for.

A girl walking up to me with a mournful look on her face.

I have a message from Leanne, she said.

Oh yeah? I said lightly.

You're packed.

I felt my heart drop through my stomach. The girl wouldn't look at me. I asked her for more but she didn't give any more. Just pointed across the room and I followed the direction of her finger until it terminated at a seated blonde girl. Leanne Morton. Her mouth was a small straight line. Her eyes were sad but at the same time fierce. If I looked really close I could see the smallest shake of her head.

For days I tried to find out what it was. Why it was. Only she would not talk, would not say a word. I racked my brains. Emptied them out. Examined them and put them back again but still nothing. I was slowly going out of my mind. How could we be so good. So close. So many hours and talks and now *this*. A cold, shocking silence. She wouldn't even look at me. It was as if I was invisible or had never existed. The mystery was debilitating. Eventually I found out it was because of the old man. *All this* over *him*. It didn't make sense yet it made perfect sense. This knowledge was somewhat a relief yet it carried with it its own torture. Now I had full-blown regret. Remorse.

I never went near that old man again. His path or his garage door. I don't think I ever saw him again. And not one word had passed between Leanne and myself, since.

The Big American Lie

I HAD A PROBLEM. Mum was throwing me a 10th birthday party at my house. She gave me a number and I had to pick.

You can have ten, she said.

Ten? I said.

Yes, ten.

Ten not counting me?

Yes.

Not counting Sam?

Yes.

Okay.

Why don't you pick five boys and five girls.

Okay.

I picked them pretty quick.

Boys: Greenaway. Moss. Davenport. Brown. And Jack Glass.

Girls: Darby. Highman. Maggio. Tromans. And Amanda Carlton.

The problem wasn't the picking. The problem was what to do with my Big American Lie.

They were bound to ask.

I cornered Mum in the kitchen.

Mum, I need you to do me a favour.

What?

My party.

What about it?

I need you to tell them all that I'm American.

She laughed through her nose. What?

They think I'm American and I need you to say that I am.

Why do they think that?

Cos I told them.

Why did you do that?

It started as a joke and got out of hand.

Well, just tell them that you're not.

I can't.

Why?

It's too far gone.

Mum was putting pots away. She was lining my mugs side by side. San Francisco 49ers next to Dallas Cowboys next to Los Angeles Raiders next to Miami Dolphins.

Robin, no. I'm not saying I'm American.

You don't have to be American. Only *I* have to be American.

She was serious but trying not to laugh at the same time.

No, she said.

But they'll make my life a misery if they find out.

Well, it will teach you not to lie then.

It will spoil *my whole party.*

She reached up and put a casserole dish at the top of the cupboard.

No, she said finally.

My mouth was dry and my palms were sweaty. It was only days away and I wanted to call it off. Fake a sick.

And whatever you do, she said, don't let your dad know. You know how he feels about lying.

I Had to Think of Something Else

SO I DID. I was going to gather them all up. All ten. I was going to come clean. Tell them it was a joke gone wrong. Only thing is I didn't want to lose my American. It's who I was. My identity. Built a whole career on this. I wasn't going to back out now. It's in the blood and would be for the rest of my life.

Instead I took Nile Greenaway to one side.

What's up, Robin?

I need you to do me a favour.

Yeah.

My party on Friday.

Yeah I know. I can't wait. You excited?

I need you to tell them all something. Everyone that's coming.

Yeah, what?

I need you to tell them all not to mention America. To either my mum or dad.

Oh, and why's that?

Well the truth is. The real reason we left America is because my uncle died out there.

Shit, really?

Yeah.

Damn.

My mum's brother.

Oh, man. Sorry to hear that.

He got ate by a shark.

Shit.

I know.

Wow.

So the last thing my mum wants is to be reminded.

Okay. That makes sense.

We never mention America in the house.

I get it.

So if you could just tell them all. Not to mention America, no matter what.

I'll tell 'em.

All of them?

Yes, all of them.

You won't miss any out?

I won't miss any out.

You know who's going?

I know who's going.

All ten?

All ten.

You promise?

I promise.

He was nodding and looking at me.

Nile.

Yeah.

You're my best friend.

And you're mine too, he said.

My 10th Birthday Party

I DIDN'T ENJOY it. Not one minute of it. I couldn't switch off. Every time a kid went near my mum or dad I watched them intensely. Feeling frantic. I watched their mouths. Trying to lip-read from a distance. The end of the party couldn't come soon enough. Whether Nile said anything or not I never knew. If he did then he must have done a good job because the kids acted normal. Natural. Like it had not crossed their minds. Not even once.

Morton & Marsden

LEANNE & Richard. I thought she might be mad at not being invited to my party but she wasn't. She didn't give a shit. She had moved on to other things. She had moved on to Richard Marsden. She was a nobody when I met her. An unpopular, unpretty quiet girl in the corner of the class. Now she was running around town thinking she was the bee's knees. So what if she was going out with Richard Marsden. I didn't care. I didn't care I was just absolutely, totally heartbroken. I wanted to do something but there was nothing to be done. At first I was going to beat him up but I didn't want to get in trouble. Then I was going to get Greenaway to beat him up but he was too nice and adult.

But I like Richard, he said.

Then I was going to get Davenport to beat him up but he would go too over the top and probably kill him. Instead I just let it all happen. Let it wash right through me. It's like I had played into their hands and pushed them together just to see how it would *feel*. And what a weird feeling it was. One I had never experienced before. It was awful and exhilarating at the same time. I didn't want it yet I craved it. Wanted more of it. I wanted to roll around in it. Drown in it. I wondered if there was a name for this. This sensation of *indulging in heartache*. Heartbreak. The torment and suffering and jealousy was an obscure kind of ecstasy. From nowhere I felt to do something. Something I had never done before. A pen and paper and a quiet room. I emptied my mind and let it flow.

Royal Rumble

IT TOOK OFF at the turn of 1991. Rocketing into the stratosphere. We were in it and on it. Kids on the concrete. Rolling around in the wet and mud. Body Slam. Elbow Drop. Supplex. Hulk Hogan and Ultimate Warrior and Macho King and Sgt. Slaughter and Mr Perfect and Texas Tornado and Tito Santana and Jake the Snake and Model Rick Martel and Barbarian and Haku. We were now going full mania on the wrestling. We fought every chance we got. Pile Driver. Powerbomb. DDT. Cobra Clutch. Clothesline. Double Clothesline. Arm Drag. Sleeper Hold. Figure Four Leg Lock. Rolling Wheel Kick. Crescent Kick. Dragon Whip. Whiplash. Suddenly I didn't care about stupid Leanne Morton and Richard Marsden. They could have each other. I had found something else.

Dances With Wolves

IT WAS LONGER and earlier than Coventry Friday. It was also overnight and it was a way bigger truck. I had to get up while it was still dark. I even fell asleep on the way to the yard. Even fell asleep as soon as I hit the lorry. Curled up on the bunk at the back and stayed there until half the day was gone. Until we were almost there at Swansea.

The truckstop was right next to a big retail park. There was an Odeon cinema and Toys "R" Us. I pretended to be oblivious but was dead excited. This excitement grew as we headed in that direction, only for it to drop when we walked right on by it and went to this public bathroom for truckers. *Ablutions*. Dad always called it ablutions.

Let's do our ablutions and then we'll go and get some snap.

We did. Body wash. Face splash. Quick brush of the tegs before making our way to the truck cafe opposite the retail park. We ate. They talked and I listened. I was the only kid in there. All the time I looked on longingly through the big window. The dense February dark. The multicoloured lights of Toys "R" Us beamed through it. I listened to the men talk and swear and perv at the waitress. I listened to them argue about Poll Tax and Maggie Thatcher. Dad defended Maggie against a load of lorry drivers from Sunderland. It got heated but Dad stood his ground. One of the men then changed the subject.

Might go pictures tonight.

What's on?

That one about the Red Indians. That Costner cunt's in it.

What's it called?

Fuck knows.

Dancing With the Wolf, or summat.

Yeah, that's the one.

Dad looked down at me. I was sucking up the last bit of ice cream.

You wanna go or what?

Where?

Pictures.

I nodded. And then went back to the ice cream.

He won't get in, said one of the drivers.

Who won't?

Your lad.

Why?

Too young. It's a mester's film.

He's my lad. I say what he can and can't watch.

One of the blokes had a newspaper open. He turned through the pages.

The men carried on slurping at their tea. One of them cracked a beer.

It's a 12, the man with the paper said.

What is?

Dances With Wolves.

How old's he? another one of them said.

How old are you? Dad said.

Ten, I said.

Right we're going, Dad said.

You won't get in.

To prove a point we headed straight there. Dad had his fists made. He stepped into the huge cinema. There was a list of all the films on the board above. Most of them I couldn't read.

Dances With Wolves, Dad said. It's not on for an hour but we'll get the tickets. Stand tall, he said.

Shall I tiptoe?

No, just stand tall.

I did.

I was expecting the ticket man to ask my age but he didn't. Just gazed over his glasses, knowing full well I wasn't twelve. I barely looked ten. Dad's simmering aggression was enough. The man handed over the tickets. It felt like a massive win. Like something big had bonded us in that moment. With an hour to waste we wandered over towards the lights of Toys "R" Us.

MY MIND had been on wrestling figures the moment I stepped inside. I wandered the aisle with a fake indifference, like I could take this place or leave it. Yet my mind and heartbeat was going 100 mph. Then they appeared. A whole long line of them. Two shelves up. Within touching distance.

Go on then, Dad said with a sigh.

They were all there. Warrior. Macho. Jake. The first thing I did was grab Hogan. But then something about the Million Dollar Man took me too. That crisp black suit with gold trim. His sharp beard. I weighed Hogan and Dollar Man side by side, before looking up at Dad.

Shall I get Sam one too?

Dad looked at me.

It seems only fair, I pushed on.

Always want more, don't you?

For Sam, I yelped.

You're a crafty little bastard.

He was smiling, shaking his head.

We walked away with both.

DANCES WITH WOLVES was long and in parts very boring. I didn't quite know what was going on. Maybe I was too young after all. What I really wanted to do was bust Hogan and Dollar out of the plastic packets and get them to go at it, right there on the cinema chair. *Dances With Wolves* was a fighting story and a love story. A love of fighting and fighting for love. I get why it was a 12 cos there was loads of blood and lots of nakedness. The dark woman who couldn't talk for most of it took her clothes off and this gave me a hot wriggling feeling and I had to readjust my trousers. All through the long film I ate roasted nuts. I didn't even like nuts but I ate them anyway to help pass the time. When it was over I was glad. Seeing the end credits was an overwhelming relief. The night air hit me and cooled my skin. I don't think I'll go cinema for a long time, I thought. Not unless it's a kids' film. Me and Dad walked back to the truck. I had already managed to squeeze the figures out of the packet and I played with them in my pocket. Dad was irritable by now and told me to go straight sleep cos we've got to be up in five hours.

Dad took to the bunk and I slept across the seats. The night got horrible cos from nowhere a queasy sick feeling came. Like I was about to be. It was the taste of those roasted nuts. I was light and dizzy in the head. Shivery, scared. It felt like all the excitement of the cinema and the figures and the ice cream was catching up on me.

Eventually it came. Sick. The nuts were back, through my teeth and out of my mouth, all down my chin and chest and pyjamas. There was loads of it. I had woken Dad up before and he had gone mad so there was no way I was going to do this again. I was just going to have to lay in it until the morning. For the next five hours. I did. I lay and lay and could not sleep. The sicky nuts was cold and the stench was foul. The smell thickened and filled up the tiny cab. The only thing that gave me peace was the song in my head. It was new in the charts and it was the best music sounds I'd ever heard. I didn't know what it was called or who it was by. A dark mysterious song, going on and on.

'Unfinished Sympathy'

IT WAS still in my head when I woke.

Fucking hell, Robin, Dad said. What's that smell?

I thought he might shout but he didn't. We were both quiet the whole time while he cleaned me up. He hated every minute of it and was nearly sick himself.

We pulled out of the truckstop at 5am. Dad was quiet and sad.

When we got on the motorway he finally said something.

I'm not that bad, you know. You could have woke me up.

I didn't say anything.

He was staring at the dark road ahead. There wasn't any other traffic. Just us.

Million Dollar Man

HE BECAME my favourite wrestler. I took the figure to school. I started talking like him and walking like him. I perfected his laugh. I practised his finishing move on Sam and then on the kids at school. The Million Dollar Dream Sleeper Hold. I drew dollar signs all over my books and Mrs Carrol went mad. Stop these Americanisms, she shouted.

Mum, can I take some money to school?

What for?

Some notes?

No you can't. I'm not made of money.

I won't spend it. Just need some notes to take.

No.

Mum, are we rich?

No.

But we have a Mercedes.

Your dad works as a chauffeur.

So will we be rich, one day?

No.

Morgan Davenport was always bringing notes to school. He was richer than me so it made no sense for me to be the Million Dollar Man. I had to pick someone else.

Another Parents' Evening

IT WAS another bad one. Mum was crying. Her head was down. She couldn't stand still.

I'm not going to any more, she said finally.

Fucking lesbian, Dad said.

On Parents' Evenings:

Duplantis was soft. Michaels was a wanker. Carrol was a fucking lesbian.

I knew this word from Davenport. I knew what it meant so I could correct Dad.

No she's married, I said.

Dad kicked off one shoe. And then another.

Still a fucking lesbian, he said.

One More Piss for the Road

IT SEEMED ages since I'd pissed my trousers at school. I had even stopped pissing the bed at night. It was long gone now and I moved about freely. I laughed and I laughed hard without fear. It was nice to not have to hide in the toilets all dinner. Pushing my crotch up at the handryer. Nice to not stink the place out and be sore all day. That horrible rash on the inside of my legs. It was good to be normal. A normal grown-up kid.

But then it happened again. A bolt from the blue without warning. One bright day at the backend of winter. We were around some of the older kids from the year above. In the hallway just after lunch. We were talking about wrestling when the goalkeeper Lloyd Christian said, that Undertaker guy looks like he hasn't slept for a week. Some kids chuckled but overall it wasn't even that funny. A cute, quirky observation, at best. Yet it took my sides apart and bowled me over. Lloyd and the others watched on as I wobbled back and felt it. That tension and then loss of control. Like the harder you fought against it the harder it came. Tall, blond and comical-looking, Lloyd stared at me with an open mouth. Utterly shocked.

Is he actually pissing himself? he said.

He does it all the time, someone said.

Amanda Carlton

SHE HAD ALWAYS BEEN around but our timing was off. She liked me when I didn't like her and then vice versa. She first liked me in the Lauren Makepeace era. Then around the time of Zoe Maggio. Then when they were gone I'd try but it's like she sensed this so she sent me packing.

But now we were going out for a bit. She was thin with big eyes and I couldn't decide if she was blonde or brunette. I even asked her this.

Are you blonde or brunette?

What do you mean?

Is your hair blonde or brunette?

Why?

What do you mean why?

She looked at me like I was dumb.

I need to know, I pushed on.

She whispered to her friend and laughed.

Disco Swim

WAS THE HIGHLIGHT of the week. Friday Night. We all went. Mostly I went with Jack Glass and Kev Moss. There was a massive inflatable dinosaur. It was like a gauntlet and you had to run from one end to the other and all the kids had to queue for it. The lifeguard would watch on. Once a kid dropped off at the finish or fell halfway he would wave another kid on. Of course we made it a wrestling thing. Elbow Drops and Drop Kicks. When we tried to wrestle with each other the lifeguard would blow his whistle and give us our final warning.

Music played over the pool and there were also other inflatables and mats to surf on. I was still going out with Amanda Carlton but barely. I wasn't all that bothered about her yet at the same time being packed was frightening. More music played. Roxanne's 'It Must Have Been Love'. Amanda kept looking at me over the pool. Crazy kid-screams echoed through the high ceiling and bounced off the walls. Light was everywhere. The big clockface was going way too fast. The night was disappearing.

Hey, Kev, I shouted over to Moss.

Yeah?

Go over to Amanda and tell her that this song reminds me of us.

This song? he said.

Yeah.

Okay, he said.

Moss did one of his epic jumps, clearing a small boat of people. Swam up to Carlton. Roxanne sang on. At the other end of the pool he leant over and spoke into her ear. This broke Amanda up. But not in the way I wanted. She said something into his ear. Moss did the same journey in reverse. Jumped and swam. Up from under the water.

So what's she say?

Moss wiped his face. Said you're pathetic.

Morgan Davenport's Older Brother

THE ONE WHO WASN'T IN PRISON. He was giving us a lift in his car to Disco Swim. He was covered in spots and had a little rat-face. Sticky-out teeth and a nasty scowl. He was like Morgan in that he could be your best friend or your worst enemy. You never knew where you stood. Tonight it seemed like the former. He bought us sweets on the way and made us laugh. Tonight it was me, Morgan and Bart Tucker. He had the windows down and music on. He was telling us about fighting and telling us about girls. All the lads he had beat up and all the girls he had sex with. He wasn't good-looking but he was hard and super-confident so I believed him about the girls. I had even seen him with some. A blonde one and a brunette one.

Both of them very pretty. The oldest brother in prison was a mythical figure. No one had ever seen him but everyone had heard of him. He was a bank robber. Apparently he had broken the World Record for being out and then back in prison in the shortest period of time. He had a party when he came out and then robbed a shop on the way home. Morgan's other brother was telling us all about it as he drove us to Disco Swim. Me and Bart listened on while Morgan stared out of the window. I guess he had heard it all before. His brother drove fast. Took bends. Jumped dips. He told us he would beat anyone up who messed with us at Disco Swim. He made us laugh and told us more stories about girls. He called them *crumpet*.

Go get some crumpet, he said.

We pulled up at the leisure centre and went to get out. We were all still laughing. Just before Bart shut his door he said, I'm off to Disco Swim to get some crumpet.

It was here Morgan's older brother switched.

What did you just fucking say?

At first we thought he was still joking so we carried on laughing.

Do I look like I'm fucking laughing?

His face was rabid. Bart's turned white and his mouth didn't know what to do with itself.

I looked at Morgan for an answer but he just put his head down so I did the same.

Get in this fucking car, his brother said. All of you. Get back in the fucking car.

We did. Part of me still thought he was joking. That he would break the spell any moment, laugh and let us free. He didn't. He started the car back up and started driving again. The same route, in reverse.

Do I look like a cunt?

His nasty eyes were narrow in the rearview.

Think you can use language like that in front of me. I'm the fucking adult. I'm the fucking adult.

Bart was white with fear. My mind was trying to work out what was going on. The sense of it. His brother turned the music down and continued to scream and threaten Bart all the way home. It felt deranged, and kind of evil. He asked Bart questions he could never answer.

Think cos I can use words like that you can, in my own car? Do you know what respect is?

Bart stuttered and stammered through all of it. No answer was the right one. Eventually he started to cry.

What you crying for? You calling me a bully or something?

He skidded up to Bart's front door and blasted the horn three times.

I want you to tell your dad why I've brought you home. And if he has a problem tell him to come and knock on my door. And I'll tell him what a little bastard you are. Now FUCK OFF out my car. I can't stand the sight of you.

Bart's hands were shaking. His shoulders were small and his walk was fast yet fragile. He struggled to open his front door. Once he was gone the music was turned back up and he went on as if nothing happened. Talking and laughing away. Morgan was still gazing out of the window. His handsome, defined face. That sharp jaw. He hadn't flinched through any of it. Like he had seen it a thousand times. When we got to the leisure centre his brother called my name.

Hey, Robin.

I took off my seatbelt.

I like you, he said.

He was looking at me over the front seat. I looked at him. Looked right into his smiling eye. When I concentrated on that eye and concentrated on everything *inside* me I knew I wasn't afraid of him. Not when I really got down to it. To the very bottom of it. I knew, in this life, with people like this, I couldn't afford to be.

Wrestlemania 7

FROM THE END OF WINTER to the beginning of spring I changed my favourite wrestler on a week-by-week basis. When Jake the Snake was my favourite I pestered my mum to take me to the pet shop.

You're not having a snake.

But why?

She was laughing at the ridiculousness of this.

Mum, PLEASE.

No.

But we never have pets.

You're not having a snake.

It'll be in a tank.

You can have one when you get your own house.

But that's AGES away. It won't even make sense then.

What won't make sense?

I sulked and moped and then changed my favourite wrestler to the Texas Tornado. I decided I was going to start growing my hair and telling everyone I was from Texas. I started walking around school with a limp.

Mum, how long does it take for your hair to grow?

What do you mean?

For me to have long hair?

How long?

I don't know, down my back, past my shoulders.

You'll look like a girl.

How long?

Dad won't stand for it.

How long?

Oh, ages.

Weeks?

Months.

I couldn't wait that long so I changed to the Big Boss Man.

Sam, where are those toy handcuffs you had?

He didn't know what I was talking about so I tipped our bedroom upside down. I looked for them frantically. Only I couldn't find them so I changed to Hacksaw Jim Duggan.

Dad, you work at a timberyard, right?

Yeah.

Can you get me a piece of wood?

What for?

I didn't want to tell him it was because of wrestling so I made something up.

I'll see, he said.

When can you get it?

I said I'll fucking see.

That took too long so I switched to the Model Rick Martel.

Mum, can I borrow some of your perfume?

What?

She looked at me really concerned.

Why?

I want to take it to school.

Robin, have you got another girlfriend?

No.

145

My bracelet is still missing and I want it back.

Can I borrow some or not?

No.

At school everyone agreed that Morgan had to be the Model cos he was the best-looking so I decided to be Earthquake.

Mum, if I eat biscuits every day how long will it take to get fat?

At school everyone decided that Phil Walton had to be Earthquake cos he was the fattest so I changed to the Undertaker. I walked around tall and stiff and tried to creep out the younger kids who ran away from me and this gave me a tremendous sense of power. I kept rolling my eyes into the top of my head. I did this all day every day and in the end I got the most chronic headaches so I had to stop and find somebody else. By this time the kids had had enough of me.

Just pick someone and stick with them, they said.

I wanted to be the Ultimate Warrior but somebody else was him. I wanted to be Rowdy Roddy Piper but somebody else was him. Then I went back to the beginning and went with the Million Dollar Man but again someone else had taken that spot. I had ran out of wrestlers to be. I sat in the centre of the playground and wanted to cry. I simply didn't know who I was.

Exile

IT WAS ANOTHER silent Sunday. It had been going well right up until the chicken being cut up. Now it was silent. Sam was shaking. I sat at the dinner table, facing the window. Watching the clothesline wobble in the wind. Can't be long until summer now, I thought. Spring at least. Can't be long until grass at school. Wrestling will really take off then. Imagine all the moves we'll be able to do.

What's up, Robin?

Dad broke the silence.

Mum looked up. Sam looked down.

Nowt, I said.

Must be thinking about something.

Dad was picking chicken from his teeth. His plate almost empty. Mine was half full.

He was glaring at me to say something so I took a breath and went for it.

Just, can't wait for there to be grass at school so we can wrestle.

Dad put the knife down across his plate.

Is that all you think about, fucking wrestling?

It never took long. Rage pushed against his words. One false move and he'll be over the edge.

I remember when it was football, he said. There wasn't a thing you didn't know. Now all this wrestling bollocks. Don't you like anything else?

Yeah, I muttered.

Dad put his hands out. What?

My mind went scratching around for something.

American Football, I said, at last.

Why don't you go and FUCK OFF to America then.

A nastiness twisted through the expression on his face. I put my eyes back on the clothesline outside. It had stopped wobbling.

Six-Man Tag

AT LAST, we were on the field so the wrestling could really take off. We could do proper moves. In class we decided upon a six-man tag team match. We squabbled and went back and forth on the teams. It drummed up attention and a lot of people were going to be watching this. Even some girls. I had somehow hustled the best possible deal. For me. I was teamed up with Nile Greenaway and Morgan Davenport. The two hardest in the class. Number one and two. We were to face Gavin Brown, Jack Glass and Kev Moss.

The match was to take place in the centre circle of the football pitch, using that as the ring.

We squared off. Most of the class watched on. Some girls were there but they wasn't really interested. Nile and I decided to be the Hart Foundation. I was Bret Hitman, Nile the Anvil. Morgan was going to be the Ultimate Warrior. On the opposing team Gavin Brown was Macho King and Jack Glass was British Bulldog and because of his jumping skills Kev Moss was going to be Superfly Jimmy Snuka.

Some pussy-square kid was going to be referee.

Straight away I pinned Gavin Brown. He was light and tricky but somehow I had managed to hook his legs away for the three-count. I was definitely the weakest in the team so getting this early hit meant

I could relax a bit. Earned my stripes. Now I could stay out of the way and let Greenaway and Davenport do the work. They double-clotheslined Jack Glass across the neck and made his glasses fall off. Before pinning him with no effort at all. He whimpered off, crying a bit. The match was almost over and we had not been fighting for no longer than five minutes.

We three circled Kev Moss. Because of his jumping skills he was hard to catch. But we had ages yet so it was only a matter of time. Nile grabbed him first. Took his arm and swung him to the floor. After that me and Morgan piled in. Knees and kicks. The crowd grimaced. Yet Moss somehow wriggled free and the chase was on again. It reminded me of the elimination game we played in PE. No one could ever catch Kev Moss. I tripped him at last and Morgan twisted his neck into a headlock. Nile threw a punch to his stomach and he groaned.

Whatever you do, I said, don't let him go.

We didn't. Morgan had his head. Nile his legs. Me his arms. We tried to flip him. Only he rolled over twice, so we couldn't get him on his back. Nile then dropped an elbow into the square of his back and I did the same. He was squirming and writhing. Morgan kicked at his legs and then I tried to roll him into a Boston Crab. Time was going and we still couldn't get the pin. Faces of Morgan and Nile was fraught with frustration. The three of us then rained on him proper. Kicks, punches, elbow and knee drops. Kev's skin beamed. He was crying and raging against it. From under the tangle of bodies I saw blood.

Just give up, I screamed.

Give it up, Kev, Nile said diplomatically.

Morgan said nothing. Just bit his tongue, jawline defined as he snarled.

Stop! one of the girls shouted. When I looked up our whole class was watching. Concerned, some scared. A few turned away.

You need to give up, Kev, so this can stop, I said.

Something was in Kev's eyes. Something had taken over.

Okay, Nile said finally. He nodded at Morgan and I and we went back to the elbows along his back. Deep, reverberating thuds. I kicked him full in the ribs. Nile now had his neck, bending him back. Say submit, he said.

We had him on his back.

The referee dived down for the three-count but only got two. It seemed like we had been at this ages. Kev was truly battered.

His face and neck covered in marks. His blond hair all over the place. His schoolclothes wrecked and torn. He had lost a shoe. From nowhere the whistle was blown. It pierced the air and sailed through the field. Dinnerladies stepping on the grass, waving everyone off.

The frustration of me, Nile and Morgan starting to leave, respect replacing it. We picked Kev up and patted him down. I stroked his hair and looked into his tear-soaked eyes. He was utterly lost. We walked him across the field. Gave him a drink. Slowly Kev came back into his eyes. There was light, and blue-clarity. The three of us took turns in looking at him and he looked at us. We nodded at him silently. And he knew what we meant.

Mrs Carrol

SHE LINED us up in class with her eyes. It was dead serious. Kev's chair was empty and I wondered if he had died in his sleep. Heard this all the time. A bump on the head and then to never wake up. She got Nile, Morgan and myself at the front of the class.

I've had enough of America, she said.

At first I didn't know what she meant. Maybe talking about that thing that was happening in Iraq.

The way you all talk, she said. It gets everywhere and now this stupid wrestling. *American* wrestling.

Her purple eyes stared us down. Carrol was normally pretty cool but she was dead serious in this moment.

Pretty cool, she said. I've told you, Robin, enough Americanisms.

I put my head down and my hands deep in my pockets.

I still needed to know about Kev, was he dead.

Kev's mum rang school today. He's covered in bruises. Black and blue.

He's not dead.

So much she's keeping him off school.

It must be bad, I thought. Kev's mum was tough. A battleaxe. She was about hundred years old. She wouldn't keep him off for nothing.

Carrol walked the room. She wore an open shell suit. Underneath a light green t-shirt.

As from today I am putting a ban on this wrestling. It can stay in America where it belongs. A long groan moved through

149

the class. Gavin Brown dropped his head. Tess Darby decided to speak up.

I saw what they did to Kev yesterday, she said. It was pretty gross.

Tess, Carrol said. Pointing an ugly finger at her. *Gross* is an Americanism.

Thought it was German, miss.

Carrol made a face, which said *don't be clever.*

A ban! Carrol went on. Any wrestling, fighting, *anywhere* on school grounds and there will be detention.

Detention was what happened at Big School. Hearing it here sounded serious and scary.

No. Wrestling, she said once more, making her position clear.

Love Bites

KEV returned the following day as a hero. We crowded him in class and he showed us his back. It was awful. He looked like a leopard. They were so vivid you could see which ones came from knees and which came from elbows. They were even patterned from the shirt he was wearing. Little white circles inside the black ones. He looked like he had some medieval disease. There were other colours on his back too. Yellow, green, purple.

They look like love bites, Tess Darby said.

She was walking by the boys. Not stopping to take any further interest.

None of us knew what love bites were but we wanted to know more. I wanted to know more. I caught eye contact as Tess walked on by and she held it. Held it until I looked away first.

Doomsday Device

WAS THE MOST DANGEROUS move in all of wrestling. So much so that no one would dare try it at school (before the ban). It was the finishing move of the tag team Legion of Doom. This involved one wrestler taking the opponent into a shoulder ride. Way up high. Then his teammate would climb onto the top rope and then clothesline him off.

Jack Glass was unsure about this. Sam sat in between us.

I don't know, Robin. We might kill him.

Jack Glass was my new best friend. He was the only one who knew just as much as me about wrestling. We three was at his house. He lived over the hill in the rough part. Behind the back of his house was a patch of wasteland. There was a tall black gate we were going to use as wrestling ropes. Jack was going to shoulder ride Sam and then I was going to jump off this gate/these ropes and clothesline Sam's neck.

He might break his neck, Jack said.

Nah.

What will your mum say?

Sam was sat on the grass. His white face looking up at us.

I don't wanna get done for murder, Jack said.

You won't get done for murder, I will.

How's that?

Well *I'm* clotheslining him, aren't I?

Yeah but I'm helping you, aren't I?

Sam was taking it in turns to look at us. Like he was watching tennis.

You'll be fine, I said.

I saw in on *Cops*.

Even though Jack was poorer than us he had SKY TV.

Saw what on *Cops*?

The person helping with the murder can go prison.

We're not murdering him. We're just going to do the Doomsday Device.

Jack looked doubtful. Sam's face was blank.

Anyway *Cops* is set in America and the law is different there.

How do you know?

Cos I'm American, aren't I?

Oh. Yeah.

Anyway it wouldn't be murder cos it would be an accident.

Eh?

It would be manslaughter.

I don't want Sam to die, Jack said, wiping his glasses.

Stop being a pussy and come on.

Okay.

All right?

Suppose.

Jack pulled up a patch of grass and then spat.

Sam, I said, clicking my fingers. C'mon.

Sam nodded and then stood up.

Jack got behind him and put his head between his legs. Put his hands on his own knees and then lifted Sam up into the grey-blue sky. A blackbird flew overhead. We could hear the echoes of kids shouting in the hall of the leisure centre below. Sam was up high. Jack walked around with him, nearing the gate. I climbed on up it, planting my feet between the bars.

Ready?

Ready.

Sam?

He nodded.

Come closer, I said.

Jack took two steps nearer.

I crouched and prepared the jump. My arm ready.

Just then Jack stepped back and lowered Sam back onto the grass.

I can't, he said.

Why?

I was so pissed off and frustrated.

It's too high, Robin. It's too dangerous. You might kill your brother. Or put him in a wheelchair at least. Your *own* brother.

I shook my head and sighed. Sat back down.

Now what we gonna do? I said.

Apple Tree

DAD was picking his teeth again after dinner. It had been another quiet one. Mum brought us apple pie and custard and put it down before us. We picked up our spoons and went to work. Plunging the silver into the steam.

In the football team this year, Robin?

Yeah, I lied.

Haven't heard you mention any games.

I shrugged.

Dad ate on. I watched his mind move. Searching for something.

Even though I never played, I reckon I'd be better than you, he said.

Nah, I said.

What do you mean *no*?

I'm too skilful. And too fast.

Not faster than me. I was cross-country champion.

I didn't know what cross-country meant. Never heard of it.

And rugby, he said. I'd definitely beat you at rugby.

Oh.

You've got to be good at fighting to play rugby and I'd beat you in a fight, easy.

Yeah you would, I agreed.

Football. Rugby. Running. And fighting. The only thing you would beat me at is swimming, he said. You're a good swimmer.

I wasn't. Not really.

But everything else, Robin, I'm better.

Denial of Nile

PAUL MARTIN loved wrestling and knew loads about wrestling and had all the figures. However he didn't wrestle cos he was a pussy so instead he was a manager. He was the manager of me for a bit. Then Morgan Davenport. Then Kev Moss. Now he was the manager of Nile Greenaway. We sat on the main table doing our work. It was a dark but warm rainy day in May. Mrs Carrol slowly walked the room while the kids had their heads down and worked. Carrol had a good balance. Our classes were never wild, but never too strict either. Occasionally she'd rant on about America but overall it was generally fine. After our tasks were complete we started to talk again. Talk about wrestling.

Why are you WWF champ anyway? Paul Martin said.

I've always been champ, I said.

Phil Walton and Morgan Davenport were listening in.

Yes, but *why*?

Paul Martin was a delicate, smart-talking little prick. He had clean blond hair and a raised eyebrow. I couldn't really answer him so I ignored him and started to talk to Morgan.

As Nile Greenaway's manager, he said, I'm setting a match between you and Nile for the WWF belt.

Nice try, Martin, I said. But wrestling is banned.

Paul Martin sniggered. Since when did you care about the rules?

I said something else and tried to die out the conversation but Paul Martin was like a dog with a bone. Nile is stronger than you, he said.

There was no point trying to deny this so I had to find something else.

Yeah, but I'm more technical.

Paul placed his ruler across the table and raised an eyebrow. Power versus skill, he said. It will be the perfect match. It is set. This dinner. Behind the top bank so the teachers can't see.

More kids were listening in now. Carrol was still moving silently through the tables.

I wanted to rip the little prick's head off.

You've had the title long enough, Robin, and you haven't even earned it.

Like you get a say, I bit. You're just a little pussy who watches from the sidelines.

I'm a manager, he said.

Yes cos you can't fight.

Maybe so.

Him owning this stripped away my power in a second.

I'm a manager, Nile's manager, and I say he is the best wrestler in the class and deserves the belt. Or an opportunity to fight for it at least.

He talked like an adult. A teacher. He was a pussy who couldn't fight or wrestle but that wasn't what he was made to do. He was made to do this. Take me apart with his words.

By playtime he had Nile by his side and a small crowd. Even some girls. Nile was smiling and friendly. He was a good friend of mine. But he wanted what was rightfully his.

I just want what is rightfully mine, Robin, he said. I just want a shot.

I'm the champ, I'm the best, I said.

I'm stronger, Nile said.

I'm more technical, I said.

What does that even mean? someone shouted in.

Look if we was in a proper ring, I'd win. I know how to use the space. I know how to take advantage of the ropes. There's a boxing club I know. They might let us use it.

It?

The ring.

All right then, Nile said quickly.

He's full of bullshit, Paul Martin said. He's just buying time.

I'm WWF champ, I said clearly. It's just the way it is.

I don't know why you always have to be the best at everything, someone else said. Nile is top dog. Just accept it.

I'm technical, I said.

Just then Nile grabbed me and slammed me into the blackboard. His strength was unreal. I could feel my face go red, then white. I tried to armlock him but it was like trying to move a tree.

Enough! Carrol said.

Kids scattered like cockroaches.

She got me and Nile under her purple eyes. What have I told you about wrestling. AMERICAN wrestling, she said. No more. It's banned. Any more and I'll be contacting your mothers.

After Nile held out his hand. No hard feelings hey, Robin. I just had to let you know. Let them all know.

It didn't count, I said. I wasn't ready and it wasn't a proper match and it wasn't in a proper ring and it wasn't official.

Paul Martin, his manager, suddenly appeared on his shoulder.

Let it go, Robin, he said. Just, let it go.

Suddenly he held up an imaginary WWF belt. Paul Martin then switched from manager to ring announcer, his voice deep and musical and uncannily American.

And here is your winner … AN NEW WWF champion of the world … the … Ultimate Warrior … Nile Greenaway.

Mr Hide

I WENT INTO HIDING. I made sure no one talked about wrestling. I reinforced the rules. I promoted the ban. I talked about the dangers of wrestling. I reminded everybody of Kev Moss's bruised back. His leopardskin skin. I brought football back. I set up games although wrestling was in the blood and football just wasn't a thing anymore. Kids wandered aimlessly around the schoolfield. Carrol had instructed the dinnerladies so whenever anyone so much as made a grab at each other a whistle was blown and there she was at the window. Mrs Carrol and her sandwich and her shell suit and her starey purple eyes.

We had to find something else so I put forward hide-and-seek.

We're not kids, Robin.

Yeah we're not six-year-olds.

Get a grip, Robin.

So I rebranded hide-and-seek as *Commando*.

Cool.

Wicked.

Good idea, Robin.

I spilt us up into two teams. One to hide and one to seek.

When it was my turn to hide I did what everybody did. Take to the trees that ran along the playground. I climbed up the tallest and within two minutes I was found. But as I worked my way down I noticed something. The smallest gap in a wire fence, leading to one of the gardens. I noted this for tomorrow.

When tomorrow came I was through it. Into the private property of a secluded garden. It was weird and scary. One minute at school, now in another world. A quiet, overgrown garden. I stared at the backdoor and expected an adult to come tearing out at any minute. I prepared something in my head for such an event, *just looking for my ball, sir.* But no one came. The flaky door stayed where it was. Peelings of paint on the ground. I wondered if anyone lived there. There were no signs that anyone did. The garden overgrown. The windows thick with grime. I put my hands up to the glass and made a tunnel with my hands. Inside it was as barren as the moon. Apocalyptic. Darkly soothing. The kids screamed on. Searched on. Only I was nowhere to be found.

Of a sudden I was the champion again. The best again.

The champion of Commando. The best in the class.

No one cared about wrestling anymore. It was banned and off the table.

People got obsessed in trying to find me.

Find Mr Hide.

By now I was so familiar with the house that I climbed upon its roof.

High on its roof I looked on down. Down at the playground, the field, the kids.

Sometimes I could hear them.

Where *is* he?

He's the Invisible Man.

Like he disappeared into thin air.

As if he walked through the walls.

We'll never find him.

Never, ever.

Mr Perfect

BECAME MY NEW favourite wrestler. He was the Intercontinental Champion. He had blond stringy hair like spaghetti and wore a leotard. When he got punched he did this great spinning cannonball move. I practised this move again and again on my bed. I got Sam to punch me and then I'd do it. His finishing move was called the Perfect Plex and I practised this on Sam too. Wrestling was slowly starting to come back at school. Carrol had forgotten about the ban and had her eye off the ball. We found a secluded part on the field and carried out matches there. We got one of the pussy kids to keep lookout for the dinnerladies. Another thing Mr Perfect did was throw a white towel over his shoulder and get his manager, Bobby Heenan, to catch it. I went up to Paul Martin and asked him to be my manager.

Sorry, Robin, but I'm already Nile's manager.

Yeah but he's Ultimate Warrior.

So?

Warrior doesn't have a manager.

Oh yeah.

And Perfect does. You can be Bobby Heenan.

Paul Martin kind of looked like Bobby Heenan too. Fair hair. Sly and cocky.

It kind of makes sense, Nile said. I don't mind.

Paul Martin considered this. Well, he said. Suppose I did get Nile his belt. I did get him to be the WWF Champ. So I guess my work here is done. And I'm always up for new challenges.

Oh and another thing, I said. Mr Perfect is Intercontinental Champion, so that means I have to be too. Nile and Martin and the others were all looking at me. I could read their minds somewhat. He always finds a way to get what he wants.

At home I asked Mum if I could dye my hair blond.

She laughed and said No.

Then I asked if they could buy me a leotard for our upcoming holiday.

Dad looked over his paper and said, you're not a fucking poof, are you?

A boy's leotard, I said.

I don't know what you're talking about, Robin.

I didn't get the blond hair or the leotard but I did find a white towel at the bottom of the wash basket. I took it to school and me

157

and Paul Martin practised it. Me throwing and him catching it. We practised again and again until we had it down. Perfect.

The Autograph Woman

MAYBE I GOT THIS FROM NANA. She told me that from the top of Blackpool Tower you could see all of France and half of Germany. Then a few years ago I had an obsession with flags. I knew our flag and I obviously knew America and I sort of knew Australia and I sort of knew USSR but other than that there was nothing. Nana knew them all and she drew them for me one Sunday evening. France. Germany. Japan. Spain. Canada. Sweden. Denmark. China. She even drew me an African flag. The flag of Africa. She drew over twenty. Every country I could think of. I brought them in and showed the kids. Most kids were impressed but Tess Darby just laughed her head off.

That, is not Canada, she said. And that, is not New Zealand. And Africa doesn't even have a flag cos Africa is not even a country.

We fought, Tess and I. So much so that the teachers got involved. Just from the smile on their faces I knew that Tess had this one. The humiliation was thorough.

Your nana, they said, has a very colourful imagination.

I was now using Nana to my advantage. She was now The Autograph Woman. A big smile appeared on her big child's face. That mole on her cheek. Her flat chocolate eyes. Her fat white fingers worked away. Making sure one autograph differed from the next. Her cunning cut into the paper. Hulk Hogan's signature was round and swollen. Bret Hart, taut and sharp, narrow like a letterbox. Sid Justice was tall. Undertaker was faded. Jake the Snake's kind of looked like a snake, swirly and serpentine. Nana had nailed it. She was an artist.

I took them to school and kids lost their minds.

But how? they said.

I had worked on my story through the night. It was a meet and greet evening in London. A friend of my dad's had found out about it. They came to the UK once a month to meet the fans. The event wasn't advertised as they didn't want crowds and crowds, just an exclusive event for the real fans. I was mobbed for days with questions about the wrestlers. I played it down and kept it cool. Everyone was my best friend and wanted an *in* for next time. I'll see what I can do, I said. This went on for a few days and then Tess Darby was back. It was always Tess Darby.

Why is Hitman spelt as two words? Hit and Man?

She stood there. Her lazy eye and pretty lips. She was not a girl but a sassy little woman. A fullness of character and body that none of the other girls had. She was put here to best me. Test my boyhood and manhood that was trying to get out.

I looked at her hard.

Luckily not too many kids were around.

Cos I was nervous, I said.

What do you mean?

I was so nervous when I met him so I split his name in two. Hit … Man. Bret thought this was funny so that's how he wrote it on the autograph. Bret was making fun of me. Bret's like that. It's just the way he is.

Tess was staring me down. A large smile spread across her face. Slowly she shook her head.

Is there no end to your bullshit, she said.

Dungeons & Dinosaurs

DISCO SWIM had closed for a while. Pretty much through the whole of spring. Now the summer holidays were here it was about to have a grand reopening. Kids were in a fever. There was to be a new inflatable gauntlet revealed. The opening was on the Friday we broke up from school. Yet another year gone by. We were all having Mrs Carrol again next year so it didn't feel like a goodbye, but rather just a long rest. A six-week vacation. All the main players were out. All the boys and girls. I was looking forward to seeing Tess in her swimming costume. Looking forward to seeing Kayleigh's hair get wet. Looking forward to all the wrestling moves on the inflatable. I went with Moss and Morgan and Glass. Greenaway and Gavin Brown was meeting us there. The inflatable looked magnificent through the dark windows. We lined up to look at it. A majestic T-rex towered above us. Almost touching the roof. Teeth and claws and tail. You had to run through its legs and then tackle a line of smaller dinosaurs. Blue waves of light and golden sparkles dazzled our eyes as the new inflatable floated back and forth on the water's surface.

That, looks fucking cool, Morgan said.

We could barely wait.

The summer was ours.

An hour later and the night was in full force. I was giddy and couldn't stop laughing. Normally lads from other schools created an edge of rivalry. An unrest and preparedness. One eye open. Watching each other's backs. But tonight there was none of that. We talked with them and had a laugh. Made new friends. We did drop kicks and elbow drops and the lifeguard didn't even blow his whistle. We were so lost we didn't care about the girls and they didn't care about us. They did their own thing and we did ours.

Then it happened.

I don't know why it happened but it did. It was the most spontaneous thing in the world. The thought had not crossed my mind until that moment but once it did I *had* to respond to it and carry it out. Almost like I had no choice. This voice, *do it*. It was at the very height of the night. In the thick of joy. The peak of fun. There was a blind spot. Under the T-rex's foot, obscured by the horns of the Triceratops. I crouched there and unclipped the key from my trunks. Took the needle in between my wet fingers and pushed it into the hard plastic. It took a few seconds but it went in. A pop and a puff of air. Before I forward-rolled over the edge and into the water. I was lit with adrenalin as I swam under the entire width of the inflatable. Out the other side to the pool's edge. Nobody had seen a thing. After that I swam to the shallow end and sat there. The noise and energy was still full frenzy. I looked at faces. I watched kids queue and run and jump. I watched all the little groups. Kids I knew and kids I didn't. I waited ten minutes, fifteen. Slowly it started to happen. A stoop in the T-rex's gait. A heavy fold in its neck. Still no one was any the wiser. Everything went on as normal. Then the knees started to go. A soft buckle. It was the lifeguard who noticed this first. From his birds-eye view. A squint in his eye. A knot in his forehead. He rocked in his seat, trying to get a better look. He stepped down and slid his foot into his sandals and then walked anti-clockwise around the pool, checking it out. My insides were hot with laughter. The silent pantomime of it all. The excruciating anticipation. This clownish juggle of cause and effect. Lifeguard was on the other side now. Squatting, squinting, confirming what he already knew. He went over to his colleague, a cute girl with frizzy hair. He pulled at her shirt and waved her over. Now they were both looking, talking, nodding and then shaking their heads. Confusion and then fear appeared on the face of a kid who got caught in the crease, as the inflatable folded in two. His limbs tangled up in the soggy plastic. Suddenly the full horror dawned on me. Of how dangerous this could be. Whistles were now screaming across the pool. Luckily the kid made it out but now it was total chaos. The lifeguard took his shirt off. Kids were toppling from the shrinking dinosaur like lemmings. I looked hard into the face of the T-rex, which at the beginning of the night was full and fierce. Now its features melted, wrinkled, sucked in like an oldperson, skull crushed. Lifeguard was in the pool. Calmly separating kids from the flattening lake of rubber. I looked around at the mayhem. Parents up at the window in the cafe above. Some running along the gangway, trying to take the steps to the pool area. Lifeguards had to stop them, taking their attention away from the kids. Their sons and daughters were confused, crying, mad. The only one staying in one place was me. I was where I had been the whole time. Sat on the tiles, by the silver steps. I was cold. Numb and shivering without realising it. Hugging my ribcage. My skin goosebumped and turning a strange grey-purple. My body looked dead.

Just then someone was at my side, Kev Moss.

Robin, what *is* this?

His question felt big. Like he wanted me to explain the end of the world. What is going on? he said.

I couldn't answer him.

Eventually we were all ushered to the changing rooms. Girls to the left, us to the right. A long mournful silence as kids shivered through it all. I couldn't tell where poolwater ended and tears started. They fought with lockers and keys and that's when I looked at mine. Unclipped and inspected it. This thin needle. This improbable spike. I pushed it into my thumb and blood appeared. A small rose of red. I watched it bloom. Kids walked heavy and stiff as they dragged clothes over damp bodies. Everything was done half-hearted and half the speed.

It took maybe an hour to leave the pool.

The Orchard Primary bunch had found a table upstairs. They took it in turns to plod up to the vending machines, rolling coins in for sugary self-soothing as Coca-Cola and chocolate began to fill our table.

They all talked about it.

Tess and Greenaway and Highman.

Why would someone do that?

The first night as well.

There goes our summer.

Morgan stared down every passing kid, hard eyes, clenched jaw. Moss moved restlessly, flicking wrappers across the table. I was the only one not saying anything. Jack Glass seemed to notice this. His big blue eye was on me. Magnified like a goldfish through the steamy circles in his glasses.

Hornet

I WAS ON MY OWN for the first week of the holidays. I walked around. I sat and felt sad. Sad for no seeming reason. Like there was a tear in my eye trying to get out. Like squeezing a drop from the desert. I got up and moved onto a huge rock and sat there. I turned to see a hornet. Hovering head-height. A low, heavy hum. I watched its wings closely. It was hardwork, trying to stay up.

Fantasy Forest

JACK GLASS was my new best friend. We were together all the time. At school and at home. His house was a bit trampy. In the sense that there was fag ash everywhere and overflowing bins. Sometimes the trash didn't make it to the bins and was left on worktops or the floor. Sometimes I found yoghurt pots in the bed and once a pair of shitty pants at the bottom of a sleeping bag when I stayed the night.

It was here I realised how clean and tidy my own house was. How *immaculate*. It was also here that I realised how complacent I'd been. How lucky I was to live in a nice and clean house. Jack Glass was the clumsiest Human Being ever lived. He was always injuring himself. He was always falling off things or walking into doors. He once smashed his head open on a cupboard. I watched him do it. I knew it was going to happen. I *let* it happen. His mum nearly had a heart attack and his dad had a massive go at me.

It's not funny, Robin. I see you trying not to laugh. It's not fucking funny. He's supposed to be your friend.

In winter Jack Glass was the first to slip on ice. In spring he was the first to fall off his bike. Autumn, first to slip on the leaves. In summer he would get really bad sunburn and he would wince

162

and cry when my mum put aftersun on him. He was a year-long casualty case. All this yet he acted so tough. To hear him you'd think he was the toughest kid in the school. He talked about fighting all the time. We'd have big debates about who was the hardest out of Nile Greenaway or Aiden Beecham or Morgan Davenport. He would rank himself right up there but he was clearly not. On the weekends his mum took us to a place called Fantasy Forest. It was an indoor playcentre for kids. They measured us at the door and we were almost too tall and old to be there. We only went there because they had a bouncy castle that we used as a wrestling ring. We got to be top dogs and bully all the little kids.

By summer we were too tall to get in. We'd try to stand in funny positions at the measuring door, stoop, sneak, anything to try and hustle our way in.

You're too big, they'd say. This is for little kids.

Eventually we were banned and not even allowed to walk through the front door. Instead we hung around at the leisure centre. Where we would lie about getting chocolate stuck in the vending machine, or we would stand over the swimming pool, taking it in turns to spit into the water.

'Summertime'

IT WAS the very height of it again. Jazzy Jeff and the Fresh Prince were all over the place. I didn't know how we got here or what was quite happening. But as the day moved and the hours fell everyone was just *out*. It was a crazy sight to see. A scene I couldn't quite hold. Girls I never saw out of school hours, Lauren Makepeace and Kayleigh Highman, were impossibly before me. Nile Greenaway on a skateboard. Morgan Davenport looking cool against a wall. Older kids, younger ones. My brother Sam. The whole Maggio family. There were some adults around too, tending to a barbeque. Handing out hotdogs. Cans of Coke sparkled on a tabletop. It was safety and freedom at the same time. Girls yoyo'd and hopscotched and turned a skipping rope through the falling sun. Kids kicked a ball but there was no game. Kids climbed a tree. Kids ran along the length of a wall. Somersaults and cartwheels. All is wild. The most wild night of my life. We ran a fever, delicious frenzy. Everyone fit and nimble, almost possessing supernatural strength. Freakish speed.

Shocking agility. Everyone could jump like Kev Moss. Something in the air. Something in the water. No one would ever get tired. There was no curfew. There was no time to be *in*. Warm dusk gathered in the soft violet light. Mowed grass, warm soil. Clean scents, lightly perfumed, of floral jasmine and lily of the valley. A quick hint of coconut.

I stood in awe and watched it all. Tried to understand it but *couldn't* understand it. Why this was or how this was or what it was because of. I looked closer at the people. I looked closely at what was around the people, in and between. Dandelion was blown across a shiny street. And the songs kept coming from a high open window.

Wolfman

I WENT WITH DAD on a three-dayer to the south coast. His lorry was bigger for the longer runs. I slept for most of it, waking as we passed the outskirts of south London. We had one drop there and then got some lunch. At the services I picked up this month's WWF magazine. July 1991. Jake the Snake was on the cover. Covered in red and yellow writing. I noticed Dad kept changing the radio station every time the news came on. I could feel something in the air. The landscape was red and flat. Pylons stretched out across it. Like giants walking the earth. In the distance traffic began to back up. A policeman wearing a flat cap was waving a piece of paper in the sky, stopping everyone. When he came to us Dad rolled his window. I couldn't hear the policeman properly, just low mumbles. Another policeman came to my side. He was standing on something, searching all around the lorry. He didn't look at me once. More focused on checking behind the seats and along the bed. After a few minutes he waved us on. Dad was taking looks in the rearview. The traffic was still slow. It was yellow, hazy, late-afternoon weather. There were haystacks all around in the fields, and a big green tractor moving through it.

What was that? I asked Dad.

Dad was quiet for a few moments, deciding what to do.

Well I wasn't going to tell you, but maybe you should know.

The intrigue made my feet move.

Know what? I said.

Well you're a big lad now. You should know about the world.

Speed of the traffic had gone back to normal.

A man has escaped from prison. He's on the run.

My feet moved faster.

So the police was trying to see if he was hiding in here?

Dad nodded. Wind was blowing through the top of the open window.

What did he do? I said.

I was staring at the side profile of his face. His long dark nose.

Some bad stuff, he said.

I knew it must be bad for him not to tell me.

Murder? I pushed on.

Worse, he said.

Worse than murder?

Dad nodded slowly.

What's worse than murder, I thought. What can possibly be worse than murder.

By the time we parked up that night I was already obsessed. My mind was alight. I wanted to know more. Hear more. I wanted to see a face.

NEXT MORNING we didn't have to get up at the crack of dawn like we always did and this was nice. I slept in while Dad read the paper. After a while he hit the bed.

Robin, up!

I sat up and rubbed my eyes, trying to hang on to the last parts of a dream.

Let's go and get some snap, he said.

We went to the truckstop and met all the other truckers. Newspapers and empty plates spread across three big tables. They told black jokes and women jokes and talked about football even though there was no football. Not at the moment.

They caught that nonce yet?

Nope.

Hope they don't.

What? Why?

Cos I wanna catch the cunt first.

Why what you gonna do?

Chop his bollocks off.

That old chestnut.

I felt to duck low and hide myself under the table. I didn't want them to notice me. Didn't want them to stop talking, or tone it down in any way.

Where he escape from?

Broadmoor.

Fucking hell.

How he escape?

Razored his way out.

How?

Bits at a time. Day at a time. Covered it with soap and shoe polish. Quite clever actually.

Clever nonce.

Gotta hand it to him. Gotta give him his due. Fucking clever.

Then what?

Then what, what?

Then what did he do?

Well he jumped didn't he.

Three stories up apparently.

Fucking hell.

From a shower room.

Then what?

Then what, what?

Then where he go?

Well if we knew that then we'd catch the cunt, wouldn't we.

Hope I catch the cunt. Chop his bollocks off.

Slice his cock off more like. With a rusty razor.

Steady on, not finished my breakfast yet.

Sausage anyone?

What he do anyway?

Raped two girls.

The table went silent for a few moments.

Bastard.

Cunt.

Bastard noncing cunt.

Hope I catch him.

How old were the girls?

I don't wanna know.

Leave it out.

Eleven and fifteen. Sisters.

I said I don't wanna know.

It was back in eighty-five.
I don't care when it was. I said I don't wanna know.
What's his name? This nonce. This beast. What's his name?
James Saunders.
Cunt.
James Wolfman Saunders.

THEY CALLED HIM Wolfman because of his survival skills in the wilderness. He had escaped before. Lasted for three weeks. Living on berries and sleeping in a bush. Dad let me listen to the radio now. They said he was HIV Positive. Highly dangerous and not to be approached. Dad kept a baseball bat down the side of his seat. I still didn't know what he looked like. I wanted to see a face.

I SAW HIS FACE. When Dad went out to make his first drop I went tearing through the *Sun* newspaper. I saw his name before I saw his face. *James Wolfman Saunders.* On Page 2. Right alongside Page 3. Although Kelly from Huddersfield could do little to take my attention away. There he was. In the flesh, on the paper. Hairlip. Blank black eyes. Staring right back at me. I stared on and on and couldn't stop. A sick-fear feeling. Underneath this mugshot the word FIEND. Just then the door went and I threw the paper down and sat up straight. My dad back in the driverseat.

　You ready? he said.
　I'm ready, I said.

FOR THE NEXT FORTY-EIGHT HOURS he was everywhere. Wolfman. I saw him standing in a crowd of people, waiting to cross the street. I saw him duck behind a wall. I even questioned the man helping Dad carry the wood. He had the same dog-blond hair. Same sallow skin. The haunted bottomlessness of his expression. He didn't have the lip though. That lump, that slant and shadowy slope in the side of his face. I know that face now. I'd know that face anywhere. Been studying it for the last eight hours, every time Dad leaves the truck.

FIEND. For ages I had read it as FRIEND and that made no sense to me. Why would a child rapist ever be a friend. It wasn't until about four hours in that I realised I had read it wrong all along. There was no R. The word was not friend. I got curious of this word. Curious and then fixated. I tried saying it out loud. I wanted to ask Dad but how when I can't pronounce it.

What does fi-end mean?

What?

Fi-end?

Dad was looking for directions and he told me to, fucking shut up a minute.

I didn't go back to it and he forgot.

That night was the worst night. I was absolutely scared to death. I couldn't close my eyes without seeing that evil mugshot in my mind. Probably looked at it over a thousand times now. I got disturbed that maybe I had looked at it so much that it was now surgically scorched into my brain. Like a tattoo. Couldn't get rid of it even if I wanted to. It was here I decided to tear out the picture and throw it out the window. It was a still night, no wind. When I looked out he was still there. Face up. Looking right at me.

Just going wee, I said to Dad.

He nodded.

I opened up and dropped down. Took the picture and ripped it up again and again. Screwed the pieces into a ball and threw it over a barbed wire fence.

LATER THAT NIGHT we met another father and son. Some bloke Dad knew from the trucklife. The son was tall and thin and blond and the same age as me. He had a funny accent and knew loads about wrestling. We had a great night at a local diner. Ate burgers and slurped milkshakes while the dads drank beer.

Who's your favourite wrestler? I asked him.

Brutus Barber Beefcake, he said.

It was an odd choice and his accent saying that sounded hilarious. He was from Barnsley.

Barnsley has a shit football team, I said.

I don't care, he said. I support Manchester United.

Oh.

What about you?

It was here I realised I hadn't thought about football in almost a year. I didn't have a team. And couldn't remember the last one I supported.

Forest, I said. Nottingham Forest.

And who's *your* favourite wrestler, he said.

Mr Perfect.

Bret's gonna beat his ass at SummerSlam.

I got my WWF magazine and showed him the preview of SummerSlam.

Oh cool.

You can take it if you like.

His eyes went massive. The magazine? he said.

I nodded.

Oh cool. Thanks.

We opened it to the page of Mr Perfect vs Bret the Hitman Hart.

Both men had long hair. Both men wore leotards.

What you looking at a pair of poofs for, my dad shouted over.

His dad laughed.

We were all smiling.

Bret's gonna win, he said finally.

No way, I said.

Bet yaa tenner.

Done.

We shook on it.

We all left the diner and headed into the dark truckstop, towards the lorries. A black wind had started. A Coke can scraped across the dirt and oil.

It was good to have a break from Wolfman. Take my mind off it. Yet at the same time I felt to bring him back.

Hey what about Wolfman? I said.

Never heard of him. Is he new?

New what?

New in the WWF.

This made me laugh. Nah, he not a wrestler, he's a …

The boy was looking at me with an open mouth.

How did I describe him … nonce … child rapist … fiend.

He escaped prison. He's on the run. That's why the police are everywhere.

Oh him, the boy said casually. They caught him a few hours ago. Haven't you heard?

Suddenly all the fear left my body. I wanted to jump up and down and clap.

Fucking nonce, the boy said.

Yeah, I said. Fucking nonce.

I didn't know this word before this trip. *Nonce*. Now it was everywhere. It was new and something I can take back to the lads at school. Teach them something.

The father and son got in their cab and we got in ours.

I waved at him through the window. Then we both started re-enacting wrestling moves. Until his dad reached over and closed the curtain on us.

DAD must have seen the hole in his newspaper. It made him smile a bit.

He turned to me before we went bed.

You know I'd never let anyone hurt you, don't you? he said.

I know, I said.

He turned off the light.

And I was no longer afraid of the dark.

RADIO was on. Brutus Barber Beefcake Boy was right. Wolfman was caught. An offduty officer spotted him walking along a road by The Fox pub in Coscombe. He called for assistance and arrested Mr Saunders without a struggle. He was carrying a fishing rod and blanket and taken to Weymouth police station. Hearing *Weymouth* made my blood run cold.

Isn't that where we are, Dad?

He just laughed.

IT SEEMED strange that the radio had called a child rapist *Mr.* I thought about that. I thought about a lot of things on the way home. As we drove through the town I looked out for the police station. It was unbelievable to think that at some point I was less than a mile away from James Wolfman Saunders. Maybe even closer. Spitting distance. As we pulled out of Weymouth for good we went through some trees, a small forest. I looked to my left and saw a man deep in the woods, taking down a tent. He looked right at me but was too far to see his features. I had to remind myself that Wolfman was caught. But then I got thinking that what if they had the wrong man. What if Wolfman was still out there. Still at large.

What you thinking about? Dad said.

Nothing, I said. Just making up a story. Just making up a story in my head.

Cleavewood Park (Part of Golden Coast Holiday Village)

CALIFORNIA. From the brochure it looked like California. Green and gold and blue. A large white house. Luxury caravans neatly placed side by side. People in the pictures wore huge Hollywood smiles. Sam and I looked at the brochure so much in the weeks leading up to it that the pages had fallen out. Even though I had taken this trip only weeks ago this time it seemed longer. Way longer. Something about being in a car instead of a lorry seemed harder. We were no longer up high and invincible. But down low with the other cars of the road. The journey went on and on. Dad had already shouted at Mum in the morning so the first half of the journey was endured in stony silence. Then at some point there was a word or two and things went back to normal. The biggest thing Sam and I was excited about was the fact they had SKY TV. This meant wrestling. No tapes or waiting around. But real wrestling on real TV. Live in the flesh. We had already studied the TV guide and worked out that we would be able to watch *Superstars of Wrestling* when we arrived at Cleavewood at 5pm.

As we drove we got nearer. To that sea-feeling. That holiday feeling. A different air coming through the back window, blue and blowy. A hint of land dropping off into the sea. Where sky meets water. Sam had already been carsick and now I was excitementsick. To see California and to watch my first-ever wrestling on TV. All the while my eyes were on the clock. Journey had taken longer than expected because of the traffic and we were an hour behind. Still we had time so I wasn't too worried. All around now there were flat white rooftops, gleaming with sun. A sea of caravans everywhere. We must be close. Although Mum had the map out and Dad was losing it again. I had the feeling that we had driven in one big circle. Landmarks I was starting to see twice. Again I looked at the clock. The thought of missing wrestling was paralysing.

AT LAST we drove into it. Just as it was in the brochure but better. The first thing I thought of was the holiday place in the film *Dirty Dancing*. A smooth sweep of road, leading to lawns of impossible bold green. Backdrop of sea and sky. The huge house at the heart of the park. A mini mansion encircled by trees. Here we were. We were here. We were here with an hour to spare before wrestling. Dad had already said it was okay to watch it. I gave him a subtle reminder by some easy comment about it.

Will you stop going on about the fucking wrestling.

We had parked outside the main door. I looked at the red of his neck through the seat.

The engine was off and the car began to cool. Dad grabbed some papers off Mum and slammed the door. Once he was gone Mum turned to me.

You need to stop going on about wrestling, Robin. It's been a long drive. We need to settle. He needs to unwind.

I know, I said. I know.

The airfreshener on the dashboard was still swaying. Eventually it stopped. The car was silent. I couldn't take my eyes off the digital. Time was going on, *and on*. Mum was beginning to fidget. Sam was looking at me, lost. I put my hands on Dad's chair and tried to see more.

Will you stop moving about, Mum said.

Some kids were coming from the pool. Shivering in swimming trunks.

I looked again at the digital.

It starts in half hour, I said.

Robin. Don't.

What?

We've been driving for eight hours.

It hasn't been eight hours.

It's been a long time.

Yeah but how hard can it be.

We haven't come on holiday to watch wrestling.

He's doing it on purpose.

Don't be so stupid.

He is. He always does.

Don't let him hear you or he'll knock your head off.

Well I'm not going to, am I.

There's more than just you in this family, Robin. Not *everything* has to revolve around you and what you want.

Sam wants to watch it too.

Don't bring him into it.

Don't you, Sam.

Sam's face was white. He tried to talk but Mum got there first.

He's here now anyway. Be quiet.

We all readjusted ourselves as Dad came storming out of the reception. Paperwork strangled by the grip of his fist.

CUNT, he said. What an absolute wanker. I've got a good mind to fuck this place off and go find somewhere else.

172

I gripped my sides. I looked at Sam.

And then there was this fat twat holding up the queue.

Luckily we drove on towards the caravans and both Sam and I exhaled so deeply you could hear it through the car. Our caravan was pretty easy to find, just two rows up from the main complex.

Are these roads fucking narrow enough or what, Dad said.

The digital had moved on. About fifteen minutes to go.

Dad took time unloading everything. Seemed like we were at the car ages before finally unlocking the caravan and stepping inside. I tried to act cool but truth is I was a silent frantic mess. First thing I saw was the TV, remote control by its side. I sat beside it.

Help with the bags, Robin.

Mum had the kettle on. Dad was moving around. Checking the rooms. Looking out of every window. All right, isn't it, Mum said.

Bit small, Dad said.

It's not small.

Well I thought it'd be bigger.

Kettle went off and Mum made the tea.

Thought we'd be able to see the sea, Dad said.

I was now glaring at the TV. My dark reflection staring back. Daring myself to grab the remote. We were now minutes away.

Let's go for a walk, Dad suddenly piped up.

Don't you want this tea? Mum said. Thought you'd be gasping.

C'mon, he said finally.

Sam shot his eyes at me. Full fear. I was starting to hate him. A hatred I had never felt before. Dad was sliding his shoes on.

I got up and grabbed the remote and put it on.

Robin, what you doing?

It's on, I said. My voice broke in my throat, a yelp.

The TV wouldn't come on and now there was full-blown panic. I couldn't look at Dad. Instead felt him there. This massive presence pushing against me. A wall of fire.

Help me, Sam.

With a shaky hand Sam took the control and fumbled with it. Beathing heavy through his teeth.

Let's have a cup of tea first, Mum said. Let these watch this. They've been going on about it long enough.

The next words from my dad would mean everything. Maybe determining how I would feel about him *for the rest of my life.*

I've not come on holiday to watch bastard wrestling every day.

I felt to say, *it's not on every day*, but, I didn't.

The channel still wouldn't show. Just an excruciating menu page. Sam was good at this shit. He was God in this moment. We were already two minutes in. Two minutes late.

Just then it appeared, 'Mean' Gene Okerlund. His all-too-familiar voice of comfort. The face of wrestling.

Well turn it down then.

We did. We did turn it down before sitting right up to the screen. Cross-legged on a cushion each. Enchanted and relieved. This had been tough. This had been fought for. This had been *achieved*.

Mum unpacked and made it home. Dad had a wash. Sam and I stayed where we were.

Superstars of Wrestling was mostly just build-up fights before the quarterly main events. You got to see interviews and previews, hype and news reports. Very rare you got to see a proper match-up. But just then a ring announcer brought in Hacksaw Jim Duggan vs Irwin R. Schyster. I jumped up and went mad and Sam clapped hard. Dad, it's good versus good, it's good versus good!

I don't care, Dad bit.

The match ended up in a double disqualification. No clear winner.

Right we're going out. We're *all* going out. I didn't listen to him. Just kept on watching. Sam was putting his shoes on, his lip out. I decided I was staying. Even if he had to drag me away. Dad opened the door and Mum and Sam filed out. The caravan suddenly had the atmosphere of home but with even less space. Tight, tense, ready for a bomb to go off.

They silently left and I stayed where I was.

Wrestling went on for another hour. Longer than I expected. All about the upcoming SummerSlam. I was sad that Sam had missed this. I had watched him through the frosted window. His little orange face, looking back. Wishing he was here.

THAT NIGHT was our first night. A Saturday night. We were about to join the Kids' Club. As a way of introducing us they were holding a Fancy Dress Competition.

Wish they'd have fucking told us, Dad said. How are we to get a bastard costume at this time? This whole place is run by dickheads.

I was heartbroken I had not managed to get a Mr Perfect leotard. The nearest I could find was some black swimming trunks with an American flag down the side.

I could wear them, I said to Mum and Dad.

Why would you wear them? he said.

Ultimate Warrior sometimes wears an American flag on his trunks.

Don't be so fucking stupid.

Sam has a cowboy hat, Mum said.

Has he got anything to go with it?

Like what?

I dunno.

I could wear my Liverpool top, I cut in. Go as a footballer.

You didn't bring it, Mum said.

We'll just have to leave it, Dad said. You'd have thought they would have told us. You thought they would have told us beforehand. What are we, fucking mindreaders.

IT WAS A PERFECT NIGHT. We walked a lap of the park and then got some fish and chips, before heading down to The Big White House. Already I could hear the pulse of music and see disco lights turn through the windows. Purple and red and green. The song playing all the time was Cher's 'The Shoop Shoop Song (It's in His Kiss.)' We stepped into the mostly dark hall and the Fancy Dress Competition was just beginning. We sat at the back and watched on.

Knew we should have got here earlier. Nowhere to fucking sit.

The kids queued and took it in turns to present their costumes. Spaceman and Ladybird and Spiderman and Superwoman and Red Indian. Back of the line and last to go was a girl wearing a wig and makeup and a handbag and a dress and high heels three sizes too big. She stepped into the spotlight and put the microphone to her lipstick lips.

And look what we have here, the compere said. And what is your name?

Angela

SHE SAID.

Angela what?

I couldn't make out her surname.

And how old are you, Angela?

Ten.

And what have you come as?

All the adults were laughing.

She flicked her brown bob and smiled some more. Perfect bright teeth.

Uptown Girl, she said.

She was looking around the room. Out into the crowd. Almost like she was giving each table a few seconds of her time. When she got here I caught her eyes for the briefest moment. It was as if the whole of my insides was lit. A round of applause before she went back to a big table with lots of people on it. Music started back up and we were told that the winner would be announced later on this evening. I couldn't stop looking over. Couldn't take my eyes off her. All the girls at school wasn't a match. Not in the same league. Not on the same planet. Way she walked. Way her hair moved. Her strong, striking features. She had kicked away her mum's high heels and put her regular shoes back on.

Go and meet the other kids then, Dad said.

Normally I was straight in. Wherever I went. But this time I entered a little cautiously, Sam in tow. Angela wasn't really in with the Kids' Club anyway. More at the table with her people. A big handsome man with the same dark complexion. He must be her dad. A thin smiley woman was asking our names and where we were from. Introducing us to the other kids. I didn't really care. My concentration was shot. I couldn't take any of it in. If I wasn't looking at her then I was *feeling* her. Feeling where she was at in the room. Angela came 3rd in the Fancy Dress Competition but really it was like she had won. She got the biggest cheers and picked her prize like a star. Walking the room. Smiling throughout it all, effortlessly and elegantly. A touch of the comic. For the rest of the night people danced to the music. 'Sweet Caroline'. 'Happy Together'. 'She Drives Me Crazy'. Kylie Minogue's 'Hand on Your Heart'. I watched Angela the whole time and dared myself to get closer to her, step by step. Mums and dads got drunk and danced with their kids. 'Agadoo'. 'The Birdie Song'. *I am the Music Man and I come from down your way.* My parents were now having a good time. Dad put an arm around me and Sam and smiled. We ate crisps and drank Panda pop. Next time I looked up they were gone … going. I saw her brown bob and glittery dress disappear out of the hall. I ran through the people, weaving in and out of the bodies on the dance floor. Engulfed in cigarette smoke. Cher's 'Shoop Shoop' playing for maybe the fifth time of the night.

I made it to the big window at the reception. Angela and her mob, laughing in the dark, heading up the steps, towards the caravans. Part of me wanted to follow them further but I knew that was just crazy. Instead I turned around and went back into the hall. Into the people and the lights and the smoke and the music.

'I'm Too Sexy'

DAD smacked Sam across the head. Normally it was a clip, but this time it was a smack. Stop walking under my fucking feet. We were out on the road in the midday sun. A burning August yet strangely grey at times too. We were heading into Ilfracombe. We were looking for buckets and spades to take down to the beach. I still had my eyes open for a Mr Perfect leotard. The people moved in a great bulk across the knick-knack shop sidestreets. White legs and sunburnt backs and shoulders. Bumbags and hats and sunglasses. Men with fat tummies and women with big bums. Hyperactive kids. Candy mouths and ice creams dripping down arms. Grannies groaning in the sun. Everywhere there were t-shirts and vests with the words *I'M TOO SEXY*. A song and a craze that had took hold of the nation. There were also football tops everywhere. Worn with pride and antagonism, confrontation. Collars up, chests out. Little laughy bits of needle as they pass on the street. Manchester United vs Liverpool vs Arsenal vs Chelsea vs West Ham vs Aston Villa. In the rare moments I saw Nottingham Forest I looked at them closely. See if I knew them from school.

The grey cleared for good and the sun came down hard. Dad was about to kick off. Mum was chainsmoking. Sam was scared to death. And I had my eyes peeled. Looking for a dark girl with a brown bob.

'Tell Me Have You Seen Her'

IT WAS ALWAYS AMAZING to me how songs would fit what was happening in real life. Like a soundtrack. I looked on longingly at the table where she had sat twenty-four hours ago as this song played. *And even at the picture show …tell me have you seen her*? An hour passed. Then two. Nothing. No Angela. Maybe this was it. Maybe that was her last night and that's why her family were really going for it.

Letting their hair down before they went home for good. I guess it made sense. Or maybe they were just going somewhere else tonight. Doing something different. Breaking it up. Either way I was depressed.

'I'm Too Sexy' played.

Cher's 'Shoop Shoop'.

Kylie Minogue's 'Hand on Your Heart'.

I haven't brought you here to mope, Dad said. Go and find some kids to play with.

His face was fuming.

Go and have some fucking fun.

Sam's Near-death Experience

THERE WAS an outdoor pool at the back and an indoor one at the front. The outdoor was small and cold and crap, so everyone went inside. It was encased in a cool crystal roof so you could see the sky when you swam on your back. It was warm. There was a jacuzzi and a sauna. Sam and I had been in it all morning and into the late afternoon. We did wrestling moves the whole time. There wasn't even a lifeguard to tell you off. I slammed Sam and clotheslined him. Did every move I could think of. Then I got bored so I decided to go wander. I was walking around sopping wet and a woman who worked there told me off but I didn't listen and carried on doing what I wanted. I walked the arcade. I wandered through the empty dance hall. I checked out the mini-cinema to see what film was playing tonight. *Grease.* When I returned to the pool Sam was as white as a ghost. Even whiter than normal. His eyes were heavy and his lips were kind of blue. His little ribcage was heaving.

Robin, he gasped. Robin, I nearly died.

What?

I nearly drowned.

I took his wrist and moved him to one side.

What happened?

I fell into the deep end. I couldn't get up. Couldn't get out. I couldn't breathe. I was under. A girl saved me. A girl gave me her rubber ring.

What girl?

I followed the direction of his shaky white hand. His finger so out of control it blurred. I followed it to a dark girl on a black rubber ring. Her tan blinding against the striking white of her swimming costume. She was looking back at us. Her eyes through her bob hair and brown shoulder. Then she went back to what she was doing.

Sam was telling me more about his near-death but I was no longer listening. I was no longer taking him in.

Gang

I WAS THE LEADER. Always. There was a kid from Coventry and a kid from Whitby and a kid from Hull and a kid from London and a kid from near us, Newark. The holiday really began in full earnest. I led them into battle against the teenagers. The teenagers who drank and smoked and had girlfriends. We dropped bombs on them. Threw words and pebbles and bits of mud. We attacked them from all angles. Roughed them up. Made sure they could never fully relax. Every time they tried to kiss their girlfriends they had it. From the beginning of the evening to the end of the night. I now knew The Big White House like the back of my hand. Every balcony, every fire door. I had a way of cutting through the kitchen without anyone seeing me. This was my secret escape route which had everyone fooled. I only shared this top information with my second-in-command, Kid from London. One night Kid from Whitby got caught and was beaten pretty bad but sometimes you had to sacrifice one of your troops. I rested him up for the night. Gave him chocolate and pop and by the next night he was back on the battlefield. My name began to travel. By Thursday everyone knew who I was. Robin the Terrible. Robin the Uncatchable. Robin Hood, Sheriff of Nottingham. The Daring Demon, taking Devon out with his dashing heroics.

For a while this actually managed to put my baby on ice. No Angela on the mind for an hour or two. Too busy with my troops, and the mission at hand.

But one night her older sister collared me outside.

You're bit of a little shit, aren't you?

From what I had gathered through the week Angela had two sisters. The younger funny-looking one with teeth and glasses. And this older blonde one, who had the same gift of genetics as my Cleopatra Angela. The rest of the kids in her crew were her cousins. All girls. It was an all-girls affair. I think this blonde one was going out with one of the teens.

She was looking right at me. Half appalled, half mystified.

You know they're going to kill you, she said.

They can't kill what they can't catch.

She laughed and rolled her eyes.

All of a sudden I was taken by nerves. My adrenalin high starting to dip. I knew how crucial this moment was. In maybe getting information to Angela, and gathering some about her.

You're Angela's sister, aren't you?

She nodded. Sucking a straw. Making her eyes big.

You fancy her or something? she said.

Felt my face go red. Hot and beaming. No, I bit.

Yeah, right, she said. You and everybody else.

That made my heart drop. A cruel reality check.

What's your surname? I said.

Why?

All of a sudden her man and his mates appeared on the brow of the hill.

There he is! one of them shouted.

Just tell me your surname.

She was smiling brightly. She knew what this was all about.

Stubbs, she said.

I was backing up, about to turn. Escape routes everywhere was lighting up in my brain like a computer.

She said it again but I didn't catch it right. Just her mouth moving, making a noise. A one- syllable murmur. The opposing force was now right on top of me. So I had to whip off into the wind, disappear into the starry night.

Awake

I LAY IN BED wide awake. Full of adrenalin and sugar and love. The Big White House was silent. The music gone and the broken murmurs of straggling families had gone to nothing. Just crickets in the night. I replayed it all. Everything. This was the best holiday of my entire life and probably always would be. It had everything. The Girl. The Gang. Unrequited love. Unending danger. Enchantment. Camaraderie and a yearning so strong I could barely breathe. It was the best of weather too. Part Californian blaze, part Floridian tropic. In the bits I heard Angela speak and the conversation with her sister I knew she was from The North. I had been on the road enough times with Dad to know the difference between a North and South accent. I also had a surname now. Or half of one, at least. What this meant I didn't know. What any of it meant, I didn't know. Probably nothing. Cos in all truth I was as far away from Angela Stubbs as I'd ever been.

Race

THERE WAS A LITTLE BLACK BOY beating everyone. A little black kid that was way smaller and younger than everyone. Yet he was racing them all one by one and beating them with ease. I was late to the game and when I walked around the corner all my gang were on me.

Robin!

Robin will beat him.

Robin is the fastest. He can't lose.

Before I decided to race him I made him race again so I could watch what I was up against. Little fucker was rapid. Great acceleration out of the blocks. Faded a little at the end but by then the damage was already done.

He's just won ten in a row, my gang said.

The boy was gasping and looking up at me.

Who you here with? I said.

He pointed over to the parents. Who were all drinking at a barbeque and watching their kids every now and then. His mum and dad stuck out. His mum looked like Whitney Houston and his dad wore big dark sunglasses like Stevie Wonder and it was here I noticed something. This was the first black family I'd ever seen on holiday. Definitely the only black family here at Cleavewood.

What's your name? I said.

Warren.

I shook his hand.

I'm Robin. I'm the leader of this gang.

So I've heard, he said.

He had a big beaming smile and a thick snotty nose. I immediately liked him.

What else have you heard?

That you're crazy and fast. Crazy fast.

I couldn't work out his accent. Not one I'd heard before.

Are you American? I said.

Nah.

He shook his head. Still smiling and breathing heavy.

So you wanna race?

Okay, he said.

I had my hand on his back. He wore a bright yellow t-shirt and a pair of oversized Umbro shorts.

Dad was looking over. Mum gave him a beer and a burger and they sat and watched us.

We now had a full audience of adults and kids. I was the last chance to beat the black boy.

While I tied my laces and got ready Kid from Whitby and Kid from Coventry was having a debate.

Black people are faster than white people.

No they're not.

Yes they are.

Look at him. He's about three years younger than us and he's beat us all.

Bet my older brother could beat him.

Yeah and I bet his older brother could beat *him*.

How do you know he's got an older brother?

You're missing the point.

Bet my dad could beat his older brother, if he did have one.

Yeah and Linford Christie could beat them all. And that's where it ends.

Kid from Whitby scratched his head.

Suppose you've got a point, he said.

Me and Warren was now lined up. He was still slightly out of breath from the last race.

I wasn't confident though, not at all. Sometimes I had a pressure problem and I was feeling it. I had lost Sports Days and not made the school team for this very reason. A pressure problem. Especially now Dad was watching me.

Hey why don't we change it up a bit, I suddenly said.

Everyone was looking at me. The parents were all now a little restless. Waiting in anticipation.

Get on with it! one of them shouted.

His black parents were stood next to my white ones.

Why don't we do a slightly different route, I said. How about we make the race a bit longer and do the last bit up the hill.

Warren's eyes were large and moist. His skin glistened green in the sun.

Okay, he said.

I was changing the conditions. Giving myself every possible advantage. I was better over the longer distances, hills especially. And this kid was already beat.

Kid from Hull ran over to the new finish line.

Kid from Coventry was ready to start us off.

My mouth was dry. My knees were weak.

Warren crouched, ready to push off from his back foot.

On your marks, Kid from Coventry said. Get set.

Go on, Robin, someone shouted.

All of a sudden I thought of Angela. Was she here? This might be my chance to impress her.

Go!

The *go* beat me to it. Angela had distracted me.

Warren was gone. Left me for dead. He started heading along the old route but then someone shouted and reminded him. Good job. Otherwise I would already be beaten. I was tracking him. Moving onto his shoulder. Only a second wind made him pull away again. The parents were all screaming like mad. Everyone wanting me to win. This gave me a boost and I was back on him. Closing down that bright yellow shirt. Now at the hill part and surely it was mine. Onto my tiptoes and now neck and neck but still he would not buckle. His arms going crazy. Kid from Hull was drawing in closer and closer and we both lunged for the finish line. Maybe I had him by half an inch but who knows. Only Kid from Hull could call it.

We both collapsed on top of each other. Panting. Laughing. Covered in sweat.

When we both stood I could see the confusion on Hull's face. His clueless eyes magnified behind his glasses. Looking hard at Warren. Then at me. The crowd on the edge of their seats, waiting for the result. Feeling the pressure on him Hull waved his arm and pointed at me.

Robin is the winner!

Cheers.

Warren still smiling. His parents too but clearly disappointed. His mum drew her little prayer-hands into her chest.

Hull shouted some more. Warren's winning streak comes to an end! Again some more parents cheered.

I felt a stone plop in my chest. Something wasn't right. Adrenalin had put out my nerves and now I was full of animation.

I took Warren by the wrist and walked him towards the people, his parents.

It was a draw, I shouted. In fact not even a draw. Warren is the fastest. Faster than me. He's already raced ten in a row and I'm completely fresh. Not to mention the age difference. Warren is the champ! I raised his arm and the parents clapped some more. His mum was smiling but his dad remained neutral. Like he had other things on his mind.

My dad wasn't happy for some reason. He turned his back on me.

Hey you wanna be in our gang? I said to Warren.

What?

My gang. I'm the leader, remember. You wanna be in it? I think you've got what it takes.

Straight away he looked up at his mum and dad. It was the first time I saw him not smile.

Nah, he said. I'm a bit too young.

The hell you are. I say who is and isn't too young. If you want in, you're *in*. Just say the word.

I better get going, he said.

He did. Joined his family. Within a few moments, they were gone.

WE WERE HEADING back to the caravan.

Well that was fucking embarrassing, Dad said.

What?

He was half your size.

So?

Half your age.

He wasn't five.

Don't get fucking cocky.

Mum shot me a warning stare.

He was fast, I said.

I'd have beat him if I was your age.

This again, I thought.

I used to beat all the black lads at school.

Thought you said there was no black lads at your school.

There was one.

Oh.

And I beat him.

Last-Night Sentiments

I DECIDED to give my troops the evening off. Last night 'an' all. Instead of ricocheting around the rooms and corridors and rooftops and courtyards of The Big White House I allowed us all to settle snug in the safety of the main hall. It had been a long hard week and we needed to say our goodbyes in peace. Just like with my mates back home all the kids gravitated towards my dad. They all wanted to be liked by him and fought for his attention. Kid from Whitby sat next to him.

It's nice up there, Dad said. Whitby. Better than shit Coventry. I have to go there every fucking week.

Kid from Coventry smiled at the banter. They all liked that he swore. It made them laugh.

Kid from Newark bought me a Mars bar and we made plans to meet.

You're not even far away, he said. Like ten minutes up the road.

Well I'm gonna draw up a plan, I said. We'll take it in turns. First month you can all come to Nottingham. Then Newark. Then London. Then Hull. Then Whitby. Then Coventry.

Cool, he said. But how will we get there?

I put my hand on his shoulder. Bus. Train. Parents. We'll figure it.

Hey you're a great leader.

I slapped his back and nodded.

Just then I noticed a kid sitting and staring at me through the bodies and music. Eyes of hate. The disco lights lighting his face up. First green, then red.

I wandered over to the leader of Teen Gang and put my hand out for him to shake.

No hard feelings, brother, I said.

He was wearing one of those t-shirts that changes colour when you breathe on it. It was blue but his armpits were yellow.

Lucky your dad's there. Otherwise I'd knock your teeth out.

Oh don't be that way. It's nothing personal, man.

Are you off your head?

We were both looking at my hand. There was no way he was going to shake it.

I tried, I said with a sigh. I tried.

I walked away. His eyes burning into my back.

Just then there was a bit of sensation. Kid from Hull had a revelation.

I love Uptown Girl, he said.

I ran cold. Felt my stomach flip.

The gang was all around him and he told them.

Loved her from the moment I saw her. She's the most beautiful girl I've ever seen.

He talked on unashamedly. He was glowing. That nothing-to-lose confidence. Brimming with it. Saying all the things I felt inside. He spoke with an openness and eloquence that was mesmerising.

I can't keep it in any longer, he said. I just have to tell you all.

I couldn't believe what I was hearing. I loved him and hated him at the same time. He spoke my mind and heart verbatim. Yet at the same time I wanted to totally obliterate him. I was his leader yet he had beaten me to it. If he didn't have glasses and great sticky-out teeth then I might be worried. He was on his feet, like he was about to do something. *Driven* to do something. Let her know. Next I got worried about his confidence. What if somehow he pulled this off. Stranger things have happened.

I had to act fast. I had to act first. So I cornered Kid from Coventry at the pinball machine.

He was shoving in coins. Pulling the spring. Lights buzzing and bleeping.

I need you to do something for me.

What?

I need you to ask Angela out for me.

What?

I need you to ask her out.

But Hull likes her.

I don't care. I liked her first.

But it's the last night.

So?

Why would you ask her out now. That doesn't even make sense.

Well tell her that I like her then.

Okay.

You will?

My voice was fast and frantic.

All right then, I'll tell her, he said. He slapped down hard on the machine.

Tell her I love her.

Love?

Yeah.

Love or like?

Kylie Minogue was playing again.

Love, I said finally. Love.

Okay.

He was a short chubby kid with colourless hair. If there was anyone for the job it was him. He spoke clear and calm and was probably the most adult out of all of us.

I sent him on his way. Watched him walk through the door.

Swimming Pool

I WANDERED OUT THERE. Upon the blue dark water. I looked at my bare arm and saw the light wave across my skin from the movement of the pool.

This is it, I thought. This is it.

I walked around it clockwise. Twice.

I pictured Kid from Coventry going up to her.

Talking into her ear. Talking through the music. Talking through Minogue.

How would she react. What would she say. On this last night.

Suddenly the hairs went up on the back of my neck as I realised I was way out in the open. Vulnerable to attack. Teen Gang was still out there. It wasn't over yet and here I was. Like Billy the Kid wandering into the aim of Pat Garrett in the final scene of *Young Guns 2*.

I needed to get back inside, and quick.

Into the hall and I expected something. I expected my gang all around me. I expected Kid from Hull to be heartbroken. Maybe challenge me. Fight for her honour. I expected Kid from Coventry to rush up and give me the news. I expected something from Angela. A smile. A frown. A warm heart or a cold shoulder.

Instead there was nothing.

Instead there was normal.

An awful, awful normal.

Everyone doing their own thing.

Dad was saying his last goodbyes to the lads. Mum was pissed, dancing with Sam.

Angela was lost in her entourage.

I managed to collar Kid from Coventry in the dying seconds before his departure.

What she say? I said.

Who?

Angela.

He started talking to someone else.

I grabbed his shirt and pulled him in. You did tell her?

Oh. Yeah. I told her.

What she say?

She didn't really say anything.

She said nothing?

Not really no.

What do you mean, *not really*?

She just sort of looked at me.

Kid from Coventry was suddenly pulled away from me. Into the crowd and gone.

The bustle out of there was intense. Like we were all carried on a great wave. The goodbyes went on and on. Parents were drunk on alcohol. Kids drunk on life. Everyone going off in all directions. Different directions. We were all going home.

Uptown Girl

I HAD TO LEAVE HER. I had to leave here. I asked Dad if we could stay one more day.

You always want more, Robin. You always want more.

He was right. I did.

I thought about Angela and it made me sick to the stomach. I hated myself for not talking to her. Not even once. Not even a word. Not even a word let alone asking her out. How come I was fearless when it came to meeting new friends. Even meeting their mums and dads. I could talk to adults better than my mum and dad could. I was a gifted talker yet I couldn't talk to *her*. Couldn't talk to The Girl. Couldn't talk to Angela Stubbs or whatever her surname was. I decided to look for her on the way out. Told Mum I'll be ten minutes.

Don't be long, Robin, cos we're packing up. And take Sam with you.

I didn't. I pretended not to hear her and bounced. Sam will slow me down. Cramp my style. I went in search for her. I did the laps. Investigated every caravan, every crevice. Places I had not seen all week. This time I'd do it. This time I'd do it right. I'd speak to her.

It was do or die and I had nothing to lose. I played it all out in my mind. How it would all go. Word for word.

There she would be. Brown bob. Stood idly next to her blonde older sister and funny-looking younger one. Her parents packing up, just like mine were. The three girls waiting around the car.

They'd see me and look up.

Can you give us a minute, girls, I'd say.

They'd look at each other.

I'd point right at the girl in question. Angela.

On this they'd leave us to it.

She'd step forward and smile. Big brown eyes.

Bit late, aren't you, she'd say. That accent of hers. I've been waiting for you.

I know.

You know?

What can I say, I'm a slow mover.

Lines right out of my America.

She'd roll those big browns and step away. Sizing me up.

I'm a slow starter in nearly everything, I'd say. You might need to wait for me to catch up.

Oh really?

But by the time I reach my prime, well, you won't be able to catch your breath.

Is that right?

That's right, I'd say.

You're crazy.

I'd look over my shoulder. Then at the floor. Back at her big browns.

Yeah I'm crazy, I'd say, with a squint.

She'd turn and leave me. Go to her mum and get a pen and paper.

Here's my number, she'd say, handing it to me.

Call me when you're ready, she'd say.

She would then lean in and kiss me on the lips.

There would be a new scent. One I wouldn't smell again. Until our next time.

THANKS FOR HELPING US, ROBIN.

The car was packed and ready to go by the time I got back. Dad slamming the door. Mum tentatively stepping inside. Sam wouldn't know what to do. We pulled off out of there. Leaving the caravan.

The Big White House. The pool. The greenest green lawn. Leaving California. There was another car just ahead of us. I saw a little brown bob in the backseat. What was real and what was imagination. At this point in the day who knew which what was what. We followed them, inching all the way along Ossaborough Lane.

Can this cunt drive any slower, Dad said.

At the busy intersection the car in front turned left. And we turned right.

Bret 'The Hitman' Hart

SUMMERSLAM. We managed to get a tape before hearing the results. I tried to stay away from Jack Glass and Gavin Brown who had already watched it on the night it happened. Bret 'The Hitman' Hart vs Mr Perfect for the Intercontinental Belt. I remembered my bet with the boy from Barnsley. A tenner. I wondered how we were going to get the money to each other. Maybe my dad knows his dad and there might be a way to meet him again. Apart from Jack Glass he knew more about wrestling than any kid I'd ever met.

Wrestling was weird. Some kids thought it was real and some thought it was fake. Mostly the older kids thought it was fake. Maybe this was a sign of something. I wanted it to be real yet certain things didn't add up. How come there was never any blood. Giant men smacking each other full in the face yet never any blood. Or rarely, at least. Boxing men wore gloves and got knocked out so why didn't wrestlers? Next was the matches themselves. A main event nearly always started with a goodie beating a baddie. You could set your watch by it. It's like they wanted to get the crowd in a good mood. Then the next match a baddie would win, then back to a goodie. The last fight of the night, the main event, and it was always a goodie who won. Hulk Hogan or Ultimate Warrior. I wanted to believe it was real but something wasn't right. Something was off.

When Mr Perfect came down the aisle I was all for him. His music. His leotard. His chewing gum. His white towel. Yet when Bret's music came on I felt a change, a sway in loyalty. He looked so cool in his pink pants and black leather jacket. Those wraparound sunglasses.

C'mon, Bret.

Sam looked at me gone-out.

Thought you liked Perfect?

I didn't say anything. Just kept on watching it. Eyes fixed.

As Perfect took control again I felt myself go back with him.

Then to Bret again.

Then Perfect.

As Perfect went for a centre leg drop Bret did something miraculous and converted it into his signature finishing move, the Sharp Shooter.

He did it. Got the submission and the win. A new WWF intercontinental Champion of the World. Bret 'The Hitman' Hart.

I jumped up and punched the air as his crashing theme music lit up the stadium.

Make up your mind, Sam said.

Oh don't worry, I have.

Sam had his head to one side.

Where are those sunglasses you got from holiday? I said.

What sunglasses?

Those long pink ones.

Dunno.

I'm having them. I'm taking them to school the day we go back.

Okay, Sam said.

Kid from Whitby

HELLO is Wesley there please?

Just a minute.

It was his mum.

Noise. Voices. Sound of the stairs.

Hello.

Wesley, my man.

Who is this?

Robin.

Robin who?

I thought of a knock-knock joke.

Forgot me already.

Robin?

I mean how many Robins do you know?

Robin from holiday?

That's the one.

Oh. Yes. How are you?

Good, good. How are you?

All right.

So I'm arranging this meet-up. Getting the gang back together.

Gang?

Yeah, all of us. Like I said on holiday we'll start at Nottingham and then take it in turns. Month by month. You in?

Oh. Well. Back at school soon.

Yeah. Well. I'm not thinking about in the week, dummy.

Dummy?

Weekends. We'll do it at the weekends.

Look, Robin, I've got to go. Football's about to start.

Really? Who's playing?

Can you call back another time?

Sure, when?

Erm, tomorrow.

Time?

He was breathing hard into the phone.

You all right?

Twelve, he said suddenly. Any time after twelve.

You got it, monster man.

See ya.

Speak soon.

Yeah.

Speak tomorrow.

Kid from Newark

HELLO is Neil there please?

Yes, can I ask who's calling?

It was his mum.

It's Robin.

Neil!

Her voice was loud and then soft. It's Robin.

I could hear them whispering from a distance.

Robin!

Neil!

Wow you called.

Yes I did.

Great to hear you.

You too.

Cool.

Nice to hear a friendly voice.

Yeah?

Just called Wesley and he acted really weird.

Wesley?

Yeah.

Remind me, which one was that?

Jesus, you guys.

What?

Don't you remember *anything*?

Ha. Oh. How you been? Forest have had a good start to the season.

Yeah, I know. Hey you see SummerSlam?

Yeah. I did. Perfect lost. Ha.

Oh I'm so over that. Kinda wanted Bret to win anyway. In my heart.

Oh. Ha.

Talking of my heart. I have not been able to stop thinking about Angela.

Really?

Yeah.

You got it bad, eh?

Just a bit.

She *was* cute.

An awkward silence took hold.

Yeah, hey you don't know what her surname was, do you? I said.

What?

Her surname. I kind of forgot it.

Nah. I never spoke to her really.

Oh.

More awkward silence.

Did you know where she was from?

Where she was from?

Yeah.

Er. No. No I don't.

Oh.

Anyway we're kind of going out.

Really?

Yeah.

Cool.

Yeah I caught her just before she was leaving. Asked her out. She said yes.

A real long pause on the phone.

Yeah we're gonna meet soon. Going over to hers for Halloween.

Cool.

Speaking of which that's why I rang.

Oh?

Our gang reunion.

Oh. Yeah.

You still up for it?

I mean, yeah. Suppose we can.

Cool.

Yup.

Well we can start with Nottingham as planned and then work our way around.

Yeah, cool. I mean I don't know how we'll all get there but—

Hey where there's a will there's a way. Leave it all to me. I am your leader. I will make it happen.

Ha, yeah.

Like you said we're only ten minutes down the road from each other.

True.

We could probably meet first.

First?

Yeah, like next week or something.

Oh. Yeah. Well. Let me ask my mum and I'll ring you back.

Cool. When?

Silence. Awkward.

Soon.

Neil then spoke for a long time. Keeping control of the conversation before softly ending it.

Kid from Whitby

HELLO is Wesley there please?

No. He's not.

It was his mum.

Is this Robin?

Yes. He told me to call today after twelve.

I see.

It's after twelve.

His mum cleared her throat with two polite coughs.

Is it okay if I ask you not to call here again, please.

I was struck, shocked. Brain got scrambled for a few moments.

His mum continued.

Wesley is very busy at school at the moment.

For some reason my eyes were starting to fill with tears.

And he hasn't really got time to take phone calls.

Oh yeah, I get it. Absolutely, I said.

All of a sudden I felt low and a loser.

It's like his mum could sense this.

Sometimes, Robin, she said, you should just let holidays stay on holiday. You should just learn to leave the magic where it is.

Silence. But not an awkward one.

Okay?

Okay.

Kid from Coventry

HE was next on my list. I had his number in my hand but I didn't use it. I didn't even pick up the phone. I didn't call Neil back either. I took all the bits of paper with phone numbers from around the country and dropped them down the drain. One by one. I said goodbye to my gang. I left the magic where it was.

Angela, Angels, Anima

LETTING GO of the boys was one thing but letting go of The Girl was another. A different thing completely. A whole new set of rules. She was around for the next three months. Still going strong as if she was yesterday. Was *this* even normal, I thought. Normal for a ten-year-old. I was premature and immature at the same time. I always had these words thrown at me. *Not Normal*. You're *not normal*. *Not Normal* was a thing I was going to endure and enjoy for the rest of my life.

May as well make the most of it.

With this I made one last attempt to reach her. I made a list of all the factual things I knew about Angela.

Age: 10.

From: The North.

Has sisters and cousins.

Looks like her dad.

Surname: Stubbs (fifty per cent chance).

I WAITED until Mum and Dad was out and then went for it.

Hello Cleavewood Holiday Park.

It was a woman.

Hello, I was wondering if you could help me.

There was a long pause on the other end.

Yes, love, she eventually said.

Yeah I stayed there a few weeks ago. A few months ago, actually. Yes.

I noticed my hand was shaking and my voice was shaking. I sounded like Sam.

Could you tell me if there was a family called Stubbs who stayed there?

Another long pause.

Oh. Er. I'm afraid we can't give out private information.

Oh. Okay.

What is it, love?

Her voice was nice. Soft. Caring.

Nah. Nah it's all right.

How old are you, love?

I hung up sharp. Slammed it down. I felt bad on the woman. I wanted to call her back and say sorry. I stared at the receiver for quite some time. I felt dumb. Desperate. A little weirdo. I looked in the mirror and laughed.

SHE was still around in November when we went to my aunt's for our annual bonfire night. I thought that leaving our city would give me a chance to see her. Maybe at the services or maybe even at the party itself. Somebody's cousin. Somebody's niece. A friend of the family. A neighbour. I stood with a sparkler and fully expected her to turn up. No longer in summer attire but wrapped up in a coat. Gloves and ear muffs.

On the drive back every yellow square of light was where she lived. I saw her on the other side of it. Curled up on a bed. Reading a music magazine. Drinking hot chocolate.

That nightdrive was so long and longing.

As I neared home I knew I was never going to find her. After months I finally accepted this. I finally gave in, gave up. Now I had a new problem. How is any other girl ever going to live up to her. A girl I didn't know. A girl I had totally made up from scratch. A girl who lived inside me. And who would do

forever.

Through A Glass Darkly

Black Satellite

I WAS SICK the morning it was being installed. Everyone else had a white one but our satellite was going to be black. It was different. It stood out. It would look cool.

I was sick again an hour before.

Oh, Robin, you're being over the top, Mum said. You need to calm down.

I couldn't calm down. This was unlimited wrestling. This was seeing it all. This was everything.

The man installing it was bang on time and I opened the door and asked him if he wanted a cup of tea.

Fucksake, Robin, let him get through the bastard door.

It's a tall house, he said.

It was. We had a garage under the bay window, making it the tallest house on the street.

There was a look on the man's face I didn't like.

Not sure my ladders are going to reach up there.

Dad and him already had friction and I was on edge. Thought I was going to be sick a third time.

Cunt, Dad said, coming back into the house. I'm *this close* from telling him to fuck off.

Heart was in my mouth. The man seemed fine. I couldn't see what the big deal was.

He's doing this on purpose, I said to Mum.

Oh, Robin, stop being stupid.

He is.

Why would he? That doesn't even make sense.

To get my hopes up.

You're just being ungrateful.

Ungrateful for what? It hasn't happened yet.

You're spoilt.

I knew it was too good to be true.

Sorry, mate, Man said. Only way this is going to work is if we put it by your window.

Dad waved him off. Nah, not doing that, mate.

Your call. I can get some longer ladders. Looking a few weeks yet though. My diary is chock-a.

I ran upstairs and noseplanted the bed. Sobbed into it. It felt like the end of the world. Hated Dad and Mum and everything. After it was all out I felt light-headed. It had been an exhausting few days, working myself up to this frenzy. As I sat there looking at the tree outside my window, something else came in. So what if I can't have SKY today. It's not the end of the world. So what if it was in a few weeks, or even a month or even a year. None of it was the end of the world. Some of my mum's words were right. I was spoilt and ungrateful and over the top. I needed to accept things more. Can't get my own way all the time.

With this revelation I headed on downstairs with a new perspective.

Once there I saw the man up outside the bay window. Screwing something in. A black satellite hovered across the glass, blocking out some of the sun.

It looks a right state, Dad said. Can't see fuck all now.

It's not too bad, Mum said. We'll get used to it.

Tom Blackman

HE LIVED over the tall wire fence. On the same cul-de-sac as Nile Greenaway and Tess Darby. He watched us from his bedroom window. Playing football on the school field. We tried to keep our shots low because if it went over the fence we were done for. He'd come down and grab our ball. Pop it with a knife and then throw it back over.

He was three or four years older than us.

Pop that ball and I'll tell Morgan Davenport, I yelled.

He was smiling and staring at us, ball in hand, about to go into his kitchen.

What's he gonna do? he said.

Get his brothers.

Something swept across his face. Tom thought about this for a moment. And then threw the ball back over.

Well go and play somewhere else, he said.

That night I had a dream that Tom Blackman fell off his bike and died.

Unsolved Mysteries

AS WELL AS WRESTLING there was *Saved by the Bell* and *Family Ties* and *Different Strokes* and *Beverly Hills, 90210* and *COPS*. A whole world of America. America every day. America at the fingertips. Going outside was happening less and less. Kev Moss would come call for me but I had to tell him *no*.

You never come out anymore, he said.

You're just jealous cos you haven't got Sky.

I don't want Sky.

Yeah right. What with all this wrestling.

People don't even like wrestling anymore, Robin. People are getting bored of it. They're outgrowing it. We're all going back to football when school starts again.

I slammed the door in his face.

Mum, can we upgrade to the Movie channels?

We've only had it a week and already you want—

More, yes I know. Look I'm just asking.

Tonight was the first time we were being left on our own. A trial run with no babysitter. *I* was the babysitter.

How much am I getting paid?

Nothing.

I have rights.

Mum was putting on her earrings. Dad was upstairs putting on a suit jacket. It always took him longer to get ready. He always looked a million bucks.

You have sweets. You have Sky. It should keep you quiet.

Part of this was exciting. Part of it was scary. Exciting in being able to do what we want. Scary because of ghosts and murderers.

No football in the house, Dad said. No wrestling.

It was weekend so we could stay up to what time we wanted.

We'll be back at midnight. Lock the door.

We locked the door and took out the key. All of a sudden it was dead weird. The possibilities were endless yet at the same time I wanted to run upstairs and curl into a ball and wait for them to come back. There were more noises outside. I checked the backdoor. After that we loaded up on ice cream and then had about a dozen wrestling matches. I gave Sam the illusion he was going to win but then turned it around at the last minute. By now I walked and talked like Bret Hart. Knew every one of his moves. I put Sam into the Sharp Shooter and did it so hard it made him cry. After he watched *The Simpsons* and then MTV. Two songs kept bringing my mind back to Angela. *Now that we found love, what are we gonna do, with it.* And U2's 'Mysterious Ways'. Then at 10pm, as Sam was falling asleep, and with only two hours to go until they came home I watched *Unsolved Mysteries*. This show was scary anyway, watching it with adults around, but on my own it was a whole new level. The theme music was chilling, ominous tones. The presenter walked through the shadows and fog, his grave voice and stony eyes.

Here, on another episode of … Unsolved Mysteries.

Why was I putting myself through this. I couldn't watch but had to watch. The show was about missing kids, spontaneous combustion, UFOs and letters from the dead. It was hard going. I was thirsty but too scared to go into the kitchen. In need of a wee but no way going upstairs. Instead I remained stuck on the chair. Watching the clock, hoping my parents would come home early. Sam was now fast asleep. The last case did me in. It was about a video tape found under a bridge. On the tape was homemade footage of a burning house. The voiceover was creepy, whispery and demented. He was saying loads of devil worship stuff. The camera shaking in his hand. He was talking about hell and Satan. Saying that this was his domain and how he belonged here. Then he told us to listen to the coyotes screaming over the sound of the approaching fire sirens. That did me. The telly was off in no time and I just sat there shaking on the settee. Too scared to close my eyes. Too scared to open them. In the end, despite my paralysing fear, I made myself put the telly back on. I didn't like this feeling. This making myself put the telly back on. It was like there were two me's. One who wanted the telly on and one who did not. It was like one self was trying to scare the other self.

Eventually I fell asleep, and when I woke up Mum and Dad was standing over me. The room was hot with the smell of alcohol and booze and another one that was like half perfume and half aftershave.

Meanwhile in Milwaukee

THERE WAS A MAN in America eating people. I discovered this in Dad's lorry. It was my last trip away with him before I went back to school. Again this was seen by reading the *Sun* newspaper.

Dad, what does Cannibal mean?

It's someone who eats people.

I looked at his mugshot. A blond man wearing glasses. A messy moustache under his nose. On the other page was a picture of his victims. All black men. There were loads. I tried reading about it all but I couldn't understand most of the words. *Dismembered. Decapitation. Necrophilia.*

I remembered Wolfman so I tried not to look at it too much. But again this created an argument in my head. *Don't look at it. Look at it.*

America was starting to change. Lots of bad things happened there. Most of the *Unsolved Mysteries* were there. Most of the serial killers were there. It was a place of guns and murder. Before it was surfing and girls and highschools and New Kids on the Block. Now it was all changing.

Changing overnight.

Changing before my eyes.

The Look

I NEVER answered Dad back. If he ever asked me to do something I did it straight away. There was no defiance from my side. When he went off at the dinner table I sat and took it. I tried to mix it up by looking away and then looking at him. So as not to be confrontational, but not ignore him either. Then he started saying that I was giving him *this look.*

Give me that look again and I'll knock your head off.

It was hard because I didn't know what this *look* was.

I tried to make my face normal. To pull no expression whatsoever but this wasn't good enough. He'd lose it, proper. Right on the edge of his temper.

Later on I'd ask Mum about it. Look, I don't know what *this look* is, I'd say.

He's right, you do. You do give him *that look.*

'I've Been Thinking About You'

DISCO SWIM was back, minus the T-rex. This made an impact. It was now flat. Boring. Pointless. The population had halved in size.

Jesus, Nile Greenaway said. How hard can it be to patch it up. A piece of tape.

Maybe they're teaching us a lesson, said Gavin Brown.

What lesson?

I don't know.

Poolwater ran off Nile's thoughtful face. His tan and round face. Just think how great the summer *could* have been had *someone* not keyed T-rex.

How do you know it was a key? Gavin said.

Well how else?

Can we talk about something else? I said.

We played on at Disco Swim but it wasn't the same. Just a few mats to surf on and one ball to pass between us. It was basically a normal swim, minus the grannies, and with a bit of music playing over it. A new song came on. I had heard it a few times and it gave me this heavy, sad feeling. A sensitive feeling like all my skin had been stripped off. 'I've Been Thinking About You', by Londonbeat. Even though we were having a good time and making the best of it the song grabbed me and twisted me up in the water. Made me get out the pool and run to the changing rooms. I was crying all the way. Doubled up and sobbing. Uncontrollable, inconsolable sobbing. Nile had followed me in.

Robin, WHAT IS WRONG?

His words and the way he said them was clear and big. He came over and put an arm across my shoulders. I cried and tried to give him an answer. Think of an answer. But overall there was nothing. I couldn't put it down to the one thing. The one reason. I was sorry about Disco Swim. Sorry for spoiling everyone's summer. I was sorry I had nearly killed that kid when the T-rex came down. I was sorry for the way I made Sam's life a misery. I was sobbing cos I missed Angela Stubbs and would never see her again. I was crying cos I had big ears and that girls didn't like me the way they liked Morgan and Gavin Brown. I was like this cos Mum will die one day. Crying for the kids in Africa and all the wars in the world. I was like this cos people were horrible to each other and I was one of them. I was crying because of all of this.

It's not the one thing, I told Nile.

I looked at him and I could tell he didn't know what I was on about. He said nothing but kept his arm there. He gave me what I needed. In that moment.

That song ended and another one came on. 'Me, Myself and I' by De La Soul. Its upbeat beat and light lyrics took me out of this within seconds. I was normal again. As if nothing ever happened.

Possession

I WAS WATCHING too many *Unsolved Mysteries*. I was still obsessing about that burning house. I began thinking about Wolfman again and that cannibal in America. I now knew what those words meant. *Dismembered. Decapitation. Necrophilia.* We were all having big Ghost Talks when we were hanging around at night. Nile Greenaway would tell one story and Tess Darby another. I was telling stories and making things up all the time. I had always thought my imagination was a gift but now I could see it was a curse. My mind would go in on itself. See things that weren't there. When I watched murder documentaries at night I went right into it. The area, the house, the murder itself. What it would all look like. I felt like my mind was working against me. I began to make rituals to keep me safe. Touch steps. Walk along lines and kerbs. Say sentences over and over again. I began to stutter in my speech and have nervous tics on my face. I tried to hide this but it made it worse. This was a dark period. I was heading into dark days. Things I knew and didn't know. Were ghosts real? Did England have serial killers too? Was it possible for a ten-year-old boy to be possessed?

I was babysitting Sam now every week. Sometimes on a Friday. Sometimes on a Saturday. Sometimes both. Late one night we had watched way too much dark stuff. Sam wanted to watch cartoons but I wouldn't let him. Then I started scaring him. Stories didn't really scare Sam cos he didn't understand the words so instead I would make noises and pull faces. I pretended I was possessed. I got more and more. More disturbing and extreme. As this went on I was finding it hard to stop myself. Like I had no control. Now I was even scaring *myself*. On how far I was taking this. How far I *could* take this. We sat side by side on the sofa seat. He was white faced and scared to death. I was scared to death too and didn't know what I was going to do next. So I jumped up and ran to the kitchen and grabbed a kitchen knife. Ran back into the front room and started wielding the blade in a repeated stabbing motion. While pulling a fiendish face. Sam was now screaming and paralysed. When I saw this I dropped the knife and began to cry. Hugged him up and told him I'd never hurt him cos he was my little brother and I was here to protect him. We were both crying in a bundle on the chair. All the time I was craving to start scaring him again. It was like there were two forces inside me, battling to get on top of each other, vying for control.

I didn't quite know what was happening.

I didn't quite know what was happening *to me.*

I was so relieved when Mum rang around 11pm.

I'll be home in an hour, she said.

Can you come home now?

Why what's wrong?

I think I might be possessed.

There was loads of pub noise in the background.

What you on about? she said.

I keep scaring Sam and I don't know why. Like I can't help it.

Oh just pack it in and go to bed.

I really think I need help. I really think I might be possessed.

Look … just stop scaring Sam. We'll be home in an hour.

When she put the phone down I felt more of the urges. They were lapping up against my brain. So I put on the first-ever wrestling tape we got and sat next to him. Put my arm around him. He was still scared. I could tell. I could feel it in his neck. Every time I moved he tensed back up. I tried to concentrate on the wrestlers and on the love I felt for Sam. I kept looking at the clock. Counting down the time until my mum came home.

The House of Jack Glass

SMASHING GLASS. We were exactly where we were this time last year. Smashing glass. Somehow I had found myself hanging around with Bart Tucker again. We three were back on. Wandering the late-summer school holidays. Putting windows through wherever we go. This time Bart and I were taking more of a backseat role, giving Sam the bricks instead. He didn't know what he was doing. We just loaded him up and pointed, sent him on his way. We decided to call for Jack Glass. See if he wanted in on the action.

I don't really know him, Bart said. Never been in his class.

Glass is going up to Big School, I said. He's all right. Thinks he's hard but he's not. Thinks he's brave but he's not.

Will he smash windows? Bart asked.

Probably not. But we'll call for him anyway.

We knocked on but no one was there.

I remembered the key he left under the mat. I looked out for his neighbours.

He's not in, Bart said.

We climbed over his backfence and out onto the wasteland. I looked back over at his house.

Sam, I said, take these bricks and put them through his windows.

Bart's eyes went big. His eyes were yellow and cunning.

Sam took the bricks and looked confused.

Do this and you can be in our gang.

What gang?

Me and Bart are the Trouble Twins but do this and we'll be the Trouble Triplets.

Sam went, wandered over. We had to help him over the fence and then pass the bricks through a gap. Bart and I then ran over to the long grass and crouched in it. Watching Sam's orange head through the tall yellow stalks.

He's fearless, Bart said.

Yeah, I said.

I agreed but this wasn't true. *Fearless* wasn't the word. It was something else.

Just then there was an almighty crash of glass. Louder than ever before. A shattering in the middle of this workday Tuesday. Sam ran back down and we helped him over the fence. We waited. Waited longer for something to happen but nothing did so we sent him back up again.

Handing him another brick.

One more, I said.

One more, Bart said.

Sam nodded.

We pushed him over the fence and back up towards The House of Jack Glass.

A FEW WEEKS LATER I was back there. On my own. New windows were put in and he was none the wiser. Some other kids got blamed. The Sharpe Family, I guess. I knocked on and waited but no one was there.

I checked under the mat and there was the key. A dull rusty silver. I picked it up and saw a key-shaped pattern on the dusty concrete. I thought about going in. I thought about having a snoop. If they came home I'd be in big trouble. They might even work out that it was me who smashed the windows. Instead I put the key in my pocket and then took it to the nearest drain.

Markus Venner

A SHADOW came over me. Just seconds after dropping the key down the drain. A big shadow moved across the tarmac and covered me whole. The shadow was man shaped. A body and a head.

I saw that, it said. I saw what you just did. A key down the drain.

I didn't recognise the voice. But I recognised the face. It was the face of Markus Venner. I froze. I couldn't believe he was here in real life. Sat on the saddle of a silver Mongoose bike. His white face and red lips. Narrow Chinese eyes and his good head of hair. I tried to speak but couldn't. He was the biggest boy in town. The hardest and most feared. He was my age but the same size as my dad. He was expelled from every school and there was a rumour he killed cats.

Whose key is that? he said.

I stepped away and turned.

Look at me when I'm talking to you.

I carried on walking. When I turned he was still smiling, hanging casually over his handlebars.

You can run but you can't hide, he said with cool menace. I'll find you, man. We'll catch up soon. Where you go, I go. I'm your shadow.

I ran on.

His voice in my ear. His breath on my neck.

The whole way home.

Six

The Last Room

GOING INTO the last year. It felt like an optical illusion to see everybody together. Two worlds in one room. A grand finale of characters. Kayleigh Highman on the same table as Tess Darby. Nile Greenaway sat opposite Kev Moss. Morgan Davenport staring down Bart Tucker. There was Zoe Maggio and Amanda Carlton. Diane Dunne and Zara Ellis giggling over Gavin Brown. I had no idea who was going to be my best friend. Who I would fancy. I had no idea what was going to happen next.

I Had Been American

NOW for almost two years. It wasn't as strong as it once was but it still needed maintenance. I still needed to remind them every once in a while. I now knew more. I could now easily distinguish the difference between states and cities. That cities were *in* states. I now had a rough geography of where places were. New York was east and Washington, DC was east and Boston was east. My hometown of San Francisco was west. So was Los Angeles and Seattle. Texas was south and that Milwaukee place where the cannibal was from was north. I had dropped using American words but still had the feeling of all things American. Like I said, it was in the blood and would be for life.

The Structure of Things

ALSO GOING INTO the last year it was important to know who you could fight and who you couldn't. Where you stood in the pecking order. It was a system that held us all together. A structure that kept order.

I looked around at all the boys and did the honest maths in my head.

Kev Moss, no.

Morgan Davenport, definitely no.

Nile Greenaway, absolutely no way.

Outside this class, in the lower year, and Aiden Beecham was an Absolutely No Way too. There was another kid in the lower year called Gary Stanley who was another hard no.

Gavin Brown was about the same level.

The rest of the school I could take. Bart Tucker was causing me some bother. He was someone I know I could take but he was acting like I couldn't and this was a glitch in the system. This was stopping the machine from running smoothly and it had to be taken care of before we could all move on.

Why do you let him talk to you like that? Nile said.

I know, I said.

Nile shook his head. Sort it out, Robin.

Goose Fair

I WAS GETTING TO THE AGE whereby I was starting to see the cycles of things. My mind was starting to categorise events with times of the year. Going back to school happened followed by Goose Fair followed by Halloween followed by Bonfire Night followed by Sam's birthday followed by my birthday followed by Christmas.

Goose Fair was when the cold came in. When the leaves stuck to shoes.

We would do the same thing every year. Park in the exact same spot. Then walk the long windy road to the lights of the fair. Music of the night getting nearer, and louder.

I knew I was of an age now cos I had started to notice the ladies. The streetwalkers of Goose Fair. In and around the surrounding area. Long boots. Short skirts. Heels. Hair. They would stand around and there was always this strange energy as we passed them on the way to the fair. On the way back there would be twice as many. Waiting on corners. Stepping out into the road. Stopping cars. I didn't fully know what this meant but I was excited by it. Sam was playing with his new toy. Eating his candy floss. Holding Mum's hand. I was old enough to walk free now. It was dark and neon. Smoke and autumn mist. Red lights driving through it. I caught eyes with one as I crossed her on the street. She kept looking at me and looking at me. I was hoping she would smile. But she didn't.

Kayleigh Highman

WAS BACK. Mrs Carrol had placed me bang-opposite her. She was as loud and as funny as ever. She was an actress. Already she had me on the ropes.

So what did you do in the school holidays? she said.
Got a girlfriend, I said.
Really, she said.
Really, I said.
Tell her you were American?
I *am* American.
And where *was* this girlfriend?
Holiday.
Where?
Cleavewood.
Where's that?
Devon.
Where in Devon?
I don't know. Just Devon.
The shy kids were moving their heads back and forth like tennis.
What's her name?
Angela.
That's my mum's name.
Oh.
What's she look like?
Brown bob. Brown eyes. Brown skin.
A Paki?
Not that kind of brown skin.
What kind of brown skin then?
Tan. Very tan.
She pretty?
Beautiful.
What she doing with you then?
That punched me in the ribs.
I'm funny. I'm fast.
Girls don't really care about that.
Oh.

An awkward pause, before breaking it by telling her the whole story from top to bottom. All the details. Fancy Dress Competition. The gang. The chases. Our goodbyes.

Kayleigh was captivated. Her head to one side. Her blue eyes gone big. In the end she had no choice but to believe me.

Give her a bracelet? she winked.

I thought she would have forgotten about that. I looked over the table to see Zoe Maggio sitting close up to Nile Greenaway.

All right, I said. That was ages ago.

The table went silent for a few moments. The shy kids were catching their breath.

So what did you do in the school holidays? I asked Kayleigh Highman.

Nothing much, she said.

Easy Rider

HE STOOD WEARING A LEATHER JACKET, admiring a tree. I was shocked he had a motorbike. Me, Kev Moss and Morgan Davenport surrounded him in the memorial park on the other side of town.

What you boys doing this far out? Michaels said.

We three just shrugged.

You're the bad boys, right? Getting into adventures.

We all smirked and shrugged. His black motorcycle helmet was cradled into his forearm like a baby.

I was just looking at the memorial, he said.

He started talking about the war but we didn't have a clue what he was on about. He started telling us about when he was in the army. Morgan was checking out his bike, looking at it from all angles.

I didn't get it cos this was not like Mr Michaels at all. Not the Michaels I knew and hated. Out here he was a completely different man. His eyes were soft. His smile was warm. He no longer despised me.

You all in your last year, yeah?

We nodded.

Then big school, right?

We all nodded.

Bet you all going to the same one, yeah?

We nodded yet again.

Band of brothers.

We looked at each other and smiled.

He was still talking that same American way.

Hey you guys gonna try out for the team this year?

Yeah.

You still number one player hey, Robin?

I nodded.

Truth is I hadn't kicked a ball in over a year. With wrestling now over it was time for a comeback.

Michaels put his hand through his hair.

Well it just so happens I'm gonna be manager this year.

Even though he was being cool and nice I couldn't help but feel my stomach drop on hearing that. Michaels knew nothing about football so why the fuck was he being manager.

But hey, he said. No one knows about this. So keep it between us, right?

We all nodded.

But as for you three … I can't see you guys having a problem making the team.

He winked and nodded again.

Anyway, you boys. I better get going. Hot date tonight.

He winked again and put the helmet over his perfect hair. Zipped up his leather and then kicked his bike into action. Some smoke rose up past the memorial. He did a cool gesture with his hand and then rolled out into the road. Put his fist into the air, before heading for the hills.

Cool bike, said Morgan.

He's all right, said Kev.

I didn't say anything. Just watched him pull a slight wheelie as he rode by the church.

Nile Greenaway & Zoe Maggio

WERE THE FIRST OFFICIAL couple in class and I don't know how I felt about it.

Nile kept singing a new song in the charts, *dizzy, my head is spinning.*

They talked with each other freely and openly and it was like they were a proper adult couple. They went for tea at each other's house and ran lines from the film *Ghost*.

See ya later, baby.

I love you.

Ditto.

Mrs Carrol had to tell them off for using Americanisms.

Mrs Carrol Had an Announcement to Make

SHE STOOD in front of the class and looked kind of serious. We wondered if anyone had died. She wore the same shell suit she wore every day. Her purple eyes held us firm.

We have a new boy starting class on Monday.

She looked slowly around the class.

Now, he had quite a hard time at his last school, so I need you all to be patient with him. He needs time and space. He needs new friends. He hasn't had an easy home life either.

I felt like she was telling us too much. But at the same time it was like she was preparing us for something. The room suddenly felt like it was shrinking. Or as if something was filling it up.

Mrs Carroll too, felt *off*. Out of her depth in some way. Which was highly unusual.

Anyway, she petered off, have a good weekend and I will see you back here on Monday morning.

The Garden Thief

KEV MOSS used his jumping skills to drop down into the garden below.

Robin, c'mon.

There was no way I was jumping that so I climbed down most of it and then jumped the rest. It was strange being in someone else's garden. A private world. We pretended to look for a ball in case anyone came out of the house.

Watch this, Kev said.

He ran towards a hedge and vaulted into the crisp autumn blue. I watched his blond and the backs of his feet disappear over the hedge. No one could jump as high as Kev. He should be in the Olympics. Just then there was a voice, *oi*.

Kev was back in the blue. Over the green. He forward-rolled and then was back on his feet.

Run, he said.

This was my talent. I ran towards the house and Kev followed. Over the other side of the hedge there was someone else heading in the same direction. There was something chasing us. We cut through the gate and was out onto the hill. We kept on running. Just then a man appeared.

Fuck, Kev said.

He's following us.

Hey, thief, the man said. Come back here.

He started to track us. Followed me and Kev all the way back to my close, then house.

You stole my property. You stole my property, he kept shouting.

We didn't know what he meant. The man was being weird and a little over the top. Kev had been in his backgarden for no longer than a few seconds and now he was following us all the way home. We took the backsteps and the backdoor. Mum was in the kitchen and I tried to tell her what had happened when this man appeared in *my* backgarden, banging on the door.

Your son is a thief. Your son and his friend just stole my property.

We didn't, Mum. We just cut through for like ten seconds.

The man had his face up to our window. He wouldn't stop talking. That's when Dad appeared. Fucking hell is going on here, he said.

Your son has been in my garden. He's a thief.

What has he stole?

My property, shouted the man. He's stolen my property.

Dad waved him away. Go on, fuck off.

But he was in my garden.

Yeah and now *you're* in mine, Dad said.

The man went to say something else but Dad swung for him. Mum was immediately in his way. The punch didn't land fully but it still knocked him back into the fence. After that he was gone.

Stay out of people's gardens, Dad said to me, before closing the door.

Me and Kev walked back up towards school.

That was cool, he said. I wish my dad punched people.

Kurt Savage

WEEEEEEEE-HOOOOOOOO.

His voice cut through the much-anticipated Monday morning. He wasn't an eleven-year-old boy but a big fat teenager. At first we had him down for *someone else*. A guest. Somebody's kid. He couldn't be our age. He couldn't be in our class. He couldn't be the boy in question. The new boy in town. He was absolutely massive. Not just in height and weight but in *everything*. The way he looked around and moved around. His overwhelming confidence. His large pink mouth, glistening with saliva. His mad-everywhere eyes, magnified behind a pair of multicoloured glasses. Eyeballs rolling around in his head like they had a life of their own. Not a word yet. Not a full sentence. Just this sound over and over again.

Weeeeeeee-Hoooooooo. Weeeeeeee-Hoooooooo.

Mrs Carrol had the same stony expression on her face as Friday. Full of worry. Out of her depth.

Kurt Savage spread across all three tables at the front of the class like something at the bottom of the ocean. Sloppy and grotesque.

All morning no one went near him. Not at lunch either.

Eventually in the late afternoon we approached him tentatively. Morgan Davenport followed by me followed by Nile Greenway. Like three zookeepers inching towards a beast in a cage.

All right, lads, he said. So, which girls do all the fucking around here?

Home

I WENT THERE and closed the door and went upstairs and fell on my bed. I felt dirty and scared. Like something had just ended and something else was about to begin. At the end of the day Kurt Savage had talked to me, Morgan and Nile. He had told us a bit about the care home where he lived. He also told us about this girl called Tracy who lived there. I had never heard anything like it. He said he was going to tell us more tomorrow. I couldn't wait to hear more, and the same time, I really didn't want to know.

Dad was away and it was just me, Mum and Sam.

So what's this new lad like? Mum said.

I held a Brusselsprout up to my mouth. I tried to think of something to say. I tried to think of a word or two but nothing would come. Instead I pushed the Brussel between my teeth and swallowed it whole. Feeling the lump stick in my throat.

Playground

KURT SAVAGE stood in the centre of it. In the centre of us, the boys. He talked and we listened. Then mid-story he started walking and we followed. He walked us towards the steps, the wall, the edge of the autumn field. He sat and we stood around him and carried on listening. It wasn't until a few minutes later that I realised he had moved us around like this. The rest of the boys were transfixed. Kurt talked on and on about the care home where he lived. He talked about this girl Tracy. We asked questions where we could.

How old is she?

Fourteen.

Colour hair she have?

Black.

She your girlfriend?

Nah, he said. Just a fuck.

He then went into it full. He talked about body parts. He talked about private parts. He mixed them together and told us what sex was and how it happened. He went into details about the clothes she wore and how she took them off. Bra and knickers. He used words I'd never heard of. Words even Morgan Davenport didn't know about. After he talked about raves. Going to a rave. Taking drugs and drinking alcohol.

I can rave all night, he said. I can fuck all night too.

Boy-boobs and rolls of fat bulged from his t-shirt. He didn't feel the cold. His eyes were mad and his teeth were yellow and his lips were covered in spit. He had spots.

All the boys were quiet on the way back into class. There was a lot of staring into space. It was strange to be around the girls again. I was finding it hard to see them in the same way.

What's the new kid like? Kayleigh said.

She was right opposite me like she always was.

Robin, she pushed on. What is he like?

It was hard to look in her eyes.

Home at Night

IT WAS HARD to sleep. I moved around in the bed. I took my pyjamas off and then put them back on again. I thought about Kurt's dirty mouth and wanted to be sick. The white slug-like scar over his lip. His soggy body and the dirt under his fingernails. If it wasn't him I was thinking about then it was Tracy. Tracy with curves and tits. Fourteen-year-old Tracy who would let *anybody* do *anything*.

Older or younger it didn't matter. Age sixteen or age ten it didn't make a difference.

Take you to meet her, if you want? Kurt had said.

This prospect was both thrilling and repulsive at the same time.

Part of me wanted to save her and part of me wanted to fuck her. *Fuck her.* Whatever that was and whatever that meant.

Kurt's words had a place in my head. Mainlining my desires.

Weeeeeeee-Hoooooooo

HE never stopped making that noise and the teachers could do nothing about it.

Why do you lot even do what the teachers say, he said. They can't *make* you. They can't hit you.

This was the logic he used in doing what he wanted. He ate when he wanted. Went to the toilet when he wanted. He never even argued with the teachers. Just laughed in their faces.

Weeeeeeee-Hoooooooo.

The sound was almost like a siren. Letting us know when he was coming and going. The girls were scared of him. The boys were scared of him.

At lunch a crowd gathered around Nile Greenaway.

What are you going to do? they asked.

They wanted to know if Kurt was the new Hardest in the School. Nile didn't back away but he didn't want it either. A ring was formed and Kurt and Nile was pushed together. The crowd demanded an answer. Kurt was smiling the whole time, his mad depthless eyes. His streetwise speech.

If it comes to it, then we'll see.

There was so much pressure on Nile in this moment that he broke. He started crying. It was a shocking sight to see. Nile Greenaway crying. It came out of nowhere.

Nile crying put Kurt straight on top, without lifting a finger. In everyone's mind Neil had given up. Forfeited his position. He had fallen.

I felt the structure of things crumble. It was like some virus had found its way in, altering the shape of our reality.

Kurt went up and shook his hand. Taking an invisible crown off his head and putting it on his own.

Morgan Davenport

WE looked at him to do something.

Can't you get your brothers?

I don't need my brothers, he said.

It was that signature scowl of his. Tight jaw. Tongue between his teeth.

I'm not scared of him, he said. Not one bit.

This was the piece of hope we clung to.

Football

I HAD one at my feet. I was rusty. Rusty but not forgotten. Some of that old skill came back. Hour by hour. Dribbles. Kick-ups. Shots. Turns. Once I was up to a certain standard I got Kev Moss back on it. He wasn't as fast or as skilful as me but his shots were harder and he was a genius in the air, headers. Then we got Morgan out. Then Greenaway. Football was back.

You know Michaels is manager this year.

Really? Greenaway said.

Hush, he told us not to say anything, Moss said.

Fuck him, I said.

Yeah, fuck him, Davenport echoed.

Us four should make it.

Easy, I said.

Yeah, easy.

Aiden Beecham will be captain.

Yeah, he is the best. We all agreed.

I wonder if Kurt can play.

Nah, I said. Too fat.

Inside the Outside

WHAT ABOUT TRACY?

Kurt was leaving the care home. They had found him a foster parent.

What about Tracy? I asked again.

He had his thick forearm inside his joggers, scratching his balls.

Guess I'll just have to find someone else to fuck, he yawned.

YOU HUNGRY?

It was afternoon playtime and we were all playing Wally against the Spiderwall. Kicking a ball at a chalked circle in the bricks.

Tuck shop's closed, we said.

Fuck that. I'll just go normal shop.

What do you mean? we said.

Gimmie some money and I'll go normal shop.

You mean, *out there*? We nodded over the Spiderwall.

Yeah.

Like you will, we said.

Why not?

Cos we're at school.

So?

So you'll be in the biggest trouble ever.

They can't hit you.

Why do you always say that?

They can't though.

You'll be expelled.

So?

So you'll be in trouble.

With who?

We wanted to say *your mum and dad* but it was here where Kurt got his superpower.

Morgan stepped up to him. Handed him a fiver.

You dare go shop and buy us all some sweets then you can keep the change.

Done, he said, whipping the fiver out of Morgan's hand.

We couldn't believe what we were seeing. He jumped the wall and ducked the beam. Dropped down into the car park. As he neared the school's perimeter I expected an invisible forcefield to bounce him back in. It didn't. Kurt walked right through it.

CAN I COME TO YOUR HOUSE?

Er, okay, I said.

I had already told Mum about Kurt so maybe this wasn't a good idea.

He was starting to follow me everywhere. I was the only one who really spoke to him. Only one who gave him time. Guess I was the only one who was intrigued. About his life. His care home. Tracy.

The raves and the drugs. I guess I was the only one who wanted to know where *all this* had started.

We'll go to your house first, then mine, he said.

Okay.

Outside of school he was quieter. There was no Weeeeeeee-Hooooooooo. He followed me home and I was nervous. Taking this *all this* into my house without my dad being there. Straight away Mum was off. Not the same as she normally was. She was quiet and moved around uneasily. I got Kurt a drink of Coke and sat on a beanbag in the living room.

Is your brother a spas? he said.

What do you mean?

I don't know. He don't seem right.

Sam was staring into the cartoons.

When I looked back Kurt had managed to fit the entire Coke glass into his mouth. I could see everything in there. Yellow teeth and black teeth. Tonsils right at the back. His giant pink tongue moving around like a slug.

WE GOING MY HOUSE THEN?

It wasn't far. Over the hill, by the cemetery. Cut through an alleyway. I was shocked to see his foster mum. She was so old it was more of a foster grandparent. She barely spoke. Didn't even really smile. It was here I felt so sorry for Kurt that I wanted to cry. I can't imagine not having a mum and dad. It must be the worst thing in the world.

WHAT IS HE DOING NOW? one of the girls said.

Kurt had thrown himself to the floor and was rolling across the carpet, convulsing.

He's doing an impression of a spas, I said.

We all did this but Kurt's impression was the best. This was the first time he'd done one and it was by far the best I'd ever seen. He was really going for it. Smashing his head against the wall and everything. We all stood around, pointing and laughing.

What's that coming out of his mouth? the girl said.

He was foaming at the mouth. Turning red and then blue and then purple. It was here Carrol and Duplantis ran in. Get out of the room, they both screamed.

Michaels came in and ushered us out.

He's having an epileptic fit, the girl said.

A what?

It was the end of the day so we finished half hour early. Everyone waited near the hall but I waited around the classroom. His image was still fresh in my mind. His head against the wall. The froth in his mouth. All the different colours of his face. I was convinced he was dead.

Can I see his body? I said to Michaels.

Go home, Robin.

I have a right to see his body.

Robin, go home.

He was my best friend, I whispered.

Robin, Michaels said. Not everything is about *you. I'm* taking care of this, he said.

Michaels turned me by the shoulders and sent me away.

The class was waiting for me in the car park, waiting for the verdict.

He's gonna make it, I told them.

Some of them looked relieved. Most did not.

Trials

MICHAELS lined us up on Monday evening. He tried to do kick-ups but the ball went everywhere. We all looked at each other and wondered what the hell was going on. Aiden Beecham was smiling to himself.

Our first game is on Friday night, Michaels said. You guys show me what you got and I will put the team on the wall.

I had been playing every playtime, lunchtime and nighttime. My skills were back. I was probably going to be the second-best player after Beecham. Michaels picked the teams and stood on the sideline and shouted loads of American stuff. He had his eyes on us. He wrote things down on a piece of paper. Then it happened like it always happened. I bottled it. I felt the pressure and got into my head and came undone. The ball bounced off my shin. I passed it to the wrong player. I got tangled up. I ran out of position and created a goal for the other team. Everyone else played the same. Beecham. Bart Tucker. Greenaway. Moss and Davenport. Everyone played with the same ability but I did not. I bottled it like I always did.

225

Piggyback Tournament

WRESTLING was still banned so we started something else. A piggyback tournament. We got into pairs and then one kid would give another kid a piggyback and we'd face off against each other. I had to pick a partner. Seeing as Kurt Savage was twice as big as everyone else and the new Hardest in the School, I picked him. There was no way I was going to lose. I was quite shocked to see Nile Greenaway team up with my brother Sam.

It wasn't the time of the year for the field but we managed to find a patch of grass near the wall, by the woods. It was kind of hidden so the dinnerladies wouldn't see us. The tournament started. Me and Kurt went through everybody with ease. He was too big and mad. He piled in hard and I barely had to do anything. Kids were falling about everywhere.

As with the wrestling days Paul Martin was referee.

While we rested, between bouts, we watched the rest. Greenaway and Sam were doing what we had been doing, taking people out with ease.

The final is set, Paul Martin announced. Kurt and Robin versus Nile and Sam.

I'd never seen Sam look so happy in the limelight. So happy and top of the world. It was nearing end of lunch and we had to decide whether to do the final now or at last afternoon playtime.

Now, Paul Martin announced.

A ring formed around us. Nerves set in. I did the quick maths in my head. Kurt Savage was stronger than Nile and I was stronger than Sam, so it should be a clear and easy win. We squared off and circled. A whistle went and dinnerladies were waving everybody in. I was looking at Sam right in the eyes. Kurt's body odour stunk but I didn't care and blocked it out. Kids shouted from the circle. Most wanted Nile and Sam to win. I grabbed Sam's wrist but Nile stepped back suddenly and yanked us forward. Kurt stumbled and slipped and we were over. My head just missed the wall.

An almighty roar. Nile and Sam in full celebration. Punching the air. Never seen my little brother so happy, so triumphant.

It doesn't count, I said.

What doesn't? Paul Martin said.

The whistle had gone. Lunchtime over.

Oh he always does this, some other kid said. Robin, you are the worst loser in the world.

We all argued about it while the dinnerladies screamed at us to get inside. Everyone was against me. I looked at Kurt for support but he was nowhere in sight. Just the sound of his Weeeeeeee-Hoooooooo heading back into class.

It doesn't count, I said again. Whistle had gone.

It was here Nile really lost it at me.

You're such a bad loser, Robin. You can *never* accept a loss, *ever*. Just cos I beat you. Your *own* brother beat you. Your own *little* brother. Well I'll tell you what, Robin, you want a rematch, you got it.

Nile was normally easy and light but something had got to him. Something deeper. Bigger. Something about beating Kurt and putting himself back on top. The structure of things. Nile had something to prove. Me and Sam will beat you and Kurt. This afternoon. It's on.

Paul Martin stepped forward and formally announced this.

I was nervous. I was scared.

I took Kurt Savage to one side. You need to take this seriously, I said.

Weeeeeeee-Hoooooooo.

I said seriously, Kurt. Your reputation is on the line.

Weeeeeeee-Hoooooooo.

Before playtime I managed to catch Sam in the playground.

Hey, Sam, I'm your older brother, right?

He nodded his white face.

I need you to lose this fight.

What?

I need you to fall off Nile's back.

Why?

I need you to let me win.

I want to win.

Yeah but I need you to let *me* win.

No.

I grabbed his wrist and twisted it.

I'll make your life a misery if you don't.

You already make my life a misery.

Something in these words stunned me.

We gonna win, he said.

Sam, PLEASE, I said. I need this.

So do I, he said.

Just then Nile walked the corner and caught us. You all right, Sam? he said.

227

Sam nodded.

We gonna win this?

Sam nodded again.

Nile held me with his eyes the whole time.

THE CROWD CHEERED. I was on my back and Kurt Savage was on his back. We were both rolling around in the mud. Utterly defeated. Sam and Nile were up in the air. Everybody was happy. Order was restored. The structure of things was back where it belonged. I watched Sam's face closely and realised this was the first time I'd seen him smile in ages. In me I broke and accepted the narrative as it was. The oldest narrative there is. Good triumphing over Evil.

Teamsheet

WASPUTONTHEWALL. Everyone was on but me. It was hardly surprising and I couldn't complain nor could anyone else. I couldn't even blame Michaels. I got what I deserved. It was crazy to think that two years ago I was the youngest to make the squad. Now I was top age and I couldn't even make the team. I couldn't make the starting eight. Lucky I was even a sub. My teammates ran onto the pitch that Friday evening. Blazing blue and white stripes of the school's signature colours and here I was on the sidelines, next to the girls.

Can you tell your sub to put a jacket on, the ref said. Can you tell him to cover up.

I did. Zipped up my coat.

Why aren't you playing? Amanda Carlton said.

I didn't answer her. Just stared straight ahead.

Mr Murdoch

ALL KIDS were terrified of him. *All* kids. Even Davenport didn't backchat him. Most didn't even look at him let alone answer him back. If he entered the room you stood up straight and stared forward like he was a sergeant major. I had yet to see Savage and Murdoch in the same room and the prospect of this had me on edge. Unstoppable Force meets Immovable Object. The physics of this was fascinating.

Weeeeeeee-Hoooooooo.

Murdoch stepped in the dinner hall as Kurt was going for it.

What is that animal noise? Murdoch bellowed.

Complete quiet fell over the hall like a blanket. Not a pin drop.

Not a pin drop but then,

Weeeeeeee-Hoooooooo.

Who is that?

Red stormed Murdoch's face. His jowls drooping and swaying as he marched to the top table. The top table where Kurt Savage sat alone. Pushing mash potato through his face. His multicoloured specs steamed up.

Was that you?

Was what me?

Don't speak with your mouth full.

Murdoch's rage was terrifying but Kurt wasn't terrified.

Well you did ask me a question. Mash was now all down his chin and all down his t-shirt.

Look at you, disgusting boy.

Kurt opened his mouth and more mash-goo dripped out.

Look at *you*, ya fuckin' nonce.

Murdoch's red face went white. Completely white.

Kurt Savage was now in the full flow of fearless hysteria.

You a fuckin' nonce, mate. I know one when I see one. And you *are* one. A fuckin' nonce.

Murdoch couldn't speak so instead he ran to the seated boy, who stood and put his knife up.

Try it, nonce. And I'll cut your nonce face out of your nonce head.

The hall and all the people in it had never seen anything like this in their life. Kurt was still smiling and having a good time. Still gulping down his mash. The knife stayed where it was. Eventually he put it down and left the hall, the school, for the very last time. His schoolbag stayed where it was. Indecipherable graffiti scrawled all over it. The rest of lunch was silent. The rest of the day, week, year.

Year 2000

1992. Yet another new date at the top of the page. Where was the time going? Writing 1990 seemed ages ago yet at the same time five minutes. A square kid kept talking about Albert Einstein but I didn't know who he was. Kayleigh Highman said if she doesn't make it as an actress she's going to be an air hostess so she can fly around the world. I kept looking at the date at the top of my page. *6.1.1992.* My pencil was smudged. I imagined the years going up. *93. 94. 95. 96.* I imagined the year 2000. How I will be a man. Maybe married with kids. The year 2000 is absolutely light years away and by then we may be run by robots. Hoverboards and flying cars. And we won't have to do anything because we can just press buttons and everything will be brought to us. I thought about it and thought about it but in the end I had to stop. It is too far in the future to even think about.

We Lost

OUR FIRST THREE GAMES under the Michaels regime.

3-1.

4-0.

7-2.

Aiden Beecham scored all of our goals. In training Michaels had us jog around the school premises chanting an army song. With the pressure off I now started playing normal again. I was now back to being the second-best player in the team.

Can Robin start the next game, sir? Greenaway said. He's our second-best player.

Sorry, Michaels said. But he didn't cut it in the trials.

What difference does that make? He's here *now.*

I can't take the risk, he said.

What risk?

I'm the manager, Nile.

But we need him.

I'm the manager, Nile.

We lost the next game 5-1. Aiden Beecham scored our only goal.

We were getting tired of Michaels. In our next training session he made us run around some cones and then got us to sit in a circle and play *Cookie Jar.*

We all had to sing the lines *Who stole the cookie from the cookie jar? Robin stole the cookie from the cookie jar. Who me? Yes you. Couldn't be. Then who stole …*

Sir, this is dumb.

Quiet, Robin.

Like what has this got to do with football?

It's team building.

It's dumb.

Quiet, Robin.

We're not six-year-olds.

This made everybody stop singing and start laughing. Michaels lost it.

Inside, Robin.

What do you mean inside?

Go inside.

The school's closed. There is no inside.

More laughter.

Right, one game's suspension.

One game's suspension, I mimicked. You don't even play me. How can I be suspended when I don't even play.

You're off the subs' bench, he said.

So I *am* playing?

Michaels was now really confused and getting madder by the second.

I mean, you're not even a sub. You're dropped from the team *completely.*

I pulled out a chunk of wet grass and threw it at him. Stormed off. Home.

Another Valentine's

SAME as it ever was. Gavin Brown and Morgan Davenport got most.

Nile Greenaway, some.

Rest of us, none.

I was going to give Kayleigh Highman one. It had to be this way. Our lessons were now full on. Every day there was something. A sparring match of flirtation. The days of making Valentine's cards with our hands were over. We were now grown-ups with pocket money. I bought her one from the shop. Penned it the night before and sealed it with a kiss. I was surprised no one else had got her one. She was pretty and blue-eyed and full of sunny radiance.

It sat in my bag.

What's up with you, she said. Seen a ghost?

People handed out their Valentine's cards easy enough.

You're white, she said.

I went into my bag but couldn't bring myself to do it.

Kayleigh sat looking at me, and then at the empty space in front of her.

AT LUNCH I went down to the bottom of the orchard and ripped the card up into loads of pieces and then threw it in a bush. I got scared of anyone looking in my bag so this way it would be gone for good.

NILE AND ZOE had gone all out. Flowers, teddy bears, the lot. Towards the end of the day Nile collared me.

How did it go with Kayleigh? he said.

What do you mean?

Give her a card?

No, why would I?

She got you one.

What?

She was waiting for you to go first.

What?

That's why no one has got her one this year. Everybody just *assumed* she was yours.

I couldn't say anything else. Nile went off with Zoe, holding hands. Morgan and Kerry were holding hands too. Kev and Diane Dunne were talking on a wall. I headed home on my own. At the bottom of the close Kayleigh was getting into her mum's car. She sat in the passenger seat like an adult, pulling the seatbelt across her little chest.

My Girl

MUM took us cinema on Saturday afternoon. Cinema then McDonald's. We was going to watch *My Girl* with that lad from *Home Alone*. We were taking Sam's new friend called Matthew Fox.

Why can't I take one of my friends? I said.

We always go with your friends. Just let Sam have *this*.

I yawned and looked the other way.

Plus, I can't afford anyone else. I'm not made of money.

It made sense. She had a point.

We went Odeon and got some popcorn. I didn't know why we were watching this anyway. *My Girl*. It didn't sound like there was going to be any fighting. It didn't sound like a film for boys. It sounded like it might be boring. We watched on. It was better than I thought. Set in America. Set in the past. I liked the feel of it. The America I knew and loved. Big white houses and hosepipe lawns. A lake. A ropeswing. I'd heard the film was supposed to be sad but it didn't look sad to me. Then it took a turn. The girl had lost her ring and the boy went back to find it, only he got attacked by bees. Earlier the boy had said he was allergic to bees so this put me on edge. He tried to fight them off. He looked so helpless, spinning around circles, trying to hit them away with his little hands. Eventually he fell in the grass and his glasses fell off. I couldn't believe they had killed him off halfway through the film. Now what are we supposed to do? This was the story of the film. Mourning the loss of the little boy. The funeral was awful. The girl came in while he was laying there in his little coffin. She was totally heartbroken. *He can't see without his glasses.* That line did me. I was done. My face streaming as I silently sobbed in the dark. When I looked over Mum was the same. The film didn't end there. It went from one heartbreaking scene to the next. Girl reads a poem. Girl given her ring back from the boy's mum. It never ends.

We left traumatised. Mute with grief. We didn't talk at McDonald's. Sam and his friend played on, perfectly oblivious. Too young to understand. Mum and me sat side by side on the bus ride home. Numb. Staring into space. Wishing the boy hadn't died. Wishing it was a different story altogether.

Paper, Scissors, Stone

MORGAN, MOSS and Me vs Tromans, Carlton and Darby. The two-part ramp of Black Path, dimming with the dying of light. A lift of dusk. March going into April. We had wrestled and ran and climbed ourselves into a delicious exhaustion. Tired in trying to impress the girls. They had their way. Turning on the cool of the railing, a flash of stomach every now and then. We were burntout but not dead. The slow hum of a soft mania. Hot and high and giddy. Now we were all lying on the moist yellow grass, thinking what to do next.

What next? Tess Darby said.

We shrugged and the other two girls giggled.

What now? Tess pushed on.

233

You're the one with the ideas, I said.

Paper, scissors, stone, she said.

What's that? Morgan said.

And for what? Kerry added.

Tess stood and pulled her top.

Boys versus girls. Girls win, boys show their bits. Boys win, and we show ours.

Whoa, Kerry laughed.

The boys all stood at once, as if on command.

I'm down with that, I said.

Morgan nodded.

Kev hung his head, a little embarrassed. All right, he said.

So how's this work? I said.

Tess was the only one wearing a dress. She stepped forward and talked like she already had this all worked out.

Morgan plays Kerry, paper, scissors, stone. Amanda plays Kev, paper, scissors, stone. And then I play *you*, paper, scissors, stone.

So it's best of three? Kev said.

I don't get it, Morgan said.

She talked Morgan through it once more. And then it was on. We faced off, three on three. Boy opposite girl.

Morgan beat Kerry.

So now you have to show us your fannies? he said.

Not yet, Tess said. Two more games. And remember, you lose and you have to show us your cocks.

That word coming out of her mouth made my head spin. Kerry and Amanda were beetroot red, looking down, not really taking any of this seriously.

Amanda then beat Kev Moss.

Tess grabbed my wrist and pulled me into her. Right, she said. It's one-all. Deciding match. Me versus *you*.

My brain was so scrambled I could barely remember how the game was played. Which hand beat which hand. To keep it simple I went right down the middle all three times.
Scissors, scissors, scissors.

I won yet Tess's face lit up like she had.

It's pussy time, Morgan said, clapping his hands. His strong smile lighting up the mischief in his face.

Kev was moving around on the spot.

I was shot, confused. A dark unknown exhilaration.

234

Kerry and Amanda were laughing like crazy. Stepping back and turning away, covering up.

Tess didn't hesitate. She didn't rush either. Up went her dress and down came her knickers.

The shock on all five of our faces, eye to eye with a full bush.

Debut

WE were already three-down. It was always the same. I wore a tracktop over the blue and white stripes. Bottom half was shorts, shins and boots. Most of the game I kicked about with the younger kids. Early in the season I stood around Michaels, hoping he would put me on. Now we were back to being sworn enemies so my chances were Jack and Shit. Second half came and our boys were walking into our 6th straight loss of the season. We were bottom of the league. The glory days of Tommy Philips, Arron Rose and Richard Docherty were long gone.

Then from nowhere Aiden Beecham scored and two minutes later Kev Moss jumped over everyone and headed in a second. We were back in it. Only a goal away from breaking our losing streak and that's when I heard my name being called out by Michaels.

My name, impossibly, coming from his lips.

Robin.

It was so far-fetched and inconceivable that I thought he wanted me for something else. I waited for his next words.

On, he said.

I stood there dumb, a kind of slow paralysis wrapping around each limb.

Captain and star-man Aiden Beecham screamed from the centre circle. Face flame-red.

On!

Everyone was watching me. The whole field. Players, parents, teachers. The Second-best Player was coming on to do the business. Fresh-legged and eager to prove. Score the equaliser. Score the winner. Become the hero and cement his legacy. Michaels eating humble pie. Okay, Robin, you may have bottled the trials but you sure did turn this thing around.

I did what I did all those years ago on my first full debut with Dad. Run on the pitch with my tracktop still on. One of their players laughed and now Beecham was losing his shit. I had played hundreds of hours of football. Probably had a ball at my feet more times than not. I had played on this pitch again and again. Playtime, lunch and after school. Up here most weekends. Yet running onto this pitch *right now* was so real it was blinding. I couldn't see. I was everywhere and nowhere. I normally played on the wing but here I was shoved in the centre. The pitch seemed so deep and busy. I was swallowed up in it. Felt like that *My Girl* kid with the bees. Disorientated and scared. Turning around in fraught, fearful circles. The game went on without me. The minute I got the ball I wanted to get rid of it. Almost as if it was going to give me a disease. A short pointless pass to Beecham who was yelling at me to run with him. Follow him. Back him up. He sweated two or three players. It was here he would normally thread me through, like so many times on the playground. But he saw me, felt me, sensed my skittishness and couldn't trust it. I was almost running under his feet now.

Fuck! Robin!

It's here that they recovered it and took it all the way to our goal. And scored.

4-2.

Final whistle.

They won.

Another loss.

Robin Goode, back on the bench.

The lads hung their heads. No one could look at me. The diagnosis had been made. It's universal. It's a fact. An exact science. The Second-best Player in School has a bottle problem. End of.

All right, Robin?

I looked up to see the owner of the voice. A face before me. Our manager Mr Michaels should be upset at our 6th straight loss of the season. Only his face wasn't sad. His mouth not so. For there was a smile there. Or if not a smile, then a cute cruel curl of the lip.

All right, Robin, he said again.

Tess Darby

HER BUSH was now all around school. It was kind of famous. Everybody talked about it. Some believed it, some did not. It took on a mythical status. Tess wasn't shy in the slightest. She walked around, chin up. She was now my favourite girl. A full crush.

Call for Me

BART told me to call for him so I did. Headed up Black Path and on to Grassingdale then Glendale.

Knocked on his front door, waited. He opened up, just in his shorts.

What?

When he told me to call for him he was smiling and friendly. Now he was staring me down like I was his worst enemy.

What do you want? he said.

You told me to call for you, I said.

He acted like he never heard me.

I'm playing with my sister, he said.

There was music in the background. Michael Jackson's 'Beat It'.

I went to say something else but was met with the slamming of the door. The sun disappeared behind a cloud and put the house in darkness. I stepped back from it and walked away. On the way home I was fuming. Nile Greenaway was right. I had let this guy get away with this for far too long.

Blue Spots on the Wall

AT FIRST I didn't know what they were. What they were for. I was in third place behind Zoe Maggio and Fat Phil Walton.

Fuck is this? I said.

Spelling, Zoe Maggio said. I'm winning.

I can see that.

How the heck are you third? she said.

Fuck knows.

Do you always have to swear?

Zoe and Nile had broken up and I was glad about that although I don't know why.

The next week there was another blue spot next to my name.

All right, Fat Phil, do you know what these spots are for?

Spelling, he said.

Yes I know it's for spelling but how do you get them?

Every time you get ten out of ten you get a blue spot.

Cheers, Fat Phil.

Can you not call me that, Robin.

Fat Phil and Zoe were way in the lead. There was no catching them. Zoe had one spot more and the race was tight. I was in third but only by one or two. All the teachers and the kids kept saying how surprised they were at my third. Because I was a naughty kid they assumed I was a thick kid. Coming third was now my full-time obsession. There were only four weeks to go and the heat was on. I had to take something else into consideration. And that was that I had a universally recognised

Bottle Problem

WE WERE given the words on Monday and then had all week to learn them. Friday afternoon was the test. Zoe and Fat Phil were head-to-head. One small slip and it was over. I wanted bronze. Only I had Greenaway, Darby and the smug Paul Martin hot on my heels. I couldn't afford one slip either. The dumb, naughty kids like Morgan, Bart Tucker and Dwayne Sharpe called me a traitor.

The Bottle Problem was here and I could feel it. Even though I was studying hours a night the test day was getting to me. My hands were shaking and my mind drawing blanks. I very nearly stumbled on a word only to change it in the dying seconds. I was *this close* from losing a blue spot. There was only three more weeks to go. With this pressure piling I decided to do something. I decided to

Cheat

WELL, not cheat. Just, *make sure*. Once all the papers were handed in I decided to sneak back into class and check. Just, check. Just, *make sure*. I would lift Zoe's paper and check that all our spellings matched.

And, they did.

I was good. I was safe.

Next week I did the same.

Yep. What's good enough for Zoe was good enough for me.

Last week. The Spelling Race had now reached full fever pitch. It was *an event.* Just as prestigious as a football match or Sports Day. People were still waiting for me to fall. Both the square kids and the naughty ones. Technically I hadn't cheated so my conscience was clear. Knowing I got to check Zoe's had eased my Bottle Problem. It wasn't so crucial now. Not so life and death. My hand was steady and my head clear.

Last afternoon and the Blue Spot positions going into the final Friday went as follows.

Gold: Zoe Maggio.

Silver: Fat Phil.

Bronze: Robin Goode.

Playtime and I sneaked back into class one last time. Rolled under tables. Ducked under desks. Fingered the test papers until I found Zoe Maggio. Lined her answers up against my own. This was the third week running. I nearly got too complacent. I only saw it at the very last minute.

The word *acceleration.*

They weren't the same. They didn't match. A hot rinse of fear washed through me. Heart drumming in my chest. I had fucked up. There was an *e* instead of an *a*. Panic and relief on the merry-go-round. Panic in my mistake but relief in that I caught it. My next task was to find a rubber. There was only minutes to go before the kids came back in. My hand plunging the insides of a pink pencilcase. Got it.

I took my paper and fixed the word. Double, triple-checking that my *acceleration* lined up with Zoe's *acceleration.* Eyes glaring at the word. Done. I shuffled the test papers back together. As I was doing this I saw something dark on my peripheries. A face at the window. White palms clean on the glass. I saw this face daily. Maybe more than any other face. The one who had sat bang-opposite me for the entire year.

Kayleigh Highman.

Her face was a mask. No expression at all and I wondered if she could even see me. I dropped to the floor quick and gasped. I was trapped. Just then the class queued at the door and Carrol appeared. That shell suit and the muffle of her voice through the window. Damn, I was caught. Just then I saw a gap leading to Duplantis's room. His class was away on a daytrip so I could make use of his room as an escape route. On all fours and I made it. Got myself into the toilets and waited.

239

Once the class was settled I casually rejoined, skipping into my seat. Almost unnoticed, except for Bart Tucker.

Where have you been? he said.

Toilet.

Why wasn't you in the queue?

I wanted him to shut up so I just ignored him.

For the next half hour I daydreamed on my third position. My bronze prize. What would it be? And the general admiration I'd get at coming so high up, against all odds and expectations.

Carrol was head down, marking all the papers.

With fifteen minutes to go she stood and cleared her throat.

Now, the results, she said.

Zoe and Fat Phil sat up.

Just then a hand shot up and stopped Carrol from saying any more.

Mrs Carrol, said the voice.

It was Kayleigh Highman.

Could she pick a better time to go to the toilet, I thought. Then I saw her eyes catch mine and my blood ran cold.

Mrs Carrol, before you make the announcement, I've got one of my own. She spoke like an adult. She spoke like an actress, which, she was.

Carrol said nothing, just waited for more.

I think I know why Robin has been getting such good marks. Why he is in third.

Carrol's purple eyes went large. Her bony white face seemed to melt in the light.

He's been cheating, she said plainly.

A gasp through the class.

He's been cheating, she repeated theatrically. I saw him through the window. Rubbing out his answer and replacing it with a new one. The *right* one.

I went to speak and deny it but Bart Tucker beat me to it.

It's true, he said. I saw him.

Carrol's eyes got even bigger. You saw him rub out his answer and write a new one?

Bart nodded.

Liar!

I looked at Bart and he put his head down. I decided in that moment I was going to fight him. Been letting him get away with it for too long.

Carrol was looking at me. A real seriousness. That's two people saying they saw you, Robin.

I started to talk. I started to deny.

I guess there's one way to find out, she said. She took my paper and held it up to the light. Her lips folded inwards with earnest disappointment.

You *have* rubbed this out, Robin. The word *is* smudged.

Acceleration

I ACCELERATED out of class. And never looked back. The shame and injustice was too much. I was immediately disqualified. I told Mum and we sat up all night, thinking how I could tell my side of the story. The truth. That it wasn't a *cheat* but more of a *justtomakesure*. Whatever way it didn't look good. Two eyewitnesses and a rubbed-out word. The next day I said nothing. Just to suck it up and accept it as it was. The biggest defeat in this was that my *acceleration* was right and Zoe's *acceleration* was wrong. She had dropped the ball, after all. If I had just trusted myself and left it where it was I could have moved into the silver position. Fat Phil got his *acceleration* right and moved into the joint gold position. My blue spots were taken off the wall. It was time to start at the beginning again.

Stars and Stripes

DAD cheered me up by buying me an American flag. He had found it at a truckstop. I was over the moon.

Really you should be having a St George, he said.

After my last performance on the pitch I was dropped as sub. It was another Home game. It was here I decided to unveil my *stars and stripes*. I waited until half-time and then went to my bag to get it. The ties that were supposed to be tied to a pole I tied on my wrists. The American flag was draped across my back like a cape. I stepped out onto the field. People started to look at me. Both on the sidelines and the pitch. It took Nile Greenaway's attention away for a few seconds and he ended up giving the ball away and conceding a goal. We were two-nil down. I walked slowly around the whole perimeter. As I got near the other team's bench this one kid shouted over to me, Hey, you American?

I nodded.

Wow.

Just then I had three or four more kids surround me. From nowhere I found myself talking to them in an American accent. I had never done this before and found it surprisingly easy. The kids were captivated.

Whereabouts in America?

San Francisco, I said.

Wow.

Soon no one was watching the game but listening to me instead. I told them stories about cities and schools and roadtrips and adventures. They asked questions but I had an answer for everything. I had an audience. I was quick on my feet. Kids wanted my number. They wanted to keep in touch. The final whistle blew. They had beaten us 4-1 but they didn't care. More bothered about the cool American Kid who was now walking away with the flag on his back. An early summer sunset, bathing the stars and stripes in a fine orange glow.

Kerry Tromans

MOSTLY she was Morgan's girl. On and off. During an *off* I made my move. I never saw the fuss but now I did. She was small and dark and strong. A quiet alpha girl. I was a bit weary of Morgan but he okayed it with a nod. Do what you want, he said.

I asked her out and she said yes but we had to keep it quiet.

Why?

In case Morgan finds out, she said.

He doesn't care, I said casually.

This certain look on her face, which closed her eyes and mouth for a moment.

Okay, she said. But let's still keep it quiet anyway. Until it dies down.

Until what dies down?

She never answered that.

I walked her home. A long walk. Up and down steps. I made her laugh a few times but mostly it was silent.

It didn't feel right. It didn't feel like Maggio and Morton or even Carlton.

You sure Morgan doesn't care? she said at her doorstep.

Not one bit, I said brightly. We're free to do what we want.

Kerry looked at me like she didn't know what that meant. I don't think I did either.

Later that night I found her number in the phonebook. Only I needed a reason to call her. I thought hard with the phone cradled in my hand, looking long into the mirror at the bottom of the stairs. Got it, I thought. I punched in her number and waited.

Kerry there? I said.

She came to the phone. Her voice surprisingly big, with some seeming expectation.

Yes, she said.

It's me.

Who?

Your boyfriend.

Who?

It's Robin.

Oh.

We have a problem, I said.

Oh?

Yeah.

What problem?

You know how you wanted to keep it a secret?

Yeah.

Well this guy who lives on my close. Daniel Holiday. Well he's only gone and found out and is threatening to tell the whole school.

I don't even know who that is, she said coldly.

Yeah but don't worry, I've warned him. It's okay, Kerry, we're safe.

Okay.

Yeah?

There was silence on the other end.

Yeah so I guess I'll see you tomorrow then.

Okay.

Bye.

Bye.

She put the phone down.

I didn't realise it but I had been looking into the mirror the whole time. The phone in my hand. The dead line still buzzing away.

Leeds United

WAS my new team. They had won the league so it made sense. They were the last-ever team to win Division One before it turned into the Premiership. They were underdogs who had not won the title since the '70s. That had to count for something. I studied the players. There was Eric Cantona and Gary Speed and Gordon Strachan. The old Arsenal goalkeeper John Lukic. Their shirt was white. I had never supported a team wearing white before. I told Mum I wanted the kit for my birthday.

What else was cool is that no one else in the school supported Leeds.

I would be the only one. I would be on my own.

A Real American Kid

ADAM Wall ran up to me at the swimming baths.

Oh my god, Robin, there's an American kid in the arcade. An actual real American kid.

I swallowed hard and was excited and curious and confused and scared and eager to meet him. I was expecting a tall blond kid or a cool black kid. Maybe a loud fat kid or a smart sharp kid with glasses. I was expecting Jordan Knight or Marty McFly or Macaulay Culkin. I was expecting one of the *Goonies*. Instead this kid was just normal. Normal looking. Normal hair, normal clothes. He was short. His face was spotty and his hair a dull brown. He wore a stripy top and dark blue jeans. His white trainers were scuffed and brandless. Adam had been talking to him for a while. They were playing the WWF game.

This is Robin, he introduced me. He's from America too. I was nodding and looking right at him. Blank and a little tongue-tied.

This is Dan, Adam said.

Dan is not even an American name, I thought. I was at least expecting a Chad or a Brad or a Chuck.

Dan turned and said something but I couldn't even tell what. His accent was thick. Not like the movies at all.

Where you from? he said.

I ... err, San Francisco, I blurted.

Thought you said you were from Texas? Adam cut in.

Dan said more stuff but I couldn't tell a word. I managed to ask him where he was from and he said a city I had never heard of in a state I had never heard of. All of a sudden I felt out of my depth and wanted to get away from him. Get away from him but I needed to be around him too. I needed more. I needed everything. I needed more of everything. I needed stories, images. People and pictures. I needed to know what the schools were like. What the girls were like. I needed his time. His phone number. I needed to be his friend. His best friend. His very best friend. I needed to meet his mom and dad. I needed to go out with his older sister. I needed to go on holiday with him. Go back home. Move in, get adopted. Then after a year I could come back and be *A Real American Kid*. Not this pretend one. Dan turned his attention back to the game he and Adam played on. I couldn't believe it. This was the first American I had ever met in real life. I looked at him like he was an alien. I zoomed in on one of the spots on his face and thought, *wow, an actual American spot*. American pus. Adam wasn't even popular. I was doing him a favour by letting him hang out with me yet somehow he had won this American kid over more than I ever could. Every time I tried to talk to him it didn't work out. It crashed and burnt. I was like a nerd trying to talk to the prom queen. This short, spotty, awkward American kid.

When it was over he said he had to go. He gave Adam a dollar bill and said it was nice meeting him. I wanted to snatch that note off him and run. Instead I just watched them shake hands. Outside a man and a woman was waiting. Again they looked completely normal. Maybe there was something slightly off, slightly out of place. Something I couldn't put my finger on. They had the sun in their eyes. One of them eventually waved Dan on.

He said something else, which again I couldn't understand. I was slowly starting to feel like I was being cheated out of my first American experience.

Dan walked casually down the steps and out the leisure centre, towards his mum and dad. Adam carried on with the arcade but I couldn't take my eyes off them. This American family. They stepped inside a small campervan. I saw the pulling of seatbelts. The engine started and they moved on. I tried to work out which side the steering wheel was on. A car waited for them to turn out of the car park and the driver, his dad, thanked them by putting an arm out of the window. I watched the sun light up the hairs on his skin, and then they were gone.

$

ADAM stood staring at it. An American president looking back.

The note was longer and thinner than ours. Bolder, brighter, better.

Give you 50p for it? I said.

Adam just laughed.

A pound then?

No.

Two?

Two quid?

Yeah.

No.

A fiver?

You haven't got a fiver.

I can get one.

Get one then.

Come to my house then.

No.

Why?

It's too far.

No it's not.

I'm not selling it anyway.

It seemed weird, buying money.

A tenner then?

Why do you want it anyway? You're already American. You should have loads of American money.

I hadn't thought of this. I watched Adam's face change. Like he had suddenly realised something.

I did what I always did. My mind going into my brain, pulling out random off-the-wall lies. We lost all our money when …

Save it, Robin, he said. Adam turned away from me and walked.

Wait! I caught him up.

Robin, I'm tired. I just want to go home.

He's not even American anyway, I shouted.

Adam turned and looked at me. Loads of mums and babies were queuing for the pool. Adam flicked the dirty blond hair out of his eyes. What do you mean? he said.

He's not American. He just had that dollar by chance and then made it up.

How do you know this?

For starters he didn't even look American. He didn't have an American name or American clothes. I didn't know his accent and couldn't tell a word he was saying. Never heard of the city he said, or the state. I don't know. Something about him was off, not right. He was a fake.

It was here Adam stepped right up to me and looked me in the eye. The dollar bill neat in his hand.

No, Robin, he said clearly. You're the fake.

Moss vs Darby

ITWASANUNUSUALPAIRING. I would never have put them together. They started playfighting on the grass and the next thing they were rolling around on top of each other. Tess kept digging her finger into his neck and Kev kept jumping away. The three of us were at the garages near school. It was a warm white Saturday afternoon.

You wanna go out with me or something? Tess said.

No, Kev laughed.

Kiss then? she said. French kiss?

A Frenchy?

Yeah.

No.

I urged Kev to do it.

You do it then, he said.

Tess put her eyes on me for a moment too long. She was wearing glasses today.

No, I stuttered.

You're both a pair of pussies.

She grabbed her bike and went to ride away.

All right then, Kev sang. I'll Frenchy you.

Tess got off her bike and threw it into some flowers. Walked up to him like she was going to fight him. Kev backed off and turned red. I felt this thump in my gut. Then this squirmy feeling settled there and wouldn't stop.

You want to or not? Tess said.

I noticed the caretaker look at us from over the field. He was carrying a shovel.

Kev stepped closer and I couldn't take my eyes off the space in between them, which was starting to get smaller as Tess got closer. Kev closed his eyes and Tess laughed a bit through her nose. She then closed her eyes too, and reached out and grabbed his collar and pulled him in. Kev tensed up and I noticed a vein in his neck. He opened his mouth and she opened hers. Her tongue came first. She forced it inside his mouth and I saw it touch his. He immediately pulled away and grimaced. Spat out and shook his head.

Now she was laughing. Laughing but I could tell she wanted more. She was still up close to him.

What? she said.

What, what? he said.

That's just the way it is.

Way what is?

That's just how you do it.

Kev was already back on his bike.

Tess now turned to me. What *do* you reckon? she said.

I didn't quite know what was being asked. My mind was kind of blown.

Lust Letter

I DREAMT ABOUT HER. I dreamt about Black Path. I dreamt about Paper, Scissors, Stone. I had never asked her out like I did all the other girls but there was probably a reason for that. She was always looking at me. Goading me. Forgetting me and then picking me back up. At night she wouldn't let me sleep. This wasn't a fancy. This wasn't a crush. This wasn't a sweet thing but something else. Something I didn't know about. It was scary and adult. I pictured her alone, between the trees. In a world where there was no one else. Just me and her. It got so much that I decided to get out of bed in the dead of the night and write her. Write *about* her. Write *to* her. I took a giant piece of paper and filled her up. With the lead between my fingertips I put words across the white. I wrote on and on until the long morning or so it seemed. I didn't hold back. I let her have it. I put it on her. The full force of my imagination. Next day I would give her this. One way or the other.

MORNING it wasn't the same. Like my brain had changed. Everything was different. I felt foolish and ridiculous. A certain shame feeling, naked and small. I felt to take the paper and rip it up. Screw it into a ball and flush it down the toilet. Just then Mum came upstairs so I panicked and threw it in my school bag.

SCHOOL. The day had that dream feel. The classroom full of thick golden light. She sat at the front whereas I was at the back. The letter was still in my bag. It was here I realised I hadn't read it over since last night. Didn't know fully what it said. Just lots of raw midnight words. It was like that dark possession feeling had come back. A deep drive. I didn't want to give it to her but I *had* to.

LUNCH came and here I was. Sneaking back into class again. Rolled under table. Ducked under desks. This time I checked at the window. Making sure Highman wasn't pressed up against it. Hands at the glass. Once the coast was clear I took my letter and slid it slowly into her pencilcase.

AFTERNOON. Somehow she had missed it. Every time she went into her pencilcase she pulled out something else. A rubber. A ruler. Then with minutes to go until the closing of the day she found it. I drew in a breath and she opened it up. Slow motion. She opened it out and started to read. I watched the back of her head. Seeing her eyes roll across my sentences. Working her way down. What I was expecting from this I didn't know. Once she was done she put the paper down. Turned in her chair and slapped the face behind her.

Bart Tucker

ALL CHAOS broke loose. She slammed the paper down on his desk and ran to the toilet.
　　What is going on? Carrol shouted.
　　Bart had his hand to his cheek. Once she came back from the toilet Bart went, taking the letter with him. On instinct I was up on my feet and following him.
　　In the dank dark of the toilet.
　　He was reading my words, or trying to at least.
　　You all right, I said.

What is this shit? he said, utterly fraught. I can't even read this. I don't know what it is.

Just then he turned his black eyes on me.

You, he said. This is *you*. You did this.

Mrs Carrol

OKAY CALM DOWN, she was saying.

The whole room was on this now. The whole class. Tess sat rigid at the front. Her arms folded. Bart was pacing. Pointing at me and blaming me.

From nowhere the letter was wafted through the air. Up high like a flag. Mrs Carrol had it between her dusty fingertips. Her mood was light, amused. The day was officially done. Kids were free to go. They had bags on and were leaving. Nile and Zoe stood around, waiting for an outcome. They too were amused, intrigued.

Tess was still fixed. Bart still frantic.

My mouth had a mind of its own. Defending myself to the death.

I couldn't believe my letter was here. For all the world to see. I couldn't take it back. Snatch it back and destroy it from going any further. I couldn't even remember what was in the letter and that terrified me. I almost didn't feel responsible for it. Like it was written by someone else. Some other mind. Some other boy.

Carrol's voice had something déjà vu about it. She said and did the very same thing as the Spelling Test.

I guess there's only one way to find out, she said. She took my letter and held it up to the light. I'd recognise your handwriting anywhere, she said.

I watched her face. I watched her face change. From lightly amused to something else. It was in the narrowing of the eyes and then a gulp in her throat. There was nothing else to say and do. Her expression told us all. Her eyes came up from the page and landed on me, as well as the eyes of everyone else.

It was here where I ran. Ran away for good.

An Inspector Calls

THAT EVENING I stayed on the sofa. It was an island and I wouldn't leave it. Luckily Dad was away so I wouldn't have to explain my face. Mum did what she does. Made the dinner. Watched the soaps.

You all right, Robin? she said.

I barely nodded.

Just then there was the door. Mum was going nowhere while *Coronation Street* was on so up I went. A momentary break from the numbness. Opening the door took my breath. It was Nile Greenaway on the top of my steps. He wore shorts and a striped polo shirt. That solid adult way of his.

You all right, Robin? he said.

I tried causal but it didn't work. I saw that in his expression.

What happened back there? he said.

Nothing, I said. It wasn't me, I managed.

Nile was nodding. I was trying to work out how much was care and how much was detective work.

I read the letter, he said. It was pretty intense.

Well it wasn't me, I said again. Closing the door some.

You take care of yourself, Robin. I'm here if you need.

Now I did close the door, fully.

I GOT BACK on the sofa. I thought about Nile's face all night. Again and again. What did it mean. What was going on. What was there. Was it care, or something else. It was here I realised that it was never the one thing. Life, people. It was never just the one thing. It was never just the one thing completely.

Windsor

WAS RED and Buckingham was blue and Balmoral was yellow and Sandringham was green. This was Sports Day and these were the houses we were in. Sports Day always filled me with great nerves. Mostly because it was the same thing for me, year in and year out. I went in as favourite and then bottled it on the day. Big crowds, great expectations. Robin Goode and his universally recognised Bottle Problem. This year, my last year. My Last-ever Sports Day and I had almost given up trying. Mrs Carrol read out the register and which house we were going to be in.

Right, Carrol said, listen up.

We sat. We listened up.

So, these are the teachers running each house. I am Balmoral. Mr Duplantis is Buckingham. Mrs Hislop is Sandringham and Mr Michaels is Windsor. Here are the teams.

Amanda, Balmoral. Nile, Buckingham. Kayleigh, Sandringham. Kerry, Windsor.

I had my eyes closed. Hands in my pockets, squeezed into a fist. Carrol read on.

Phil, Balmoral. Morgan, Buckingham. Bart, Sandringham. Paul, Windsor.

The tension was crippling. Like she was leaving me last to drive me out of my mind.

Zoe, Balmoral. Kev, Buckingham. Tess, Sandringham. Robin, Windsor.

FUCKING KNEW IT. I turned and stepped away. Wanted to scream at the glass door I was staring at. My reflection looked mad. I was heartbroken. I was devastated. My last-ever Sports Day and I was in Windsor. Windsor and Mr Michaels.

He

SMILED when he saw me. Michaels combed back his hair and jumped down from a desk. Doing that clickety-click hand thing of his. He welcomed us in and looked us over.

So here is my team, he said. He was wearing red. Windsor red.

My team of champions. We gonna kick some ass or what!

The kids inched forward and murmured.

Michaels opened his shirt and threw back his head, exposing a muscular neck. His Adam's apple bobbed up and down while he screamed at the ceiling. Spit everywhere.

I said we gonna kick some ass!

Now the kids were screaming with him.

Yeah!

I sat and looked through the window at Duplantis and his Buckingham. The mood very different to in here. Calm and light.

Hey, Robin, what you looking out the window for? Michaels roared. Not being a traitor, are you?

Jesus Christ, I thought.

Duplantis

I COLLARED him the following morning.

Mr Duplantis.

Robin.

Sir, I need to be in your team.

What?

Sports Day.

Ah, yes.

I need to switch. I need to be in your Buckingham.

He smiled his wide warm smile. Adjusted his glasses.

Let me guess, he said. You're Windsor. You're Michaels.

I nodded.

That's rough.

Why would they even put me in his team. They know he hates me.

It's not on purpose, Robin. It's just the run of the register. It's pure luck.

Yeah bad luck, I mumbled.

This made Duplantis smile.

Why you smiling. It's not funny. Why can't I be with you?

Something came to Duplantis's eye.

Why don't you see it as a test, he said. It will make sense one day. When you're older.

Duplantis was always saying this. *It will make sense one day. When you're older.*

I didn't care about older. I cared about today. *Now.*

Duplantis and I were late. Kids were waiting for us in classrooms.

I've got to go, he said.

Duplantis started walking away.

Can't you get me to switch? I said.

I'll see what I can do, he said.

Please.

He was walking backwards. I said I'll see what I can do.

Michaels

WAS ALREADY getting us to chant silly army songs. He was getting us to play *Cookie Jar* again.

Sir, why are we doing this?

Team building, he said.

Next we had to decide upon a captain.

Who wants to nominate themselves? he said.

Nine out of ten times my arm would have been straight in the air.

Instead there was just a sea of silence.

Oh c'mon, said Michaels. There must be *someone*.

Heads began to turn, one by one, towards me. Eventually a kid spoke out.

I say Robin, he said. He's the fastest in the school and he's in the last year. Makes sense.

Before I could say anything Michaels took a step towards me.

You feel up to it, Robin? Feel like you can handle the pressure?

I looked up to him. Those smiling, spiteful eyes.

Yeah, I said. I can handle it.

Cos I know the last few Sports Days haven't worked out for you.

Just then Paul Martin spoke out. I'll do it, he said. I'll be captain.

There he was. Smug little fuck. Blond hair. Blue eyes.

Okay, said Michaels. Paul Martin it is.

No I'll do it, I said.

No, me, said Paul Martin.

You can't run. You can't fight. You're crap at *all* sports.

What has fighting got to do with it? he said.

Yes, what has it? Michaels joined in.

Paul Martin sat up and cleared his throat. I have organisation skills, he said. I'm a manager. And managers are captains.

Why don't we put it to a vote, I said.

This made all the kids nod their heads. I knew I'd win.

No, Michaels said. No voting. We're not singling people out. I've made my decision.

Based on what? I said.

Based on your attitude, Robin. Talking about fighting. This is Sports Day. A *team* event. Not your bullyboy tactics in the playground. Paul Martin is captain. End of story.

The Fall of America

FALL meant autumn. And sometime later this would catch me out and be a part of my undoing. By now it was about fifty-fifty on those who believed in my American Blood. Orchard Primary was becoming a swing state. Tess didn't. Greenaway did. Zoe didn't. Moss did. Highman didn't. Come to think of it most of the girls didn't and most of the lads did. Paul Martin didn't. He brought this up in one of our Windsor meetings.

Robin can't be your captain because he lies. Reckons he's American but he didn't even know that *fall* means autumn.

Buckingham

DUPLANTIS COLLARED me at playtime.

Some good news, Robin.

Oh?

I've had a word with Mrs Carrol and some of the other staff. We're gonna let you switch.

What?

We're gonna let you come onto my team.

Oh.

You don't sound so happy.

No, I am.

Duplantis was watching my face, and watching my mind go. I must have been caught in a daydream. Looking at all the kids on the field.

You know what. I think I'm gonna stick, I said.

You sure? Duplantis was smiling some. Say the word and we'll have you from red to blue in no time. There's a place for you in Buckingham if you want it. We've got a pretty good team this year. Greenaway. Beecham. Moss. Morgan. We're going to be unstoppable.

He was making the offer more tempting with each passing sentence. Switching would guarantee me gold.

Yes was on the tip of my tongue.

Nah, think I'm gonna stick. Stick with what I've been given. Think I'll see how this one plays out.

Duplantis was looking right at me. Like he knew what was on my mind.

Linford Christie

CAN'T BELIEVE it's been four years. I remember the conversation after the last Olympics. About Christie having to wait *all this time* to get his gold. One Olympics was at the start of Orchard Primary and now there was one as I was leaving. People talked about stories having a beginning, a middle and an end but I often found that life wasn't like that at all. I found that it moved in one big circle. One big circle or sometimes lots of little ones linked together. Bit like those rings on the Olympics.

Beat Bart

I WAS starting to dream about it. Most nights. Most nights I was fighting Bart Tucker in my sleep. Fights he started but I couldn't finish. It my heart I knew I could beat him but in dreams I always lost. My fists would become balloons, empty and powerless. It was like punching through heavy water. It was always in front of a crowd and the experience was humiliating.

At school, in reality. And most people now just considered Bart to be harder. I had let him get away with so much that people just put him above me. The end of school was getting nearer and nearer and this was how the legacy would end. Robin was above Bart. Bart pushed it and Robin gave nothing back. Bart goes above. The simple mathematics of the pecking order. I wouldn't even mind this so much if it wasn't for Bart's bullying and nastiness. His turn of mood and unpredictable behaviour. One minute best friend, next, worst enemy. Maybe he was this way with me because it was unresolved. A glitch in the system. *Sort it out, Robin*, Nile had said. He had called this again and again throughout the year but nothing was done.

I knew the morning it was going to happen. Another horrible dream. A fight on the field in front of the whole school. The dream so real and raw that I had to listen to it. I had to pay attention.

All day I watched him. His movement. His snapping, snarling temper. Then at lunch I made my move. A playfight turning into a real one. I pushed him hard in the back and that was all that was needed. He was at me and on me. He kicked out but I stepped away and then came back with a fist. A punch to the side of the face. And then it was on. A crowd came in. Not a dream crowd but a real one. Nile was alive with adrenaline.

All right, Robin, sort it out, sort it out.

Most people wanted me to win. I heard my name.

I twisted Bart into a headlock and put him on the grass. Choked him as tight as I could go. Just then his nose appeared above my grip. A tiny triangle of pink. Morgan Davenport was now staring me down. Nodding at his nose.

Smash him, he said coldly. Bust it.

I had an arm free and it would have been so easy. Bring this fist down and end it.

A yelp ripped from Bart's chest. Tears appeared and a slow, scared whimper.

We done? I said.

We done, he said.

You sure?

I'm sure.

Mrs Carrol

ALWAYS GAVE US A TALKING-TO after a fight. In front of the class. Yet at the same time she always had to know who won. Like she had to have knowledge of where we all stood. She was also fair and wanted to make sure no ongoing bullying was around. Morgan Davenport ripped into Bart after our fight. He never liked him after Bart had stolen his Nintendo game.

All right. Enough now, Morgan, Carrol said. I think he's learnt his lesson.

Bart's face was white and small. His eyes large and soft. Gone was the scowl.

Have you, Bart? Carrol said. Learnt your lesson?

Bart nodded.

Nile gave him a tissue and things went back to normal again.

Running

IT WAS OUR LAST MATCH of the season. An Away game. My last-ever appearance for Orchard Primary. Somehow I had found myself on the team. The starting eight. All season we had lost. All but one. I couldn't understand it because the years previous I had watched us win trophies and tournaments but now in our final year the team didn't work. We had individual players but together we didn't come through. I blamed Michaels. He made it about him. Shouting from the sidelines in this dumb American accent. He dominated the games and one time the referee even had to call him out and calm him down. At half-time his teamtalks made no sense. He had no idea about positions or tactics. The only thing he kept saying was, Aiden Beecham is a one-man team. *Aiden Beecham is a one-man team.* He said it so often it even began to piss Aiden off. So now we were on our last match, deadlocked at 2-2, going into the second half. Aiden had scored both goals and he was really going for it. He'd been booked for nearly breaking a kid's leg. Morgan Davenport had also been booked for a reckless clash of heads. Their striker was scared to death of our defender Nile Greenaway. We were all fighting to the death on this one. I was starting to feel something. *Space.* My speed was opening up room on the left. Aiden could sense this and was pinging over passes with mind-blowing accuracy. A goal was coming. Threat was in the air. I could feel it. I'd hit the outside of the post and the chances were coming. I had yet to score a goal for Orchard Primary in the whole time I'd been here. I dreamt of how good this would be. How legendary. Last goal in the last game in the last minutes.

With about ten to go something happened. Michaels stopped the game and waved me off.

Robin, off.

I was too shocked to speak so the team did it for me. All of them. Moss. Davenport. Greenaway. Even Aiden Beecham going at him wasn't enough to reverse his decision. The other team watched and waited. Parents. Teachers. Michaels now had his head down waving me off. I wanted to walk slow, slouch away insolently yet at the same time I didn't want to waste time for my team. We were on the edge of winning. Only our second win of the season. So with this I ran, started running. Off the pitch.

Yes, Robin, Greenaway shouted.

Aiden Beecham and his team started clapping. I was lit with rage at the pure spite of Michaels. Wanted to spit at him on the way out. Deplorable. Putting his personal revenge before the needs of the team. I ran. I was running. Ran right past him and all of the onlookers.

Where's he going? someone said.

I didn't know myself. Ran down the bank and into another field. Gavin Brown was circling on a bike.

Go on, Robin! he shouted at the top of his voice.

I could feel all eyes on me. Maybe I was no better than Michaels. Taking attention off the game and onto my defiant, dramatic heroics. Powered by adrenalin, I kept on running. Tears down my cheeks. Teeth clenched. I was surprised by how far I could go before getting tired. Still I felt eyes upon my back when in reality they had probably restarted already. I ran the length of the low field and through a fence connecting to the Big School, the large comprehensive. A gravel athletics track opened up before me. I ran into it full pelt. I was tired now. A burn in the throat. A roar of fire in the chest. I managed a full lap. I managed two. I hated this feeling yet I needed this feeling. An internal pressure to push on and not stop. I was running against Michaels. I was running against the world. I was running *for* me. It was a hard, scary feeling. Like it was something to be conquered. Not just conquered but understood. Conquered by being understood and maybe vice versa. I ran another lap before falling onto my knees, rolling over onto my back. The white featureless summer sky spun. This god-awful feeling. This was something new. This was something that wouldn't end here. Something I was going to have to carry with me, into the future.

Denmark

I HAD ALL OF MY SAVED POCKET MONEY across the table. I counted it up and pocketed it. Left the house and headed to Black Path. Grassingdale, Glendale. It was a warm orange night.

I stood at his door and knocked on.

Bart's face dropped as he opened. Straight away he looked over my shoulder. His face was white and his hair was sticking up. He still had that defeated look in his eyes.

I went into my pocket and pulled out the five note. Mum had let me swap it with my piggybank coins.

Your winnings, I said.

Bart took the note automatically but was confused.

What winnings? he said.

Denmark *did* beat Germany tonight.

They did, he said. But our bet was ages ago. Before our fight.

A bet is a bet, I said.

Some life came back to his face. His eyes got clearer.

There were rumours that his mum and dad were splitting up and I could almost feel that behind him. Through the open door.

The underdogs won, he said.

They did, I confirmed.

Who would have thought it.

Schmeichel is great, isn't he?

Bart nodded. Then he looked away, awkward.

I would let you in, he said. But …

Nothing else came after the *but* so we just stood there.

You could come out for a bit? I said.

Yeah, Bart said. But it's late, you know?

I know, I said.

Well I'll see you on Monday then.

Yeah, said Bart. You will.

Morgan Davenport

TOOK MY BROTHER Sam to one side and then lined up his class like he was a teacher or something. He stared at them all with cool menace. That lightning-strike scar on the inside of his eyebrow.

Now, he said. We're leaving this dump soon, so we won't be around.

The kids were looking at Sam then back at Morgan.

But trust me when I say, if *anyone* touches him, we *will* be back.

Sports Day

DAYS LEADING UP TO IT WERE BOLD, bright and blue. A sweet yellow burn. But today was not that. It was a nondescript afternoon of warm grey. Summer through a sheet of tracing paper. A bland sun got high but did little else. A dead wind every now and then. White lines were painted on the grass a week before. I noticed they had made the lanes a little longer than the previous years. This pleased me cos the longer the race the better. Many of my defeats came from running out of track. I was a slow starter. In it always for the long game.

We were told to wear the colours of our house. I was Windsor red so on the morning I had to choose which football top. Liverpool or Forest. Neither felt right so I went with the red of San Francisco 49ers. At lunch I caught Michaels and Paul Martin writing on a massive piece of paper. They were putting way too much into this, I felt. Acting all important. Why did you need battleplans and maps and diagrams. It was Sports Day. You turned up and ran. How hard can it be.

They both stood when I entered the room.

260

Paul Martin looked at Michaels to say something, so he did.

Robin, we're taking you off the Sprint.

What?

We're putting you on the Obstacle.

They were both looking at me hard. Waiting for my expression to change. It did. I felt my face go white.

You are joking, right?

Michaels was shaking his head. You're racing Obstacle.

I'm shit at Obstacle.

No you're not.

Yes I am.

I had never felt such a built-up rage as this.

I can't skip a rope, I said. I can't do egg and spoon. It ends in a sack race and I'll never out- jump Kev Moss.

Paul Martin turned his back on me and wrote something down.

Robin, Michaels said. This isn't about individual glory. This is a *team* event.

I tried to speak but something caught my throat.

He's right, Paul Martin said. A team event.

You're not even racing, I said. In *anything*.

I had a hot finger pointing right at him.

I'm organising, he said. I'm captain.

Sorry, Michaels said. But the decision has been made.

I was shaking. Tears came to my eyes. They had broken me. I was ready to snap.

This doesn't even make any goddamn sense, I said.

Don't swear at me, Robin.

I said goddamn. Goddamn is not swearing.

Don't shout at me, Robin.

Michaels and Martin were standing side by side. Staring at me.

I'm not shouting, I shouted.

Right you're out, yelled Michaels. He did the motion that referees do in American sports.

You're outta here! He pointed to the door.

What?

You're out, he said. No Sprint *or* Obstacle. No Windsor and no Sports Day for you.

You can't do that.

Yes, I can.

He can, Paul Martin added.

My mum and dad are coming to watch. They're on their way.

Good, said Michaels. And you can tell them why you're not racing, when they get here.

Paul Martin turned and wrote something else down.

What are you writing? I said.

Mr Michaels stepped into my space.

I will not be shouted at *or* swore at, he said calmly.

Goddamn isn't swearing, I said. *Fuck you* is swearing.

NEWS spread. I was out. I sat in the toilets and cried. I hated Michaels so much I decided I was going to get him beat up. As soon as Dad was here I was going to tell him all about it. Dad *would* beat him up. At the very least give him a slap.

Banners and balloons and chairs and refreshments were set up all around the school field. Kids went into the changing rooms and got ready. Wearing their respective colours. My face was raw from crying and my muscles were tense from this constant hatred. I was exhausted and isolated, disorientated. All the teachers were with their teams. I was alone, walking the orchard and the woods and the field. Now parents were appearing. Filling the school.

Michaels then walked into view. I thought about pleading with him to let me back in but I couldn't bring myself to do it.

What shall I do? I said.

He was looking for something so just gazed right through me.

Where shall I go?

You're not running, he said coldly.

But where shall I go?

Sit in our pen. The Windsor pen. But sit at the back so no one will see you.

IT WAS NOW. The field was full. I managed to see Mum but Dad wasn't there. I couldn't get to her even if I wanted to. Mr Murdoch stood in the centre of the field and gave a massive speech. He then presented the Opening Ceremony, where some girls did a dance.

Back of the pen, Michaels said. He shoved me and told me he didn't want to see me until it was over.

DUPLANTIS. I saw his face through the crowd. First he mouthed something but we couldn't hear each other so he came all the way from the other side of the field. He was wearing all blue.

Robin, what's going on? Why aren't you dressed? Where are your shorts?

Under my trousers.

What are they doing there?

I'm not racing.

Why?

Michaels has stopped it. Stopped me.

Why?

I shrugged.

Why, Robin?

I really don't know.

It was the first time I saw him mad. Really mad. So mad I thought he might actually do something. He swore and turned on the spot. Looked at the grass and then at the sky. He stepped away and then looked over his shoulder at me.

You got your shorts on, right?

Yes.

Right.

I didn't know what was happening. All I could do was wait. The races came and went. Starting with the youngest and then getting older.

Apart from the relays, my race was the last of the day. As the boys got up Duplantis was back with me.

Robin, he said quickly. Trousers off. Quick.

I kicked off my shoes and then pulled them off. Hands shaking a little. I looked up to see Nile Greenaway, Morgan Davenport, Gavin Brown, Bart Tucker and a few others head towards the start. There had never been nerves like it. Not a moment like this before.

Duplantis put his arm around me and walked me across the face of the pens. His large hand on the small of my back. Then up to my neck. I expected him to say something but he didn't. We then both looked over towards the start. I saw Nile's face change. In his eyes and mouth there was this one thing. Simple fear. Morgan too shook his head in disappointment. Seeing this gave me a bolt of confidence. There was something so solemn about all of this. The whole field had to wait. Parents in the crowd. It was funny cos I craved this attention my whole life but now it was here I didn't want it. I just wanted to go back to my pen. Sit at the back and watch.

Duplantis then dropped his hand and his long arm swung across the empty lane.

He turned and looked me dead in the eye.

This was here. This was now.

I didn't look at the crowd, my mum, or Michaels.

Just down that long corridor of grass. The bumpy earth of an uneven field. A ribbon appeared at the bottom of it. One girl holding one end, a second girl the other. Together they pulled it tight across the finish. It looked about a hundred miles away.

Mrs Carrol stepped off the track and then raised her voice.

On your marks.

Hairs on the back of my neck.

Get set.

Fire in the gut.

Go!

I was gone.

For the first time ever nerves left my body. Already the three main players were decided. Morgan to my left. Greenaway to my right. We three were away. Deadlocked and going for it. Then the blur to my left started to drop but the one on my right stayed where it was. Of a sudden I was taken back to the playground all those years ago. Racing Nile. Thinking I'd won but I hadn't. Didn't want to leave anything to chance this time. Halfway and something happened. We turned at the same time and looked at each other. It was a similar expression on his face when he came over after the Lust Letter. The curious acknowledgment of a deep friendship. Nile and I had had years of this. Up against each other daily. Edging, testing, bringing the man out of the boy. This look on his face knew that and I know he was seeing the same in me. He gave me a little nod as if he was telling me to *go for it*. Yet at the same time I know he was doing everything in his power to beat me. On any given day we could beat each other. Yesterday might be his day. Tomorrow too. Today was mine. We were well into the second half now and this was where I was always going to pull away. I had never won an official race in my whole life. Lots of playground victories, but nothing like this. I broke the ribbon to a crazy cheer. Mum was somewhere in all that. So was Duplantis.

Winning the War

MICHAELS had won battle after battle but this was it. This was where it ended. I was pacing towards him. Ecstasy and fury together as one. Love and hate. The sweet bliss of revenge. Just then something caught me by the collar and pulled me back in.

He put his hands on my shoulders and looked at me fully in the face. Felt like the first time I had ever been looked at.

You did it, he said.

I did.

You're heading to Michaels, aren't you? he said.

I am, I said.

What you going to say?

I'm going to tell him to *fuck off.*

Are you?

Sorry to swear, sir, but it's the way it has to be.

Is it?

I mean, I'm never going to see him again.

That's true. You're not. So I guess you can.

I started to walk but something made me stop and turn.

What would you do? I said.

Me?

Yeah.

Well, I'd go right up to him and look him in the eye. And then I'd shake his hand.

I felt my stomach flip at the mere suggestion.

That hand. Shake *that* hand. Sorry, sir. I'm afraid I can't do that.

That's all right. You only asked me what *I'd* do.

I was stood on the spot.

Let me guess, I said. *It will make sense one day.*

Duplantis didn't need to answer that one, just smiled.

I started to walk away from one man, and approach another.

Don't forget, Robin. To look him in the eye. That is always the most important part.

San Fran Scarborough

I HAD A NEW GANG. They stood around me and listened, open-mouthed.

What part of America?

By now I had perfected the accent.

San Francisco, I said.

265

There was Kid from Leeds and Kid From Manchester and Kid from Newcastle. Kid from Newcastle was hypnotised. He was staring at me as if I was from the moon.

I've never met an American person before, he said.

I wore my red San Francisco 49ers cap.

Are you from America too? they asked Sam.

Nah, I answered for him. He's my cousin.

THIS TIME we had a caravan of our own. Not a luxury static but one we had to fit onto the back of our car and drag through the mud. There was always something wrong with it. Dad screamed at it. Threw things. Before our last holiday he couldn't close the window so he put his fist through it. Sliced his arm open and got rushed to hospital. The worse part about the caravan was putting the awning up when we first got there. No matter how many times he tried he always ended up losing it. Either the pegs were missing or the poles didn't fit or we put it up wrong. Then Dad was off. Raging, throwing things. Threatening anyone who happened to be walking past and look over.

Fuck are you looking at.

This time he promised to keep his cool. We'll take our time, he said. Doesn't matter if it takes us all day.

It was raining when we got there. Which made the whole ordeal twice as bad. Mum suggested we wait until it stopped but Dad had to do it *now*.

Amazed he kept his cool for so long. For once I thought he might actually pull it off. Then I noticed a pole hanging over his head. The more Dad yanked at the awning the looser it got. I watched it drop, fall, float. Like watching the weightless movement of a feather. I could have warned him at any time but I didn't. Part scared to speak out, part pure amusement. I watched it drop across his head. At the moment of impact I was off and running. This was a new method I had devised. The minute he starts, I run.

I ran and ran. Two hundred yards away and I could still hear his madness over the caravan park.

KIDS told more kids and now I was a tourist attraction. *The American Kid*. They crowded me at the arcade to get a peek or hear a word. Stories came. Highschool. Hollywood. A trip to New York. I acted cool and casual. In my own world. This chewing gum nonchalance got the girls on board. At night we hit the disco. I was a bit too old to be getting chases now but still there was the edge of trouble. I had my entourage. Occasionally Mum and Dad would come over but I handled this with skill and deft manoeuvring. Kept my distance. Camouflaged my accent in the music.

That your uncle and aunty? they said.

Yeah.

Where are your parents?

Back home. Back in the States, man.

MORNING routine. We had breakfast in the caravan. Cereal and toast. After Dad went for his ablutions we had about fifteen minutes to clear the pots, wash the pots and put the foldaway table back. The table was a nightmare and the tension in putting it away before Dad got back was intense. Sometimes it was really exciting. Seeing him through the window. Coming closer. We would balance and jostle the table, slotting it back in the nick of time.

Why are you all out of breath? he'd say.

Nothing, we said.

KID from Newcastle was now introducing me to anyone he could find. He was a cute little dark kid with enthusiasm. I had promised him a trip over to America and now he wouldn't leave my side. He was with me all day and all night. Football in the daylight, disco in the dark. Keeping up my accent was getting tiring. Sometimes I'd slip up and he'd notice.

Guess I must be hanging out with you guys too much, I'd muse.

It was also exhausting keeping Mum and Dad away. I had to devise reasons for why none of the kids could come to call.

The younger kids were impressed and loved having me around but some of the older ones hated me. Rough kids from Liverpool. One came up to me and blew cigarette smoke in my face. Fuckin' Yank. You all think you're God's gift.

With two more days to go I couldn't wait for this holiday to be over. It was now very stressful. The lying and the hiding. The sneaking. My brain always on high alert. Thinking five moves ahead. Kid from Newcastle idolised me and I felt a great responsibility towards him. Then one day, when he wasn't around, his sister turned on me out of the blue. She too was dark and cute. And frighteningly smart.

I know you're full of shit, you know.

Her words stunned me.

You might have fooled this lot but you don't fool me. Your accent is ridiculous.

Of course I fought her off but her smile was everywhere. Her eyes reached right inside me.

Our James won't have a word said against you, but we all know.

What do you mean *all*?

My mum and dad. We've heard your accent and your story and it's just, she said that word again, *ridiculous.*

I DON'T KNOW why I agreed to it but I did. Kid from Newcastle introduced me to his dad and he asked me if I wanted to go back to his caravan for chips. It was the very last night. Tomorrow I go home. Really I should have hidden away until this was over. His mum and dad were lovely, quiet people. The mood in the caravan was so different to ours.

We sat around the table and ate.

His parents listened to my accent but never asked about it.

Tell Mum and Dad where you're from then, Robin. His sister wasn't letting me off that easy. She was smiling over the table. A dark brown bob profile and for a mere moment I was met with a flash of last year. Of Angela Stubbs.

San Francisco, California, I said.

Amused looks played over the table.

San Francisco, Sister said. Isn't that like the capital of California?

No that's LA, I said. That's Los Angeles.

Sure it's not Sacramento? she said with smug playfulness.

C'mon now, Becky, Dad said. Eat your chips.

They all knew but I talked on anyway. It was the longest, most painful hour of my life.

BOWLING. Dad made us go bowling on our very last morning. Insisted on it. He took me and Sam and led us along the windy shiny path.

Last bastard day, he said, and the sun decides to come out.

He walked us through the holiday complex. This was the first time I was out with Dad. Wide open and fully exposed. Vulnerable to attack. Kid from Manchester then swooped on us from nowhere. I felt my insides twist. I was done. Busted for sure. Kid from Manchester talked about America constantly but somehow Dad never heard.

Hey do they play a lot of bowling in America? he said. I bet the alleys in San Fran are cool.

We played a few frames but the tension was too much. It was only a matter of time before this whole thing came crashing down. Eventually I took myself to the toilets and hid there. I had a full headache and my breathing was getting faster. Something was happening inside me but I didn't know what.

Once the coast was clear I made a run for it.

I got home and hugged Mum, cried a bit.

What's wrong, Robin?

I don't know, I said.

She stroked my head and I was soothed for a few moments until I saw his oncoming figure through the window. A small orange boy trailing him.

YOU CAN'T ALWAYS FUCKING WIN, YOU KNOW. Dad had kicked the door open and was staring at me with mad red eyes.

Bad fucking loser, you are.

I was confused. I didn't know what he meant. I was sure the Kid from Manchester would have said something at some point. But Dad seemed nonethewiser.

It was here I felt the pressure to do something. Say something. I had been sitting on this all week and it needed an *out*.

It's not the losing, I said.

What then?

They think I'm American.

Dad's face twisted up. Ya fuckin' what?

They think I'm from America.

I told them more and more. I told them it all. How it started as a little joke but got out of hand. I told them about the accent, my story, everything.

Who do they think *we* are then?

My uncle and aunt.

It was here where Dad went mad the most.

Fucking lying. Being a fucking liar. And why do you want to be American anyway? What's so special about America. Aren't you proud to be English?

Mum tried to make light of it.

Oh he just wants to stand out, she said. He just wants to show off.

KID FROM NEWCASTLE came to call. I told him he could cos I had nothing to hide anymore. We walked and went away and sat in the long grass and ate through a bag of sweets.

I knew I had to break this to him but I wasn't sure how. Then he got the ball rolling for me.

Mum and Dad and Sis don't believe you, but I do.

This broke my heart. Looking at his big brown eyes. Full of loyalty. Full of trust.

James, I said. They're right. I'm not.

It was here I dropped my accent altogether. I thought he might notice but he didn't. Maybe my accent had waned over the week and I didn't even notice myself.

Yeah I know you don't live there now, he said. But you *are* American, right? I mean that part is true. It *must* be.

I went to answer but he wouldn't let me finish. It's like he didn't want to hear it.

I can't wait to tell my friends, he said. They'll never believe me that I had a holiday with an *actual* American kid. My friend from San Francisco.

In the end all I could do was look at the wonder in his eyes, and agree.

Sure, I said. Sure.

And I can still come and visit you, yeah?

You betcha.

The afternoon was here. It was time to go home. Him back to Newcastle, me back to California. We shook hands and parted ways. He wandered back towards the caravans whereas I decided to walk awhile. Towards the high cliffs, over the water.

I WALKED TO THE VERY EDGE of the earth. Took off my cap and skimmed it into the white. Wind took it to the waves.

Hell

SAM'S ONE AND ONLY friend was over. Matthew Fox. They were playing in our bedroom. I crept up the stairs and listened in. Watching them through the crack in the door. Matthew was the one doing all the talking.

I like playing with you cos I only have a little sister, he said.

Sam said nothing.

Wish I had a brother, Matthew said.

Sam put his toy down.

Trust me, you don't, he said.

Yeah but your brother is cool. He hangs around with Morgan Davenport. No one can bully you.

It's worse at home, Sam said.

Matthew Fox was looking right at him.

Trust me, Sam said. Having an older brother is hell. It's like living in hell.

The floorboard creaked and Sam looked up so I stepped over into the bathroom. I pretended to wee, flush, wash my hands. I found myself staring in the mirror. There was a smear on the glass which made my skin look weird. I rubbed it off and then looked at myself again.

Sam, I said on the landing.

The boys stopped talking.

Sam, I'm making a sandwich, do you want one?

The silence lasted long.

Matthew, I said. Do you want a sandwich?

Yes please, Robin, he said.

I'll fetch you both one.

When I got to the kitchen Mum was there. I took out the bread and the butter and some ham. A few chocolate bars from the fridge.

What you doing? she said.

Making a sandwich.

When I turned she saw my face.

Hey have you been crying?

Nah, I said. Just had a wash.

Darby vs Goode

IT WAS AT THE SAME GARAGES as Moss vs Darby. I caught her there by accident.

Why are you on your own? she said.

Same reason you are.

She said she had been with Kerry Tromans all afternoon but now she had gone home. Her hair was big and curly. Something I had never seen before. All of a sudden there was this scary, intimate feeling. This claustrophobia. Just the two of us. I had been thinking about this moment for the last year and now it was here I didn't want it to be.

I should get going, I said.

Me too, she said.

We could see her house through the high wire fence but we had to walk the long way round to get there.

You gonna walk me home or what?

I nodded and we started moving. Past the caretaker's and then up Black Path.

I ripped my kneecap open here, she said.

This made me look down at her thick pink leg.

What are you looking at? she said.

Nothing.

It was a late-afternoon dark. The best of summer was over. I was talking a lot. Talking fast. Tess was a talker too but now she said very little. And what little she did say was cold and abrupt.

What's with all the questions, she said. You my therapist now?

I didn't know what this meant. She was one month older, plus ten years.

As we touched on her close she slowed the pace of our walk.

I know you sent that letter, she said.

What letter?

That love letter. That *lust* letter.

Another word I didn't know. I decided to change the subject.

We're going to different big schools, aren't we?

She laughed, snorted. Please stop saying *big* school, she said.

Okay.

Big school is only what *small* people say.

I began talking again. Lots of talking. Naming all the kids and what schools we were going to. Moss. Davenport. Carlton. Overwood. And Woods. Are going to mine. And Greenaway. Walton. Martin. Marsden. And Maggio. Are going to yours. The rest are all going to that shithole one.

Yes, I know, Tess said plainly. She was clearly bored.

But you did send me that letter, didn't you?

I did something with my head that was neither a shake nor a nod.

We were on her doorstep now. A place I had never been before.

Nile Greenaway lived slapbang opposite and I wondered if he could see us. It didn't matter now cos school was over. There was nothing left to tell.

Well, she said. I guess I'll be seeing you.

Music played through the walls of the neighbour. The song 'Finally', by CeCe Peniston.

Wonder if I'll remember you in the future, she said.

I couldn't think of anything to say so I didn't.

She put her eyes down and said more.

Don't you know that we're always the oldest we've ever been.

It was an odd thing to say. For a few moments I drifted off and thought about memory. How some people have great ones and some none at all. Before I could say anything there was a soft closing of the door. Tess's face disappeared and I watched the brown blur of the back of her head move away, into her home. I stood staring at the glass. The separate panes made me look as if I had about ten different faces.

Pep Maggio Caught Me on Black Path

WHAT WAS YOU DOING with Tess Darby? he said.

He was sitting across his bike. He was chewing like he had just finished eating something. Pep had been at Big School a year and he looked bigger and sounded older.

Which school are you going in September? he said.

I told him.

I'm glad you're not going to mine.

Oh.

He was at the one Tess was going.

You going out with her or what?

Tess?

Yeah.

No.

You went out with my sister, didn't you?

I put my eyes on his front wheel.

Yeah about a hundred years ago, I said.

That's what I remember about you the most.

What?

That you never stick with anything.

What do you mean?

Always supporting a different football team. Always a different girl. You never stick with anything.

I thought about saying, I stick on your mum. Only his bike was blocking me. I was kind of backed into a corner.

You're a gloryhunter and a cheat, he said.

Pep was talking quite calm but I could tell he had things to get off his chest. So I let him. He said more things but by now I had switched off. Instead I looked around and felt the air on my forearms and face. It was as if in that moment it had turned from summer to autumn. When I tuned back in to Pep it was as if he had gone to being nice. Or if not nice, normal.

Can you remember that ghost we saw? he said.

What ghost?

In the window.

You're at big school, I said. You should be outgrowing stuff like that.

He smiled but carried on talking through it.

That summer. Classroom window. It was on a Sunday night. You don't remember?

Suddenly it came back to me. Oh yeah, I said. I remember.

What *was* that?

I put my shoulders up and turned my mouth down. Beats me, I said.

Pep was smiling a big one. Shaking his head.

Anyway I'm hungry, he said. Better get going.

I watched his slow walk up Grassingdale. Why he didn't ride his bike I didn't know. Pushed it alongside him. His big bum and the creak of his trainers. He was humming a song. A tune that was familiar but one I couldn't quite put my finger on.

As I Lay in Bed that Night

I THOUGHT about what Pep said. I thought about what Pep said about *sticking*. It had never occurred to me before but I guess he was right. I never stuck. So I got out of bed and turned the light on and took a pen and a piece of paper and wrote:

Football Team, Leeds United.

American Football team, San Francisco 49ers.

274

Colour, Green.
Wrestler, Bret Hitman Hart.
Food, Pasta.
Best Friend, Nile Greenaway.

I will stick with these until the end of time, I thought. I kept the light on and took my list back to bed. Lay on the bed instead of in it. I thought about my best friend Nile. He was going to a different Big School but we had made a pact to stick together. His mum and dad were splitting up and I knew I had to be there. For him. Yes, from now on I am going to stick. I am going to be a sticker. Pep Maggio had taught me something. I turned off the light and lay in the dark and thought some more. Thought about my list. Maybe I should cross out the wrestling bit. Getting a bit old for that now. Next my mind wandered to girls. I hadn't put them on the list. I thought about them all. Tess. Zoe. Kayleigh. Lauren. Leanne. Diane. Zara. Kerry. Amanda. Angela Stubbs. They seemed like they were gone now. All of them. This made me feel really sad but I guess there'll be more. I guess there'll always be more.

September

Sunday Service

I SAT at the bus stop even though I wasn't waiting for a bus. The people looked like they had been waiting a long time. An old man wearing a flat cap, standing, reading a book. Sat down was a large African woman in a bright yellow dress. Down her dress was a line of silver disks. Like little circular mirrors. They kept reflecting off the sun, making the man squint every now and then. For a brief moment two rainbow diamonds appeared on the page of the book he was reading, lighting up some of the words.

I couldn't see the words.

But I knew it had to mean something.

Ouroboros Umbilical

MORGAN DAVENPORT and Kev Moss came to call. We didn't look right in our blazers and tie. Didn't look old enough or responsible enough for such a picture. Mum took it with a camera. A long thin thing with a flash. Mum always said Morgan was going to break hearts when he got older and that had always made me jealous but it didn't anymore. He took the wheelie bin out for her and put it out front. Kev let a spider run over his fingers. Mum was still looking at us as we walked away, slowly at first. Perhaps wondering who was going to take the lead. Down my backsteps and out onto the close. Crossed the main busy road and onto that big steep hill opposite. It was still warm. The days still light. We didn't walk in a straight line but rather snaked our way over. Side by side. Higher and higher. At the top I could still see my house and my kitchen window. In my mind's eye I could see my mum at the sink. Not really washing the pots, just the soap on her hands.

What are you looking at? one of them said.

Nothing.

We kept on. Until we were over the brow of the hill. And gone.

www.ingramcontent.com/pod-product-compliance
Lightning Source LLC
Chambersburg PA
CBHW022000010726
47494CB00003B/815